BOOM TOWN

NIC STONE

SIMON & SCHUSTER

New York   Amsterdam/Antwerp   London
Toronto   Sydney/Melbourne   New Delhi

Simon & Schuster
1230 Avenue of the Americas
New York, NY 10020

For more than 100 years, Simon & Schuster has championed authors and the stories they create. By respecting the copyright of an author's intellectual property, you enable Simon & Schuster and the author to continue publishing exceptional books for years to come. We thank you for supporting the author's copyright by purchasing an authorized edition of this book.

No amount of this book may be reproduced or stored in any format, nor may it be uploaded to any website, database, language-learning model, or other repository, retrieval, or artificial intelligence system without express permission. All rights reserved. Inquiries may be directed to Simon & Schuster, 1230 Avenue of the Americas, New York, NY 10020 or permissions@simonandschuster.com.

This book is a work of fiction. Any references to historical events, real people, or real places are used fictitiously. Other names, characters, places, and events are products of the author's imagination, and any resemblance to actual events or places or persons, living or dead, is entirely coincidental.

Copyright © 2025 by Logolepsy Media Inc.

All rights reserved, including the right to reproduce this book or portions thereof in any form whatsoever. For information, address Simon & Schuster Subsidiary Rights Department, 1230 Avenue of the Americas, New York, NY 10020.

First Simon & Schuster hardcover edition October 2025

SIMON & SCHUSTER and colophon are registered trademarks of Simon & Schuster, LLC

Simon & Schuster strongly believes in freedom of expression and stands against censorship in all its forms. For more information, visit BooksBelong.com.

For information about special discounts for bulk purchases, please contact Simon & Schuster Special Sales at 1-866-506-1949 or business@simonandschuster.com.

The Simon & Schuster Speakers Bureau can bring authors to your live event. For more information or to book an event, contact the Simon & Schuster Speakers Bureau at 1-866-248-3049 or visit our website at www.simonspeakers.com.

Interior design by Wendy Blum

Manufactured in the United States of America

10　9　8　7　6　5　4　3　2　1

Library of Congress Control Number: 2025941363

ISBN 978-1-6680-5627-1
ISBN 978-1-6680-5629-5 (ebook)

For Brittany Marie Hogan,
who told me to "write that next bestseller."

And . . .

For Angel, the story midwife of my wildest dreams.

BOOM TOWN

THURSDAY, JUNE 5

ALL LADY JOSEPHINE WANTS is to get back to her camp. She got turned around somewhere, and all the trees look the same here. Also, her stomach hurts. She stopped getting her monthlies a long while ago, so that's certainly not the issue... Plus, her head hurts too.

What had the guys at the Lee Street Bridge given her in that bottle?

There's a noise behind her, so she turns around. Too fast. Her arm brushes something scratchy, and then there's a dull throb in her shoulder as the wind is knocked from her thin frame. The dusky sky blurs into focus overhead.

She's gotta find her camp before the sun's all the way down. She's a tough ol' broad for sure, Lady Josephine. But it don't feel safe out in these woods at night.

She shuts her eyes then, even though she shouldn't. The river's nearby. She can hear it.

Her camp is near the river. Just inside the tree line a small ways up from the little alcove where she takes her baths.

She can follow the river.

She struggles to her feet, and as she stumbles along—zigzagging a bit, though she tries to walk a straight line—her gut swims. Maybe she shouldn't've drunk that stuff. Those guys seemed nicer than most, but maybe they thought she'd hang out for a while and they'd get lucky. Most men are like that. At least the ones she's met.

She drifts left and slips into the water but catches herself. Only her shoe and pant leg get wet. Up to the knee. There's a crop of pines ahead on the opposite bank that look familiar . . . she thinks.

She gets to humming. "Sweet Love" by Anita Baker. It's been in her head for some time now. Heard it when coming out of the convenience store where she spends most of her daytime hours. The owners are real nice and don't mind her presence, so long as she stays outside. Even let her use the bathroom from time to time.

The car playing the song had been turning into the parking lot of the "gentlemen's club" across the street. Lady Josephine had done some dirty dancing back in her day, but rarely for gentlemen, and never in a place as fancy-looking as that Boom Town. Even had a neon light in the shape of a girl holding on to a pole. She can't remember ever seeing the parking lot empty.

She was really something back in the day, Lady Josephine was. Slender and brown-skinned with a head full of "good hair," as they used to call it. One of the most sought-after call girls in all of Atlanta (though even with that profession, she tried to always do the right thing).

"Sweet Love" had been her favorite song.

She doesn't like to think about the old times, but reminders sneak up. Just the other day, Lady Josephine overheard a woman talking on her cell phone about girls going missing. Said that if the girls were Black, no one would look for them.

Made Lady Josephine real sad. It was certainly true that nobody had ever looked for *her*.

She wishes she had another drink.

Lady Josephine trips over her own feet and goes down hard. Right into the ice-cold water. The burn in her nostrils kicks her will-to-survive into gear. *That* is something she's never managed to shake no matter how bad things got.

The water is shallow here. If she could just get her feet up under her ...

Her hand reaches for something jutting up out of the water on her right, and by the time her senses have caught up, she's sitting on a rock ledge, soaked and shivering.

Something red in the water catches Lady Josephine's eye. It's bigger than the average piece of junk that washes up on these Chattahoochee shores, and trapped in an outcropping of rock that some part of her recognizes. She looks over her shoulder and sees the bright blue of her tent just beyond the tree line.

Well, look at God.

Her attention is pulled back to the red. It's fabric, she realizes. Ballooned so it's all she can see above the waterline.

The current pushes it against the rocks, and more of it breaks the surface.

An arm.

Lady Josephine leans over and vomits into the river.

PART ONE

THE LOVELY LADIES

MONDAY, MAY 26

Lyriq

I KNEW FROM THE MOMENT Damaris Wilburn walked in that she didn't belong in a place like Boom Town. Sure, the inside of the club was a sight to behold. It was a lot bigger than it looked from the street, and had a show floor shaped like a half circle: the two long, curved bars set on either side of the entrance at the front wall made the room look like it was being hugged, and the three stages—each with a shiny, silver pole at its center—stuck out from the rear of the building like depraved rays of sunshine. Behind the middle one, *BOOM TOWN* was displayed in black letters, all backlit in neon green, with the pole lady bold and bright between the two words.

But still: it was the way Damaris stopped dead to take it all in. Eyes big as dinner plates and mouth all open—wasn't a person on earth who could convince me she'd been inside a strip club before.

Couldn't tell if she was amazed or horrified.

Either way, the girl was so busy gaping around like she'd just landed on another planet, she didn't notice Guapa and me sitting beside the center stage, waiting for her to climb her little ass up there and show us what she was working with.

"Excuse me?" Guapa finally called out to her. "Over here."

Damaris almost jumped out of her skin.

The audition went *real* bad. Not that Damaris had a clue: she'd danced her little heart out. It just . . . wasn't exactly the kind of "dancing" people came to our establishment to see. There hadn't been a lick of body-rolling, dropping, twerking, or popping. In fact, there was a point when homegirl launched into a series of ballet-like spins *around* the pole before abruptly dropping into a wide-legged squat and swinging her arms like propellers. It gave very *interpretive dance.*

If I hadn't known the girl had zero experience, I would've thought she was making fun of our profession and been ready to knock her pretty teeth out. But she clearly had a dance background. No, she wasn't busting the type of moves that would make men cash in big bills for singles and throw them in the air. But there was something about her ease of motion and how attuned she seemed to the music. Made her real hard to look away from. The maple syrup skin tone, gravity-defying titties, snatched waist, and naturally fat ass certainly didn't hurt either.

Not that any of that mattered: I knew I would hire the girl from the moment the doors closed behind her. Even if it meant I had to train her myself. For one, I owed my life to the person who'd requested her audition—a cousin of hers named Tink. (Also owed Tink money, but that was neither here nor there.) More importantly, though, Damaris's resemblance to someone else was so "uncanny," as they say, it hit me like a punch to the ribs. After telling her we'd be in touch with a decision, I had to excuse myself from Guapa and Astro (our DJ) so I could run to the bathroom and sob. Hadn't cried like that since my pawpaw died when I was eleven.

Scared the shit out of me.

What Damaris didn't know (yet . . . because someone was sure to tell her): she looked a whole hell of a lot like one of the club's former headliners: Felice Jade Carothers. Though only I called her by her given name.

To everyone else, she was Lucky.

Everything had been different when Felice was around. Not to toot my own horn (especially since it don't really *blow* like that anymore), but she and I—*Lucky* and *Lyriq*—were legendary in the world of erotic dance. We moved as a unit: the Lovely Ladies. And with us in the building, Boom Town was the most notorious and highly patronized strip club in the city of Atlanta six nights per week.

If DJ Astro was on the turntables and we were on the stage, it was damn near guaranteed that whatever song 'Stro was spinning would eventually climb to number one on multiple Billboard Music charts. She and I *literally* helped make hits. One "Best New Artist" Grammy winner even thanked us in his acceptance speech.

We were everything.

But then I started having some issues with my health and had to take some time off. And by the time I got back and took over as dance manager, Felice was gone.

I never stepped onstage as a performer again.

And she never came back.

She'd been gone just over a year when Damaris ballerina-spun us into her orbit. And though I clearly *knew* the girl wasn't Felice, I also knew there wasn't a world where I would reject her.

So, I hired the little hoe. Very much against my gut and in defiance of the GM's *minimum two-years erotic dance experience* requirement. Whole thing made me nervous as hell. She was young—barely twenty-one, according to her ID. And even though I had a feeling she would learn the ropes real fast once we started training, I also knew she had no clue what the hell she was getting herself into. There was a certain level of *I-don't-give-a-fuck* a woman had to possess to thrive in this industry, and I wasn't sure Damaris had enough to survive her first dance with actual customers in the building.

But even with the red flags twerking in a holographic G-string at the back of my mind, I took the girl under my wing and taught her everything I knew. Not that I would ever say it out loud, but I'd failed Felice in so many ways, I guess I felt like setting Damaris up for success could be my chance at redemption.

Thankfully, she was truly on her shit. Damaris was a perfectionist when it came to moving her body, so she trained hard. Too hard sometimes: there were mornings when I would get a call from the guard at six a.m. asking if he could let her in the building. "She says she needs to practice," he would say. (I think the dirty bastard had a crush on her.)

It did surprise me how enthusiastically she shook her ass once she learned the ropes. I thought she would need time to get used to dancing nude—most grown women aren't comfortable doing that even when alone—but two weeks in, when I had Astro turn on a song and take a seat beside the central stage so ol' girl could show off what she'd been working on, she put on a performance so insanely sexy, even *my* shit got to tingling.

When she was done, 'Stro sat statue-still, eyes as wide and mouth as open as Damaris's had been her first time in the building. Which was saying a lot: the man was surrounded by butt naked baddies six nights a week.

I'd seen that look on men's faces before when they managed to snag a private dance from Lucky.

At Boom Town, a new hire typically chooses her own stage name, and then management—myself and Bones, the GM—either approves or disapproves. But as I watched Damaris move, I could see what she'd be called as clearly as if it'd been flashing over her head in neon green: Charm.

I thought to myself, *This one will bring us good fortune.*

Wish I knew how wrong I would be.

I HAVE NO IDEA how to approach the boy. Because Guapa was right: his vibe is definitely giving *childlike*.

When Guapa came banging on the bathroom door to tell me there was "somebody here lookin' for Charm," I'd rolled my eyes. Figured it was some guy who'd seen her on the daytime shift and come back for more. She had that effect on a handful of them.

"You ain't tell him she's not here?" I replied through the door.

"Of course I told him that, Lyriq. And he responded by asking to speak to the manager, like some disgruntled, middle-aged white lady. I was about to tell him to take a hike, but then it hit me that he used Charm's real name."

My whole body went hot. I quickly finished my business, pulled my dress down, washed my hands, and came out, pulling the door shut behind me. "Come again, now?"

"It's some lil dude."

"Huh?" A "lil" dude? Had the girl been seeing someone? Or what if it was worse? What if she'd gotten herself caught up in some shit?

"One who's never been in a strip club before," Guapa went on. "The way his eyes damn near jumped out his face when Knight walked past naked made that clear. Can't be more than twenty-one, and I only give him that cuz you gotta have ID to get in here."

"You said he used her real name?"

"Yeah. 'I'm looking for Damaris,' is what he said. She ever call after not showing up for her shift this afternoon?"

Normally, I would've told the truth: Nah, she didn't. Which meant that if she happened to show up tomorrow, she'd get sent right back out the door. No call/no show equals no job.

But somebody showing up and asking for a dancer by given name wasn't normal.

I looked at my watch. Most would assume I do it for the clock, but nine times out of ten, I'm checking my heart rate and ECG. The former was higher than it needed to be.

I took a deep breath.

"So, you gonna go talk to the kid?"

"Can you chill? Damn." Nosy ass.

Though whoever the dude was, I definitely had to talk to him. If for no other reason than to find out how he knows Damaris.

I just didn't expect him to look . . . the way he does.

He's definitely man-*shaped*. Maybe six three, broad-shouldered and solid, his long locs neatly styled in a low ponytail of rope twists.

It wouldn't surprise me to learn he's some sort of athlete. Though nothing like the average one I encounter. There's a purity about him that irritates me to no end. It's in the way he stares straight ahead with his hands behind his back. Like he's *choosing* not to indulge in the abundance of bare flesh baddies scattered about the space, doing hella impressive shit with their bodies.

He clearly ain't here for a good time.

I lift my chin as I approach. "Lemme guess," I say, crossing my arms (mostly to conceal my own flat chest; it's been over a year since my breasts were removed, and yes: I'm still a little insecure about it, especially up in here). "You think one of my dancers stole your wallet?"

"Oh, umm..." He almost looks away as I step into his space but seems to think better of it. "No, ma'am. This is my first time visiting your establishment."

Ma'am?? "Whoa now, honey bunch, you can't come up in here and have bitches feeling old. You did ask for a manager, didn't you?"

"My apologies. Yes, I did."

"Well?"

"I'm looking for my friend. She's one of the... dancers? I believe she goes by 'Charm' here—"

"And who the hell are you?"

That snaps him to attention. And my fury is real: I hate when people hesitate around the word *dancers* to describe the women— myself included—who've worked as entertainers in clubs like this one. Literally, that's all the Boomer Baddies are doing: moving their bodies in rhythm to music.

Dancing.

How anybody else feels about that don't have nothin' to do with us.

I'm not sure what the kid sees when he looks into my eyes this time, but he deflates like a pin-poked balloon. "My name is Dejuan Taylor. Damaris— sorry, *Charm*—rents out the basement apartment at the house I live in with my mom. She hasn't been home in a few days."

He says more, but I don't hear any of it. Because the small crowd near the entrance parts and I see the last person on earth I'd want around at a time like this.

The siren in my head is even louder than the music.

BEFORE

Lucky

HE WAS AN ANOMALY at first. Not that white men never came into Boom Town—it was within five minutes of two different university campuses, so senior frat boys frequently stumbled in after parties, already drunk as hell. They were often some of the best-paying customers when they managed to actually get our attention.

What made T different was his bearing. I always hated the word *swag* because it felt overused and ill-defined, but there was really no other way to describe T. He was a smooth, but swaggy-ass white boy. Like the type who would have gone to an Ivy League school, but joined a Black fraternity.

He was tall-ish, dark-haired, and bearded. Green-eyed and well-built. Whatever cologne he wore screamed *generational wealth*, and even dressed business casual—blazer, button-down, dark jeans, Air Jordans—it was clear he was a man of means.

Didn't hurt that he moved with the type of solidity that could part a sea of designer-draped hip-hop artists *and* their entourages without a single person realizing they'd moved. T was Important, and there was no denying it.

Though relatively young—mid-thirties at most—T looked like he would be more at home in an NBA box suite chatting up old money team owners than hanging out in a Black strip club. But there he was. He'd come in alone that first time—another thing that made him stand out. It was a Town Hall Tuesday, the club's most "boomin'" night of the week. Called such because Micah Michelle Johanssen—Lyriq—and I, Felice Carothers, shared a headline set that DJ Astro would use to premiere whatever record he'd taken a liking to from his Hit Box the previous week. It was a literal wooden box—painted green, like everything else in Boom Town—with a slot in the top where aspiring artists could drop in thumb drives with music on them. Astro would listen to every submission.

Which is why Tuesdays were so packed: if you'd been one of the people to shoot your shot, you had to be in the building in case your song got chosen. And of course, you brought your whole crew.

Thomas, however, walked in unaccompanied.

Knight—tall, thick as butter, and the color of the hazelnut chocolate at the center of a Ferrero Rocher—was the first dancer to notice him. At Boom Town, the rule of first contact was something we took very seriously: the first person to interact with a newcomer got dibs on offering a private dance. Which frequently led to being requested—aka guaranteed money—whenever the customer returned. T oozed affluence, so bagging him on sight should've been a no-brainer.

But Knight didn't approach.

None of the dancers on the floor did.

According to Knight, Thomas, hands in pockets, had looked around—"to get the lay of the land," she supposed—and then made his way to the bar. The bartender, a honey-hued trans woman named Clutch, chatted with him for a second as she poured whatever he'd ordered, then she smiled and went to tend to the next set of customers. He turned around on his barstool and resumed taking in the space, drink (bourbon sour, Clutch told me later) in hand.

"All right, all right, all right," came Astro's thrumming baritone over the loudspeaker. "It's about that tiiiiiiiime!" The crowd erupted. ("That white man ain't even blink," Knight said later. "Just took another sip of his lil beverage.")

The call-and-response began—Guapa, Twizzler, and Shyne's cues to get into position. Each of poles at the centers of the three Boom Town stages disappeared into a wide hole in the ceiling. The three of them, plus Micah and I, were standing *above* those holes, preparing to make our Boomer Baddies entrance. *Y'all come down like angels outta the only type of heaven I wanna go to*, a guy once said to me, hand over his heart.

It was ridiculous.

"You bitches ready?" Guapa asked as she grabbed the center stage pole.

"Is *your* ass ready?" Twizzler rolled her neck out and stretched her arms. "You the one who had knee surgery. You stretch today, Grandma?"

"Oh, fuck off."

Astro: Y'all ready?
Crowd: YEAH!
Astro: I said, Y'ALL READY?
Crowd: HELL YEAH!
Astro: What y'all ready for?
Crowd: TOWN HALL TUUUUUUUUUESDAAAAAAY!

I could picture it: the houselights going dark as all three Boom Town stages lit up in bright green. A low, humming bassline filled the air.

"I got a straight-up *slugger* for y'all from the Hit Box this week," 'Stro announced. All of us dancers had heard the song already—Town Hall Tuesdays were the only night of the week we rehearsed for—and it really was a good one. "Big Whoa and crew, if y'all in the building, make some noise!"

A burst of *whoops!* and hollers shot up through the holes.

"We gone work on that artist name, but the song slaps!" Astro continued. A ripple of good-spirited laughter ran through the space, and Micah rolled her eyes. She had quite the attitude that evening.

"Let's get it!" from Astro.

As he increased the volume of the music, the energy in the building rose with it. And when the beat dropped, so did Guapa, Twiz, and Shyne. All scantily clad in similar shades of forest green.

The crowd lost it.

Astro's voice rang out again as he introduced each of the first three ladies. Which meant it was almost go-time for Micah and me.

We stepped up to the center pole. When it was our turn, she would drop first, and I would follow. Usually at this point, she would wink at me, and I'd lick my lips in response. It would drive her wild—"I love it when you remind me of what that tongue can do," she'd say. Which would get *me* going. It took our shared dance sets to another level, all that throbbing with want and hyperfocus on each other once we were onstage.

But that night was anything but usual. She wouldn't even look at me.

Astro: "And now the moment you've all been waiting for! Introducing the divine dy*nas*tic duo ... the queens of your *wildest* dreams and Boom Town's *loveliest* ladies: Lyriiiiiiq annnnnd Luckyyyyyy!"

The lights on the central stage turned white below us, and Micah made her descent. Once she was halfway down, I followed suit.

The set itself was a blur. We did our regular twerking/grinding/

clapping/touching ourselves while stripping naked—seemingly for each other—but my heart wasn't in it.

In fact, my heart wasn't in anything at that point.

It couldn't be.

Because just days before, Micah had begun to break it.

I COULD SEE T, though I didn't know his name yet, coming towards me as I moved away from the stage once the set was over. With the mood I was in, I hated him on sight. His presence felt like an invasion. Not that I had anything against white men in general, but I'd had more than enough encounters with ones like him—who moved as though nothing was immune to their will—to last a lifetime.

"Excuse me," he said from behind me as I went to speak to a group of attorney guys who frequented Town Hall Tuesdays. "Excuse me, miss?"

I ignored him.

As I laughed and flirted with the regulars, he hovered like Casper the Friendly Fucking Ghost. All pale and conspicuous. I'd hoped he would take the hint and buzz off, but he wound up doing the opposite.

"Excuse me . . . Lucky?" he said, taking a step closer.

I looked over my shoulder. "Yeah?"

"My name is T. I'd like to request a dance from you—"

"I'm not available right now." And I turned back to the group.

"Understood," he said. "You mind telling me if you intend to avail yourself before the night is over?"

Avail myself? Who the fuck did this man think he was?

I turned to face him fully. "To you?" I said. "No, probably not."

His eyebrows shot to his hairline. It gave me a little thrill—there were few things as satisfying as making it *clear* to a man who thinks he owns the world that he doesn't own me. "I have a number of regulars here tonight that take priority."

"Well, how do I get on that list?" He stared into my eyes. And though it was deeply unnerving—most guys I encountered at work couldn't keep their gaze above my neck for more than a couple of seconds—I also had a hunch he regularly used eye contact as a coercion tactic.

But I really wasn't the one. "Sir, I mean you no disrespect, but nothing about you says *I should be a priority.* Not over customers I've been entertaining for years."

He held up a wad of money. "Thousand bucks for a single dance," he said. "Come on."

Would the money have been great? Of course. But I refused to even look at it.

"I'm good," I said. "Appreciate the offer, though. I hope you have a good night." And I turned to take my leave from him. The attorneys had moved to a booth and were throwing singles in the air while Twiz, Guapa, and Shyne danced their asses off, the last making it clap over the table as a server delivered multiple orders of lemon pepper wings (had to love Atlanta). I moved to join them—that shit I said about regulars hadn't been true at all . . . I just had no interest in sating this white man's tawdry little *I'm-totally-into-Black-women* visual fantasies.

But the motherfucker grabbed my arm.

He realized his mistake when I whipped around, rage first. His hands went up in surrender, but I still stepped right into his face, finger raised. "Don't ever put your fucking hands on me without my permission, got it?"

"Okay, okay. My bad—"

"Is there a problem here?" One of the guards had approached us.

"Nah, there's no problem, Randy," I said, looking right into T's eyes. They were the murky green of a succulent plant. "This patron and I just needed to come to an understanding. Right, *T*?"

His head cocked just the slightest bit, and this time, he did give me a once-over. When he met my gaze again, he looked . . . impressed. "Yeah, that's correct," he said. "Another time, then?"

It was a question I wasn't expecting. A challenge, even.

I'd never been one to back down from a challenge.

"I think not, actually," I said. "Though again, I appreciate the offer."

I turned and walked away, knowing his eyes would be on me the whole time. And the more distance I put between us, the more bothered he would be that I hadn't given him what he wanted.

What I didn't expect was the feeling that overtook *me* as I went. Because that challenge had sparked something inside me.

And I really hoped he would come back.

TUESDAY, MAY 27

Lyriq

FOR THE SECOND AFTERNOON in a row, my not-so-Lucky Charm was a no call/no show.

And if *that* wasn't enough to drive a bitch to smoke—Bones was definitely looking at me crazy ("So this the type of bitch you hire when I'm not lookin' over your shoulder?")—creep-ass Thomas McIntyre showed up last night, looking like a Great White shark in a tank of black angelfish.

I only ever had one encounter with the man, and that was more than enough. He creeped me the fuck out. Reminded me a smidge too much of some of the rich, powerful, and sadistic sons-of-bitches I'd encountered in a previous life I had no interest in reliving.

I did notice him from the stage his first time in the club. And that only happened because Lucky and I had begun to fall out and weren't as focused on each other as usual. After the dance, he chased her down, and I went about my moneymaking business. But within fifteen minutes he was interrupting my time with a different customer, asking if he could be next. I told him I'd already committed to a handful of others, but I would try and get to him when I was done. "If I don't, rain check for the next time you come in, okay?"

I'm still not sure when that next time was because I was out sick for a while after that night. But by the time I saw him again, the rain check was moot because he'd taken to someone else.

Seeing him last night after talking to Damaris's little boo thang (I guess?) brought up some shit I try to keep buried. But there it is, staring me in the face and grinning like a toothless crackhead. Not giving a single fuck about whether or not I want to deal with it.

I take in another deep pull from the cigarette—*so* disgusting—and blow the smoke out my cracked car window. I chose this brand, American Spirit, because the word *organic* on the packaging made me feel a little less guilty for lighting up. But it ain't doing a damn thing to calm my nerves.

The ironic part is that my reason for quitting all those years ago now feels like my reason for starting again: Felice Jade Carothers.

I take another drag and stare out the windshield.

I'm parked outside the Purple Unicorn: a squat, black-painted brick building that stands out from its run-down surroundings. The next lot over has a multi-business strip: a liquor store, a pawn shop, a beauty supply store, and a vegan café—all with metal netting over the windows—and directly across the street is a "paid parking" lot that looks like it could be an impound.

Almost two years ago I came here with Felice. Boom Town got slapped with a health code violation—cook blamed it on "them stankin'-ass chitterlings y'all had me in here making for Juneteenth." Club got shut down for a week, so Felice, lemons-to-lemonader that she was, decided she and I should "explore some other erotic dance establishments" with the free time. We started here because of the goofy-ass name. "I bet it's a tawdry shitshow inside," she said as we parked, excitement twinkling in her big brown eyes.

She was right. Not only did the musty interior give the feel of walking into a disco porn scene from 1973—complete with mirror ball—the place reeked of cigarette smoke, hair spray, and unreached potential.

And that was before we saw the dancers.

The front door to the place opens, pulling me back into the present, and a raggedy-looking white woman with a flower tattooed on her face steps into the sun.

Daisy.

When she reaches her car, instead of getting in, she leans against the driver's side and lights a cigarette.

I frown at the pack in my cup holder.

When Daisy took the stage after being announced all those years ago, Felice had spit out some of her drink. In addition to having skin the color and texture of a reused paper lunch bag—"Tanning bed much?" Felice whispered in my ear—the woman looked like her bones were sloppily draped in vegan leather, and she "danced" like her joints needed WD-40.

It's wild to see her now.

After Daisy's (terrible) set, Felice had taken my hand, led me into a corner with empty chairs, and given me a show of my own. I'd seen her dance before, obviously: we'd been practicing and performing together for a few months by that point. But with the full force of her . . . *Feliceness* aimed at me, I started feeling things for her that I'd never felt before. For anyone.

It caught me by surprise at first, the fluttery-gutted lightheadedness taking me over. And it wasn't just her body. We'd gotten close over the handful of months we'd been dancing together, and there was a sense of safety I felt with her that was new to me as well. She truly cared for me, Felice did.

When the tacky-ass song ended ("Pour Some Sugar On Me"),

Felice knelt between my legs, leaned in close, and asked, "So how'd I do, Hot Girl?"

And I kissed her.

It took me a minute to get *and* admit it, but the way I felt about Felice scared the shit out of me. Trusting people had never come easy, and I had no idea how to accept that she could *see* me for real, flaws and all. But still wanted to love me.

So, I threw it all away. A couple months into our little love affair, Bones caught wind of "some funny shit going on between y'all"—there was a strict "no fraternizing" policy at Boom Town. And I took the out.

A few days later, I got sick for the first time—sore throat, fever, a left breast that was swollen, warm, and hurt to touch. But that was just the tip of the iceberg. I eventually wound up being out for seven months. And by the time I came back, Felice was gone.

My phone rings.

"Hello?"

"Your girl ain't coming back, Lyriq," comes Bones's voice through the receiver.

Heat spreads through my (breastless) chest like an overturned glass of liquor. "Huh?"

"Charm. We gotta cut our losses. Whatchu wanna do?"

Crawl into a dark closet somewhere and dissolve into the carpet, is what I'm thinking as I stare at the Unicorn's purple doors.

I pull more mentholated poison in deep and blow out the smoke, not bothering to turn towards the cracked window this time.

This puff centers me. "I'll be there in thirty minutes," I say into the phone. "Go ahead and cut the lock off her locker."

"**THIS SHIT MIGHT BE CURSED.**" Bones is hovering over me as I take Damaris's meager belongings out of locker #22 and toss them in the reuseable Trader Joe's bag I pulled out my trunk. "I'm surprised you gave her that one."

His tone is giving *passive aggression*, and the shit is irritating. "It's just a locker, B."

"Yeah, all right. If you say so."

Guapa said something similar when I tied a *Congratulations!* balloon to the handle of this locker on the day we told Damaris she'd been added to the schedule: "Wow, you're giving the little weirdo Lucky's old digs?"

"It's an empty metal compartment, not a home nor a headline set," I fired back.

"I'm gonna get rid of this stuff," I say to Bones now, shutting the door with a *clang* and hanging the bag from my shoulder.

He doesn't reply.

"Okay, then." I take a step towards the exit, but then he grabs my T-shirt from behind, hooks an arm around my waist, and pulls me back into him.

"You good?" He licks my neck.

The words—and the warm breath attached to them—ghost over my collarbone in a way that would usually get my juices flowing. Which I hated but also loved: it was both terrible and titillating to be the object of Bones's desire. At just about any other time, moments like these would lead to me being bent over the desk with one of his hands over my mouth to keep me quiet and the other one holding both of my wrists behind me as he rails me from behind.

Not today, though. Today, I want to get the hell out of here.

"I'm good." I wiggle free from Bones's grip. "Be back in a few hours."

I'M NOT SURE why I decide to rifle through Damaris's things. It would make more sense to reach out to Tink. Let her know her baby cousin stopped showing up for work and had to be let go, then drop off the stuff she left behind.

But I can't stop thinking about the boy. Well . . . *young man*, technically. Dejuan. How innocent he seemed and how concerned he was about Damaris. It couldn't be denied that the dummy had caught feelings for the girl. And as he clearly hadn't met her in the club, he was proof that Ballerina Barbie had other shit going on.

Just like Felice did.

Once safely inside my condo, I dump the bag with Damaris's stuff on my bed. There's a small pouch of basic cosmetics—foundation, powder, blush, black liquid eyeliner, mascara, and clear lip gloss—as well as a comb, a Denman brush, an old toothbrush, a mini jar of edge control, a handful of hair elastics, and a pack of bobby pins.

A tin of spearmint Altoids. A little drawstring sack with three crystals inside: carnelian, citrine, and fire agate (seems the girl was looking to feel empowered). And rounding it all out, a pair of well-worn sweatpants. And that's it.

Wildly disappointed by the lack of *anything* juicy—had Damaris really been *that* green?—I start putting everything back like it was.

But as I'm refolding the pants, I see a lump in one of the pockets. It's a small leather coin purse. Inside are a few quarters, a bracelet with two charms (a heart and a cross), a folded piece of paper with handwritten instructions for using a washer and dryer (Did she *really* need these?), and a pair of photos, laminated together back-to-back.

On one side is Damaris at maybe ten or eleven, standing in front of a man and woman I'm guessing are her parents. They're dressed in their Sunday best and posted up beneath a *Happy Easter!* sign.

Basic.

The flip side, however, makes my eyebrows rise. It's Damaris again, but at fifteen or sixteen. Smiling like the damn Kool-Aid Man and holding the arm of a white dude who is definitely older than her. Maybe early twenties.

Could be just because of where my head is at, but the dude in the photo reminds me a smidge too much of Thomas McIntyre.

I put the picture pair back where I found them and decide to check the other pocket.

There's a rubber-banded stack of business cards.

This isn't odd in the least. Many of the men who come in during the day shift do this thing where they include a business card when they give a dancer a wad of money. Felice used to comment on how "self-incriminating" it seemed. (She was such a smarty pants.)

Most of the girls I know—myself included—would toss the cards.

But not Damaris (because of course not).

In fact, Damaris had built quite the collection during her two-and-a-half months onstage. And as I flip through them, I can't help but be impressed by the variety—there are a few attorneys, a residential *and* a commercial real estate broker, a private practice chiropractor, a pediatric orthopedist, a veterinarian, three general contractors, an insurance agent, a certified financial and estate planner, a restaurateur, and the CEO of a chain of coworking spaces.

There's only one that gives me pause. It's got glossy black lettering against a matte-black background, and there's no business or occupation listed. Just a number handwritten in black Sharpie on one side, and a name on the other.

Thomas J. McIntyre.

A highlight reel from one of my worst nightmares clicks on in my mind: Felice laughing and dancing; Felice popping a wandering hand; Felice being pulled into a lap; Felice trying to move two paws from places on her body they weren't supposed to be; Felice looking panicked; Felice crying; Felice saying stop; Felice pinned down; Felice going quiet . . .

Before I can think too much about it, I go into my closet, open a tall cabinet, pull a box down from a high shelf, and carry it back to the bed. *FELICE* is scrawled across the top.

Despite being the person who emptied locker #22 once I came back and learned she was gone, I've never taken the time (read: had the courage) to see what's inside.

Thomas's card in Charm's belongings, though?

That changes things.

I close my eyes and take a deep breath.

Then I open the box.

BEFORE

Lucky

TWO WEEKS. THAT'S HOW long it took T to return to the club to collect on his "rain check" dance from Micah. Which was essentially a lifetime: the number of visitors who flowed through Boom Town on any *single* night was more than a dancer could keep track of.

But I'd been deliberately keeping track. In fact: I hadn't been able to stop thinking about the self-important white man (within the walls of the club at least) since I walked away from him. I checked for him nightly.

Though I wasn't sure why. Definitely wasn't attraction. Not in the traditional sense at least. I rarely felt attracted to men. In fact, the only dude who'd ever truly gotten my motor running had been the super sweet one who changed my life at fifteen. And that whole thing only happened because I'd been so caught off guard by the way the sight of him and the sound of his voice melted all the tension from my muscles.

Unfortunately, the fact that I *couldn't* figure out how or why T had grabbed my curiosity by the throat and pinned it down just made me that much more anxious to get eyes on him again. I only knew about the "rain check" Micah offered—which hadn't been a real thing; she was just trying to get rid of him without bruising his ego (a gift I didn't have when it came to men)—because I overheard her mention it to Shyne in the locker room as we all got ready to leave that night.

When I saw him two Town Hall Tuesdays later, I almost broke my damn neck. Literally. I was in the thick of a slow-spinning inverted descent from the top of the pole on the center stage when he stepped right in front of my anchor spot—the green neon sign behind the bar of a woman bent over at the waist with her skirt up; it was the only thing bright enough to keep me from getting dizzy. The sight of *him* startled me so bad, my muscles went slack just long enough for me to lose my grip on the pole.

I dropped.

Barely caught myself in enough time to flip off backwards and land in a split.

Of course, the crowd went apeshit.

As Astro closed out the set and I made my way offstage, I kept an eye on T. What grabbed me this time was his face: all traces of cool, calm, collected, confident, and cavalier were gone. He looked, I knew from a myriad of experiences both positive and negative, like a man with an objective that required immediate fulfillment.

He made his way towards the bar the same way he'd done two weeks prior, but this time, his head was on a swivel. He was so distracted, he didn't notice the dancer who'd stepped into his path—Marvel, a deliciously thick and glistening, amber-skinned new addition to the night roster—until he literally crashed into her. One of her ankles rolled, which sent the other one wobbling, and within half a second, Marvel looked like she was doing some strange boogie-down dance as she fought to stay upright.

Which worked out in my favor: the mini commotion and subsequent move to a less crowded part of the club—near one of the side stages—provided just enough time for me to get within listening range without being spotted.

"Whoa," T said, putting a hand on his forehead. "Are you all right?"

"Yeah, I'm fine." Marvel adjusted her bikini top—which barely covered her nipples—and shifted the sides of her G-string up higher on her hips. "You were looking a little lost . . . just wanted to make sure you found what you're after." She gave him a once-over and licked her plump bottom lip.

I rolled my eyes. You could always tell a *new* Boomer Baddie by the magnitude of thirst she displayed. Had to stop myself from yelling, "Let 'em come to *you*, honey!"

"I was looking for Lyriq, I believe her name is. She and I have a prior arrangement."

If Marvel was annoyed—and I presumed she was: the most frequent complaint from new nighttime girls who'd been dancing for years and worked their asses off to get hired at Boom Town was that they "couldn't compete with the website girls": those of us who'd been working *here* for years and were featured on the homepage—she hid it well. "Ah, I see," she said. "Unfortunately, Lyriq isn't in tonight—"

"When will she be back?"

His question set me on edge. Micah had been out for six days at that point, and I'd resisted reaching out again after she said, "You can't help me, but thanks," when I called on day two. Nobody knew what was going on with her but Bones, and I certainly couldn't ask that asshole anything.

I hated how unsettled I felt all of a sudden. It was knocking me off my game.

Marvel's voice pulled me back to where my feet were planted. "Really wish I knew, sugar." She took a step closer to T. "But as she's not here, and you and I both are—"

I couldn't take it anymore. "Hey, Marvel, baby?" I stepped out of the shadows. "There's a man in a green baseball cap searching for you high and low." I leaned closer and lowered my voice. "And he look like he got *money*, honey."

"Oh!" Her eyes went wide and hungry, and her whole demeanor changed. *There* was the bad bitch Bones hired. "Hope you find what you're looking for, Saltshaker!" she said over her shoulder to T as she sauntered away, booty bouncing like a slow-motion drumroll.

When I turned back, T was smirking at me. "That was the best you could do?"

So, we were going there already. "Excuse me?"

"'A man in a green baseball cap'? You could've at least given her a shirt color too."

I didn't know how to respond to that.

"Glad you rescued me, though." He shoved his hands in his pockets and lifted his chin.

"Excuse—?"

"You already said that. You're excused."

And I was done. In all my wondering about him, I'd *clearly* forgotten the smugness. I turned to walk away. "I hope you have a good night, *T—*"

"Ah, so you *do* remember," he said. "I was right, then."

I whipped back around. "What the hell are you talking about?"

He stood up tall and clasped his hands in front of him. "There is no man in a green baseball cap, Lucky," he said. "And if there was, somebody else would've come to tell her. You're far too important in this place to be playing messenger."

I couldn't come up with a damn thing to say.

"So, you wanted to get me alone, then?" he went on.

"Oh, fuck all the way off."

He laughed.

I glared at him and crossed my arms.

"I mean . . ." He gestured behind him to an empty chair. "We are *here* now, aren't we? What do you say?"

As he looked me over head to toe and bit his lip, I stared at the face I'd spent two weeks searching for in each new nighttime crowd.

Arrogant son of a bitch.

"Game on," I said.

Within ninety seconds, good ol' T was putty in my hands. "Jesus Christ," he breathed as I wound my hips in front of him. "You are *immaculate*."

I draped my bikini top around his neck and grinned when those green eyes lit up like the club's spotlights at the sight of what was beneath it. I'd been a perfectly perky D-cup with "Hershey's Kiss" nipples since my second year of college.

It felt good to hold a man by the balls without touching him. So, I got into my groove. The sensation of his eyes waltzing over my curves was the perfect fuel. With him staring at me, slack-jawed, I fixed my awareness on the soles of my feet and allowed the pulse of the beat to push up into my legs and hips and torso and shoulders until it took me over.

I'd just slipped off my G-string and was bent over, making it clap in his face, when he spoke.

"So, where's your friend?"

It snatched me back to earth with so much force, I stopped moving and turned around.

His eyebrows rose. "Sore subject?"

"Not sure what you mean." The clapping resumed.

"Lyriq," he said (as I figured he would). "Aren't you two supposed to dance together on 'Town Hall Tuesdays'? Keep the club going up?"

I bent deeper. Grabbed my ankles and lifted my chin so he wouldn't see me roll my eyes. "My god, you are corny."

He laughed again. "Seriously, though, what gives? Where's your partner?"

"She's not my partner."

"Turn back around, please. Your ass is beautiful, but I'd really like to look at your face."

But I didn't want to. At all. Not that he could've known, but the mention of Lyriq and her conspicuous absence—*while* I was naked and actively dancing—had not only killed the vibe . . . It'd poked an open wound with a filthy fingertip and filled it with bacteria.

I forced myself to comply. (Had to get paid, right?)

"How many songs do I get?" he asked.

"What?"

"With you," he replied. "How many songs do I get?"

"Oh. Two."

He looked me in the eye. "Let's double it."

"Huh?"

"I'd like four songs. Beginning with the next one."

I leaned in so close, I was sure he could feel my breath on his lips. The Micah questions knocked me off my square, but I was determined to get back on it. She didn't deserve that sort of power over me. "Not sure I can give you four songs, T," I purred. "Can't spend too much time with one client or the other ones get jealous. Boss doesn't like that."

It wasn't true at all: to Bones, money was money. But I knew I needed to get *away* from this man to fully regroup.

"What happened between you and Lyriq?" he said then.

And I stopped. Completely. "Listen, Mr. . . . ."

"McIntyre," he filled in. "Thomas McIntyre."

"Cool." I was livid. "I mean you no disrespect, but I'm here to dance. This Barbara Walters interview isn't part of the package."

Which, again, wasn't true. Yeah, the men—and sometimes women—who came into Boom Town wanted to see asses, titties, and labia. But a lot of them also wanted to talk. About themselves, mostly, but many were genuinely curious about the women making their dicks hard (and/or pussies wet) with minimal contact.

I just wasn't in the mood.

The first song ended, and a new one began. "I would like four songs, please," Thomas repeated.

"I—"

"And I'd really like for you to re-dress and start over. You may remove your top, but please keep your panties on for the duration."

I let the fight drain out of me. "As you wish."

I held it together and did my thing through Astro's "throwback track"—"Bad and Boujee" by Migos. It was the perfect song to get lost in.

But when Rihanna's "Skin" came pouring out next, I could feel little fissures snaking through my composure. Micah and I had done a number of filthy things to each other's bodies with this song playing in the background . . . on repeat.

I still managed.

The third track, though, "Mind Numb," by a guy who called himself Toby Diesel—it leapt to the top of the Hot Hip-Hop chart two weeks after Astro chose it for the Town Hall Tuesday spotlight—blasted the vault inside me the rest of the way open. As the lyrics filled my head and the beat pulsed over my skin in waves, bursts of memory overtook me.

The way she move—

A flash of full lips and a perfect smile before the sting of teeth against the skin of my throat.

It blow my brain—

Warm, freckled flesh dimpling beneath the pointed tips of my shamrock-green fingernails.

I can't see sense—

Eyes the golden brown of tree sap popping wide above flushed cheeks on a sharp intake of breath.

Logic in chains—

A sharp tug at the roots of my hair and a silent scream from my scalp as my head drops back.

Feel like she love me—

Burning breath and a gorgeous mouth tracing wet kisses down the center of my chest.

I'm overcome—

A dress strap ripped as bodies flip, revealing the firm, brown peak of a perfect, paler-skinned mound.

No words, no reason—

Slick, soft warmth enveloping my fingertips, and a shin scar vanishing from sight as knees drop wide.

Got my mind numb . . .

An earthquake against a tongue and an instant tsunami—

A hand wrapped around my wrist, snapping me back, and T's face swam into focus beneath me. I was fully straddling his lap.

And he looked nervous. "Are you okay?"

Was I okay? (The hell kind of question was that?) "What do you mean?"

"You're crying," he replied.

Once his words set in, I touched my face. It was wet with tears.

"Oh my god. I'm so sorry." I got up too fast and stumbled. He reached out to steady me, but I pushed his hand away. "I, umm . . . I need to . . ."

It was too much. Micah's absence. The fight we'd had. Not knowing what was going on with her . . .

All too much.

I had to get out of there.

"I need to go." I made a beeline for the side door that was miraculously nearby. It would spit me out next to the dumpsters, but I didn't care.

"At least let me pay—"

The door clicked shut behind me, trapping the rest of his sentence inside the building. Fall was settling over Atlanta, and I couldn't have been more relieved as the cool, night air caressed my face.

I dropped into a squat with my back against the building. Thankful that the music inside was too loud for anyone to hear me scream.

WEDNESDAY, MAY 28

Lyriq

THE PHONE NUMBERS ARE different. Even down to the area code. Which seems like it shouldn't be a big deal—there has to be at least a year-and-a-half of space between when the two cards were handed out.

But something about Thomas McIntyre giving Damaris a different number than he gave Felice hooks itself on the rope of my red-flag meter and raises that shit to the top of the stripper pole.

Today was Damaris's third no call/no show. Now I can't stop looking at the damn cards. Even now, I'm standing in front of "cursed" locker #22, staring back and forth between them.

I'm irritated as fuck about not being able to let the shit go— definitely the only person in *this* building who seems to care about Damaris's absences at this point. But: finding a card in Felice's stuff that was near identical to the one in Damaris's . . . And mere days after Damaris stopped showing up for work and the supplier of said cards *poofed* back from what I *hoped* had been the nastiest pit of hell?

Whole thing slapped me into a memory: couple weeks after the Purple Unicorn field trip, I came home from an extra shift and found Felice in my bed, wearing nothing but reading glasses. She had her face in a James Bond book that looked very old. "Oh my god, listen to this," she said (as though there was nothing strange about going to someone's condo, stripping down, and getting in their bed to read naked without telling them?). "*'Once is happenstance. Twice is coincidence. The third time, it's enemy action.'* Doesn't that give you a chill??" And she shuddered like she was cold.

That was the thing about Felice: she was smart as hell and would get this fire in her eyes when some intellectual shit excited her. I didn't always love how she was always trying to get me to think about things I didn't want to, but there was no denying the sexiness of her mind. So, I took my own clothes off and climbed in beside her. "I'll show you enemy action," I said before disappearing beneath the comforter to go to work. And yes, it was a lame line—the one thing I've never had is game—but it didn't matter: within a minute, the book had hit the floor, and she was holding my head with both hands and grinding against my open mouth.

Anyway, enemy action: while the matching-card thing is definitely suspect, what's *really* bugging me is the fact that Thomas McIntyre snaked his way back into *my* place of employment without me knowing. For Damaris to have the thing at all suggests that she danced for him. And as her last known day at work was Friday, that was the *latest* they could've met.

How long had he been coming up in here again?

I'm obviously not in the building 24/7, but realizing he could've been moving in and out of it for months without my knowledge makes me feel like the world has flipped upside down. I can't remember the last time I was inside the club during the day shift for longer than a few minutes, but still: If that country club sewer rat had returned from the dead, wouldn't I have known it? I could've warned Damaris—

"Whatcha got there?"

Bones's voice knocks me out of my thoughts, and as aggravating as he can be, I'm thankful. There's a hole in my memory from last night: one minute, I was holding the cards side by side at eye level, and the next, I was sitting upright on the floor with them near my feet.

It'd been a long time since I passed out like that. Happened pretty regularly during chemo. But now, so long as I stay rested-up, well-hydrated, and moderately unbothered, I stay standing.

Or at least I *did*. The fact that some damn *business cards* took me there is . . . I don't even wanna think about it.

"Nothing important." I stuff the little death rectangles (at least that's how they feel to me) into the kangaroo pocket of my hoodie, then spin and kiss Bones. "Ready for a great night?"

"Whoa now, you can't be kissing me on the mouth in public," he says. Because of course he does. "We got a business to run in this hoe. You know how I feel about blurred lines between—"

"'Pussy for paper and pussy for pleasure.'" *Though wasn't this motherfucker licking my neck in this exact spot just yesterday?* It's a fight to keep my eyes from rolling.

"All right, then. Take that raggedy-ass sweatshirt off and get ready to hit the floor. Keep them bitches in line."

He walks away.

And I exhale. Last thing I need is Bones asking questions. Especially not tonight. Tonight I plan to have a chat with "Thomas J. McIntyre." Who has come in every night since Damaris went M.I.A.

Coincidence? Maybe. But I won't be able to let it go until I know for sure.

I hear voices in the hallway and pull myself together. Need to ask the other dancers if they've heard anything from—or about—Charm, but I can't give the impression that I'm in the dark.

The dressing room door opens, and in walk Guapa, Knight, and Lush. Lush, a new-ish, young-ish Boomer Baddie (like twenty-three) with a figure that explains her stage name and skin the same golden-brown as the violin I played in middle school (and then smashed to pieces when my mama got fed up and took herself out), has fully been welcomed into the fold by the veteran dancers.

It makes me smile.

"The hell you grinnin' at, Mellow Yellow?" Knight says, giving me a (mostly) playful shove. She didn't love that I'd gone from headliner to dance manager and she officially had to answer to me.

"Oh, fuck off, bitch," I reply.

"Ooh, I'm calling the Better Business Bureau!" Guapa, now nude from the waist down, folds the sweatpants she just took off and shoves them in her locker. "You not supposed to talk to your *subordinates* with such *disparagement*—"

"Can you even *spell* them words you throwin' around like that wagon you draggin'?" from Knight.

"Oh my god, why do you sound like a two-bit rap aspirant?" Lush cuts in.

"Ahh, I get it now, Guap!" Knight replies. "You been hanging out with SAT-Prep over here! Done got cute with the *vernacular* and shit!"

"Excuse you, it's G-R-E," from Lush. "And I intend to ace it, thank you *very* damn much. Master's degree, here I come!"

I drop my eyes. Another random reminder of Felice.

"You know, Lucky had a master's degree," Knight says.

My head snaps up. *Is this bitch reading my mind?*

"In *education*, of all things," Knight continues.

Guapa: "That's riiiiight! I remember when she told me she only stayed working here because teacher salaries were a joke in comparison."

"Hear that, Lush doll? All that schooling shit for what?" Knight. "You know men only wanna pay women if they can get themselves off on what we're doing."

"It's the pessimism for me," Lush replies.

Guapa: "I mean, she not really wrong, though."

Lush: "What you think, Boss Lady?"

Takes me a sec to realize she's talking to me. "Huh?"

"The education thing," she says. "Is it worth it?"

All that goddamn money spent on fancy degrees, and I still make more shaking my bare ass for a living. The fuck is wrong with this world?

The memory grabs me by the throat and squeezes tight. Felice and I were in bed together after a super fucked-up night at work when a celebrity visitor made his entire entourage masturbate while we Lovely Ladies performed for them in a VIP suite. Whole room smelled like baby oil.

Felice cried in my arms before we shared a long, hot bath in my condo's claw-foot tub.

I couldn't answer Lush's question right now if I tried.

"You young ones be a lil too bright-eyed and bushy-tailed for me, Lushy Poo," Knight says. "Not tryna kill your dreams but—"

"Oh, speaking of young ones!" Guapa turns to me as she adjusts the grass-green top that's basically a set of pasties attached to strings. "Word around the pole is that your little protégé couldn't take the heat!"

"Ooh, teeeeea!" from Lush (of course). "Spill, spill, spill!"

"I mean, it's not exactly *hot* anymore," Guapa goes on. "But *allegedly* some dirty old man made a comment about how young she looked and how much he liked it. Threw her little ass into a tailspin."

"Honey, we all knew that girl wasn't really 'bout this life," comes a new voice. Marvel has entered the room (and apparently the chat). The addition couldn't be more perfect: she does day shifts three times per week. "She was talented for sure, but it was clear as the sky is high that she wasn't gonna last long."

"She doesn't have the *range*." Knight mimics the voice of a grumpy old lady.

Everyone laughs.

"To be honest, I'm glad she stopped showing up," Marvel. "That split personality thing she had going on was exhausting."

Lush: "Split personality? Girl, what?"

"Yessss, I picked up on that too!" Knight adds. "Like she would pop her shit onstage, but then go cry in the bathroom."

"*I* think that white man got in her head," Marvel jumps back in—

And I've had enough. "Okay, okay!" I clap twice. "Not to shit on the 'spill' shindig or whatever, but I need your pretty heads in the game. Rumor has it there might be a celebrity visitor tonight—"

Works like magic: they all scramble to get ready.

Which I take as my chance to dip. I'm hot now, and I know my skin is turning red. This is the *last* place I can lose my composure.

Someone grabs my wrist as I open the door.

Guapa. "Won't say I told you so."

I clench my jaw to keep from swinging on her. On the list of shit I hate the most, being grabbed like that is at the top. Catching me by the shirt is one thing, but my wrists? Gotta take a deep breath to recenter. "You just did, hoe-bag."

I snatch away and escape into the hall.

———

THOMAS DOESN'T SHOW.

The moment I'm in my car with the door closed, I grab that box of "organic" menthols I should've thrown away.

I think that white man got in her head.

The first time I saw Felice with Thomas was the night of our supposed "comeback." It wound up being our last dance together.

After a spat following a near catastrophe during a shared spin move on the pole, I'd gone looking for Felice to apologize. But seeing her bent over in front of Thomas—who she clearly had a vibe with . . . a sore reminder that she and I were done—broke something inside me. Especially since he was gazing into her glory hole like it was a goddamn kaleidoscope. I knew from experience that it was glistening.

I left early that night.

I think that white man got in her head.

The one time I broke down and asked someone if they knew anything about where Felice had gone, the girl said Lucky had "fallen in love" with one of her regulars. "One day he stopped showing up, and she got real sluggish, like her battery was dying. Looked like her luck had ran *out*, chile."

I never brought it up again. To anyone. Bones made it clear that Felice called to say she wasn't coming back. So that was that.

Damaris's ass wasn't ready, and Felice left while I was out.

Both women were gone because they *chose* to be.

Right?

Still, though . . . When I get to my condo, I head straight to the closet and pull down the Felice box. There's an old flip phone and charger inside it. One I purposely ignored when going through it yesterday.

I plug it in and put it down on my bedside table, and while I'm getting ready for bed, it powers on.

There's still cell service.

Even wilder: there are a slew of numbers in the call log and texts, but only one saved contact—*Jeff*.

I open that text thread and instantly see *Felice* in several of the incoming messages. Whoever *Jeff* was, he knew her outside the club.

The last text in the thread is outgoing:

Just found out I'm pregnant.

I read it again. And a third time. And a fourth.

There's no way in hell . . .

On a whim, I open Jeff's contact info and pull out the pair of Thomas's business cards. Breath held, I flip the Lucky one—marked by a hole I poked in the top right corner with a safety pin—to see if the numbers match.

They don't.

Neither does the number on the back of the other card.

My vision goes fuzzy.

Lucky was *pregnant*? And who the hell was *Jeff*?

How much else do I not know?

As possibilities fill my head like popcorn, my vision goes dark at the edges.

A Bible inside Felice's box is the last thing I see.

BEFORE

Lucky

SOLID REFLEXES, HALF A SECOND, and a literal inch: a combination of miracles that would go down in Boom Town history as "the Lucky trinity."

Because in the middle of *The Lovely Ladies' Raging Reunion* headline show, which we rehearsed extensively for, Micah flubbed a shared pole trick, and the six-inch heel of her green platform stiletto came terrifyingly close to impaling me through the eye.

It would be the nail in the coffin of our . . . dealings with one another.

Even if I'd been willing to forgive the bitch for the grossly dismissive way she acted when Bones asked about our "*extravocational relationship*" (fool stayed making words up), Micah's iciness towards me when she returned to work—after being out for ten days (not that I was counting . . .)—was something I valued my*self* too much accept.

And now she'd tried to end my life?

I knew as soon as the set was over that it had been the last time we would ever dance together. Did I also know that the sudden threat to my eyesight hadn't been deliberate? Of course. But it was easier to digest *She hates me and wants me dead* than it was to face the truth: the woman I'd stupidly fallen for no longer loved me. If she'd ever loved me at all.

And I was pissed.

As we exited the stage, adrenaline still humming in my veins from the brush with death-by-stripper-heel, I could feel my rage rising. So, I clenched my teeth to hold the flames in.

But then Micah spoke: "Certainly not the best set *we've* ever done, but the floor is packed, so Imma make *me* some money tonight—"

I grabbed her upper arm and yanked her into the dark mouth of the hallway to the locker room.

"Oww! What the fuck—"

"That *set*," I hissed, shoving her into the wall, "was the most terrifying seven minutes of my *life*. Your sloppiness almost cost me a goddamn *eye*!"

Micah drew back. For half a blink, she *almost* looked stung. But then her face closed down like a metal security gate. "Bitch, who the fuck you think you talking to?"

"I'm talking to *you*, Micah!" Six weeks of pent-up hurt boiled over. I leaned in so close I could feel her breath on my lips. "There was no *we* anywhere in that set. Only a *you*. As usual. *I* just cease to exist once you're sick of me. Out of sight, out of mind, out of heart. That's how you prefer things, right?"

Micah's eyes narrowed . . . but when she opened her mouth to respond, a look of terror washed over her face, and she gasped.

I looked over my shoulder, but no one was there. When I turned back, there were tears in her eyes. All my fury dropped away. "Micah, what's going on with you?"

Her eyes went cold. "Other than being called *sloppy*, I'm fine, thanks."

She stepped around me and headed to the floor.

T found me with a woman in a veil and a *Bride* sash motorboating my breasts as her bridesmaids cheered her on. To say he'd become a regular felt true, but not quite: after that second Town Hall Tuesday visit, he'd come in two more times *that week* and three the following one, but I never, ever approached him. He had to seek me out.

Two songs. Occasionally three if it was a slower night. Perfectly paced out so that by the final half of the final song, I was totally nude. Once it ended, he would watch me re-dress, then hand me a folded stack of crisp bills that I would tuck somewhere in that night's getup to be counted later. (So far, it'd been five hundred dollars per song. Every time.)

I'd kiss him on the cheek and be on my way. And as I sashayed off, he'd call out a day of the week.

When he walked up on *this* night, I couldn't have been more grateful. Though nothing about working in a place like Boom Town was ever predictable, the idea that *something* tonight might go as it typically did was a huge relief.

Or at least I thought it would be.

"You're late, little leprechaun," he said, looking at his watch.

So he was in a mood too. *Wonderful.*

"Awww, come on, Tommy baby," I purred, flipping back into performance mode. "Don't be mad at me—"

"Never call me that again."

The intensity of the rebuff caught me so off guard, I couldn't form a response. Just took a step away from him.

"Ah shit, I'm sorry." He put a hand on his forehead and pushed his hair back. "I didn't mean to snap at you like that."

"Bad memory?" The words were out of my mouth before I could catch them, and I cringed inside as they hit the air. Was it against the rules to learn a thing or two about the lives of the individuals paying me to dance? Of course not. In fact, I often felt like I was providing a form of debauched psychotherapy, based on how perfect strangers poured their guts all over the floor while I took my clothes off.

But T was different, and I knew it. He wasn't like the sad, middle-aged men who'd spent decades working the same meaningless jobs to provide for wives and children they felt didn't appreciate them. He was young and rich and vibrant. He moved through the world in a way that I wanted to be able to.

Which made learning more about him dangerous. Because the more I learned, the more I'd want to know, and the more questions I would have. And if there was one thing I knew from experience, it was that the more interest I showed in who *he* was and what he had going on, the more likely he was to get the wrong idea.

"You could say that," he replied. "Either way, it doesn't have anything to do with *you*. So my reaction was inappropriate. I hope you'll forgive me."

"Lighten up, Buttercup." I slid back into character and took his hand to lead him to a seat. A new song began, and I got to work. "Two songs tonight, yeah?"

"Yeah, sure."

It wasn't his typical response, but I tried to ignore it. Settle into my body and do my thing.

"I saw why you were late," he began.

The idea of me being "late" when there wasn't an agreed-upon time was endlessly aggravating. Especially *that* night. So, I turned around and dropped my ass into his lap, shoving back with more force than usual.

"Whoa," he said.

I shut my eyes and smiled.

But he didn't let up. "I see your friend is back."

"She's not my friend." I unhooked my top. Slipped it off while circling my hips so he wouldn't notice. Worked like a charm every time.

"Well, tell me how you really feel—"

"Nah, I don't think I will." I stood and turned to face him, topless now. His eyes went wide, just as I'd hoped they would. "I can give you something else to focus on, though."

"You two seem really close, is all," he said then.

It was the same way Bones had put it, *You two seem close . . .* "Nah, B, we just dance well together," Micah replied. Which was the *right* answer, considering the circumstances. Any other one would've lost us our jobs. It was the finality with which she'd said it that slid beneath my skin and grew thorns. The statement was as much for me as it was for Bones. And once I saw the tension ease out of his shoulders at Micah's words, I knew.

Bones *wanted* Micah, and despite him being a shitbag she'd complained to *me* about, she was totally into it.

She chose him over me.

"Nah," I said. "We just dance well together. Or at least we used to . . ."

"Yeah, that close call looked pretty scary," T went on. "It was a wild thing to see from a distance."

I body rolled in an attempt to get him to stop talking (it was one of my favorite tricks once I'd heard enough about the dissatisfaction of mediocre living from other clients).

But he didn't. "One second you two were in perfect sync, but then it looked like she got hit with a lightning strike or something. Her eyes went wide and her whole body jerked. It's good you have such great reflexes—"

I stopped dancing and dropped down so we were eye-to-eye. "Are you done?"

For a moment, he just stared. It was a little intimidating, for sure, that bizarre gaze boring into mine. In that moment, the color screamed *envy*. I wondered what all he could see.

But I refused to flinch. Didn't even blink.

Within seconds, his shoulders dropped and he covered his face. "I'm doing the most tonight, aren't I?"

The rhetoric—and the vulnerability attached to it—so surprised me, I burst out laughing.

Who the actual hell was *this guy?*

He sat up straight and again looked me in the eye. "I need to tell you something."

And boy did the alarm bells get to ringing. Which I did *not* have the bandwidth to navigate. I stood and resumed my gyration. "Two-song max tonight, remember? Place is packed."

The first song ended.

"Now down to one."

"Okay, well, sit and talk to me for the last one, then?"

I returned to his lap and leaned my head back against his shoulder before I shook it. "Can't. Optics and all that."

"You're really giving me a hard time tonight, aren't you?"

"I mean, that's certainly the goal." Down to just my green thong, I dropped into a squat before popping my ass into the air. A gluteal round of applause for the white man. "How 'hard' we talkin'?"

"I've been coming to see you so frequently because my wife and I haven't been getting along."

"Ah, you're married?" I hated it, but I was disappointed. His marital status officially matched that of most of my regulars. It knocked off some of his shine.

"Yeah, and I want a baby. But my wife doesn't."

"Tough call, for sure." We were almost at the halfway mark of the second song, which meant it was time for the grand finale. I slid a thumb beneath the snapping waistband of my G-string—

"Wait." He grabbed my hand.

It took everything I had not to snatch away.

"Will you leave that on this time?"

"Oh, we're back to that now?"

"Just this time," he said. And he looked up into my face. "Please."

And so I finished out the dance only topless. Which, on a night as busy as this, made me so conspicuous, I felt more exposed than if I'd been naked.

By the time the song was over, I couldn't have been more ready for the encounter to end. Honestly, just wanted to go home. So, despite it being out of the ordinary, I was relieved when he stood as I was getting dressed and said he had to leave. "Thank you." He held out the usual stack of folded bills.

There was something sticking out of it this time.

A card. Matte black with rounded corners.

Thomas J. McIntyre leapt off the front in glossy letters, but there was no email or occupation. It was the strangest "business" card I'd ever seen.

"Friday," he said.

"Yeah, okay." I flipped the card over as he walked away. It'd been premeditated. Because there, in black Sharpie that barely stood out from the background, he'd handwritten a phone number.

THURSDAY, MAY 29

Lyriq

T. THAT'S THE NAME Felice used in the messages she exchanged with the number on Thomas's card.

And as excited as I got when I typed said number in the search bar, and the thread popped up, the messages themselves were so fucking vanilla, I wanted to flip the folding piece of shit into another dimension.

Speaking of the flip phone, it was apparently the one Felice used exclusively with Boom Town patrons she kept in contact with outside the club. Most of the threads began the same way:

> **Hey! This is Lucky.
> Got you locked in.**

**Awesome! Glad you decided to
actually use the card.** ☺

In many of them, "Lucky" is the only name mentioned, and only in the initial text. And though there are a handful that get explicit,

Felice's responses are so forced, I laugh aloud a few times while scanning through them.

The more I read, the clearer it became: the flip was a burner that little Leecy-Poo used for a sexting side hustle. Whether or not she was charging for the messaging sessions, I couldn't tell... it wasn't like how on a smart phone, someone could send money through text. But it *was* evident that just about all of the message exchanges began after the person on the other end had received at least once dance from Felice at the club. And many of them appeared to be regulars. So even if Felice *wasn't* being paid directly for the smuttier chats, staying engaged with the customers between their visits—thereby keeping the flames of anticipation lit—certainly couldn't've hurt when it came time for her paid dances. **Damn, you really brought it tonight... did what you said you was gon do**, one messenger professed (the previous text from Felice, sent twelve hours earlier, mentioned giving him a dance that would "transport" him "to another dimension"). **Glad I had some extra cash on me cuz you earned that shit.**

Clever little bitch.

Felice and T, though, seemed to have developed a short-lived friendship. Felice made first contact, but barring one additional time, Thomas sparked every other text interaction. He would occasionally make single-line complaints about his wife (and he and Lucky couldn't have gotten *too* close, because he never used the woman's name), then follow with **But not gonna dwell on that** and change the subject. For the most part, everything was super pedestrian. He would reach out **just to say hi** or **check in** to see how she was feeling, or he'd send pictures of random stuff—like a video of a ceiling covered in plants. **Looks like Americano isn't the only place with one of these**, that message read.

Almost three months of going back and forth, and not a lick of anything remotely spicy.

In fact, based on the date their correspondence stopped, I'm pretty sure I know what ended it. That's why I'm currently parked across the street from a condo building in Old Fourth Ward—one with an under-construction ground-floor shop. The sign in the window says *Coming Soon: America the Brewtiful* in big letters over a steaming mug of coffee. (Who comes up with this shit?)

After a sweep through Felice's flip provided no further information regarding Jeff or the pregnancy she mentioned solely to him, and T's texts proved themselves useless as well, I decided to sift through her stuff again.

To my surprise, this time I found a photograph.

It was tucked into a Bible. The one object I did my best not to even touch during previous searches. They creeped me the hell out, Bibles did: people shaping their entire existence around a text written at a completely different time in a completely different part of the world just felt *weird* to me. The Constitution gave me a similar ick.

I forced myself to pick it up and flip through it this time.

It jarred me at first, finding the picture of Felice and me tucked between the thin pages. The photo had been a sort of gift from me to her: after Toby Diesel's "Mind Numb" hit #1, he returned to Boom Town to do a live show. Felice and I danced our asses off that night. The following one, a photographer who'd been in the building returned to give me a print of one of his shots. He'd caught us in our bikinis, holding on to each other and laughing.

As I remembered that night, even though the photo had clearly been balled up and then smoothed out, a strange warmth spread beneath my rib cage at the thought of her carrying the photo with her anywhere she took her Bible . . .

But then I noticed what was highlighted on that page: *The old life is gone; a new life has begun!* And there was a date written beside it.

One that, when cross-checked, led me to a requested meet-up with Thomas in their text thread—the only one they appeared to have outside of work before they stopped communicating.

Looking up at the building now, all I really feel is frustration. No idea what I'd hoped to find at the address "T" sent Felice all that time ago, but being in front of it just brings up more questions I can't answer. There was a grand total of seven messages exchanged on that day: the first was from T on the morning of the rendezvous, resending the address and expressing his excitement about seeing her. Then two from Felice: **Here.** and **Want me to order for you?** Before one more from him: **No thanks. Be there shortly.**

The final three were from Felice. And then they didn't text again until two days later.

What happened in this building? I wonder as I stare at the covered-over windows. Felice mentioned a "chat" in her final message that day, but was that literal or some sort of code word? It was hard to tell in an industry like ours.

It's unnerving as shit, not having any answers. Especially after spending almost a year and a half refusing to ask any questions. What's worse, the one question I can't shake is the one only *I* can answer:

Why hadn't I looked for her?

When I returned to work for good—after half a year of being pumped full of drugs that made me feel like I was halfway to hell and *then* still having to get my titties chopped off—I learned that Felice had been gone for two months. Why hadn't I reached out to make sure she was good? And more importantly, why hadn't I let her *in*? Told her what was going on with me. Allowed her to be the friend I needed and *knew* she wanted to be to me . . .

Why had I shut out the woman who would've done anything for me? Especially at a time when her love and care were what I needed most?

Like... what the hell was *wrong* with me?

Also, why the fuck am I *here*? Felice Jade Carothers is long gone and clearly not coming back. And anyway, there were obviously things she didn't let me in on either. (Like a whole fucking *pregnancy*?? I still can't believe it.)

We had separate lives and different priorities, and there's not a planet in the universe where things could've worked out between us.

So why am I wasting my energy with this?

My phone rings. Bones. "Yeah?"

"Well, hello to you too, MJ."

"Please don't call me that. Is there something I can help you with?"

He doesn't reply immediately, so I know he's going to say I "overstepped tonally." Not now, though: Bones's calls mean business and business only. And I'd really like for this one to end. "You still there?"

"Some kid came in here looking for Charm."

My chest tightens. With both alarm *and* irritation. Can ol' boy not take a hint?

"Guapa tells me it's not the first time."

I roll my eyes. Of course Guapa narc'd. Ol' face-ass, teacher's-pet wannabe. "He tell you his name?"

"His name is irrelevant, Lyriq. Word is, *you* were who he asked for the first time. *And* y'all had a whole conversation that *I* know nothing about."

"The girl decided not to show up, and some lil nigga she was likely fucking came looking for her because she ghosted him. It's a tale as old as time, Bones."

"Well, the 'lil nigga' claims he told *you* he thinks there's something wrong. Also claims *you* said *you* would look into it. Which is why, according to him, he came back today: to see if you'd 'found anything out.' Fuck is going on with this girl, Lyriq?"

My vision goes dark for a second. I was already worked up enough from staring at this under-construction coffee shop with no clue why it matters. Definitely don't need *this* shit on top of it.

I inhale deep and blow it out slow. "There's nothing going on, Bones."

I think that white man got in her head.

Another deep breath. In . . . out. "The girl couldn't handle dancing naked for strange men. She's not the first young bitch to get in over her head by taking a job like this, and she won't be the last."

"*You* hired her, Lyriq."

"Yeah, I'm aware." It's starting to grate, the way Bones keeps emphasizing *you*. "It was a bad hire. They happen. Remember that friend of your cousin's—"

"Don't get off topic. What we're talking about *right now* is the fact that a dancer you put on my roster has vanished. And now it's somebody looking for her, claiming there's something wrong. Which *you* knew but didn't tell me."

I want to yell, but it won't do me any good. For one, Bones is already pissed. Adding fuel to the fire is a no-go. I know that from experience.

For two, what would I even say? I haven't the vaguest idea of why the girl stopped coming to work or where she might be. The easiest thing—*smartest* thing, even—for us to do is presume she stopped showing up because she wanted to and keep it moving. I know from my *own* unfortunate experience of "going missing" in my early twenties that law enforcement won't take something like *this* seriously without undeniable signs of foul play. And there aren't any.

"My apologies. It genuinely didn't feel like anything to tell."

"You need to fix this, Lyriq. Like, immediately. This man's got to talking about filing a missing person's report and reachin' out to her parents, and he slipped up and said she was only nineteen."

I stop breathing.

"Now maybe she'd gagged him, and homie was confused. Why a twenty-one-year-old would lie and say she's *younger* is beyond me, but whatever. My point: what I'm *hoping* is that my dance manager—who I've seen high, low, and in-between and taken care of every step of the way—didn't go a leap *and* bound beyond shitting on my 'minimum two years of experience' policy and also hire a bitch who lawfully can't even *enter* my club, let alone work there."

"The boy got got, Bones. You know I would never do that."

So why is my heart beating so fast?

"I'm not gonna ask any more questions because I don't wanna implicate myself in case some shit goes down. But if there winds up being an investigation and *anything* blows back on this establishment, Imma be on that ass, Lyriq. Like I said: you need to fix this."

I don't respond.

The phone *boops* three times as the call goes dead.

No clue how long I sit, staring at the door to the coming coffee shop with my mind full of static. But at some point, a Black guy comes out. It snatches me back into my body. As he crosses the street to the lot I should've pulled into instead of sitting here at the damn stop sign, looking lost, I lower my window and wave him over.

"Excuse me," I say. "When is that place opening?"

"Another couple of months. New owner wanted the inside gutted and the name changed."

"Damn. *America the Brewtiful* was the best y'all could come up with?"

He laughs. "I think he just wanted to stay on-brand. Old name wasn't great either."

"What was it?"

"The Real Americano."

"Wow. Yeah, definitely worse."

He looks up and past my car to the next intersection over. "That's actually him right there," he says, lifting his chin. "The new owner."

A massive black EV pickup truck hangs a left onto the street, then signals to turn into the parking garage. When it does, I can see the driver.

"Kind of a strange guy. Real intense," the guy continues. "But he's decent. Lives in the building."

One of T's messages to Felice pops into my head. **Looks like Americano isn't the only place with one of these.**

I look back at the café's papered-over windows. Felice and Thomas McIntyre really had been inside that place together.

"*That's* the new owner? The guy in the pickup?"

"Yep," the man says. "Everybody calls him Mr. Mac."

I scowl. I can't help it. "That jumbo truck makes me think he might be overcompensating." I turn back to the man. "Thanks for the info."

"Sure thing." And he continues to his car.

I know I have to do something. I've come this far, and I won't be able to live with myself if I don't. But what pops into my head is outlandish. And there are infinite ways it could go wrong.

I just can't really think of an alternative, considering my limited resources.

This is my only option, and time feels of the essence. So I pull Felice's flip phone out of my purse, tap out a message, then copy, paste, and send it to two different numbers: T's unsaved one from the business card . . . and Jeff's.

Then I toss the damn thing in the glove box. Even if there are immediate replies, it'll be better to wait a bit before checking and responding.

I reach for my cigarettes, but instead of lighting one as I turn onto the street in front of the shop, I lower the passenger window and throw the whole pack out. It lands right in front of the door.

I smile and pull off.

Congrats on your new coffee shop, Thomas McIntyre.

BEFORE

Lucky

I WAS IN TROUBLE, and I fucking knew it. Knew it as well as I knew the weird little café I was in—which had orchestral remixes of early-2000s trap music floating through the air—was owned and operated by queer-friendly, millennial white people. They'd made the top of my cappuccino look like a bird carrying a leafy branch in its beak and offered me raw goat milk yogurt with "farm-to-fork granola." *Made in-house from fresh ingredients purchased at the Old Fourth Ward Farmers Market!*

I looked out at the street through the window at the front of the little café. I'd planted myself in a back corner, as far from the massive panes of floor-to-ceiling glass as possible. People underestimated how frequently an erotic dancer got recognized outside the club. Which was the *last* thing I needed. I'd heard more than enough horror stories about male customers treating dancers different after seeing them in public with other men.

No one could see me with T. Not fully clothed, in broad daylight. It's the only reason I agreed to meet inside a place called the Real

Americano. Which at the moment had a string quartet remake of Project Pat's "Chickenhead" pouring from the ceiling.

Not that I could see the speakers: said ceiling was obscured by a canopy of hanging plants so dense, it created the disorienting impression of being in some sort of repurposed section of a jungle.

This was a terrible idea.

I knew it'd be best not to think too much about any of it . . . which of course meant I was thinking about *all* of it as much as possible: T sharing something deeply personal two visits ago; me breaking my own fourth wall—completely unprompted—and sharing something personal the next time he came in; the idiotic decision to randomly shoot him a text in the middle of the afternoon the next day; him immediately calling, me sending him to voicemail in panic, and then later lying about why I "wasn't able to answer"; him suggesting we *grab a coffee to chat more*; me stupidly saying yes . . .

Then stupidly not canceling.

Then stupidly getting up and dressed two hours before I typically would, so I could navigate my way to the address he sent, with some spare time to change my mind and jet if I didn't like the location (or, you know, came to my senses).

"Fancy meeting you here." The voice—moderately pitched and not the least bit *sexy* by what I understood to be straight-girl standards—hit my thought spiral like a record scratch. How men of *any* echelon managed to get women to like them was beyond me.

"That's the best you could do?" I said.

I was nervous. That was really the only time I got snarky when not working. At work, the snark was a defense mechanism that helped me feel in control. Besides: it was mighty difficult to bruise a man's ego while dancing naked to earn his money.

I wasn't at work, though. And he was staring at me with an expression I couldn't read. Which made it hard to breathe.

(*WHY had I come here??*)

But then: "You look..." and his eyes dropped to my chest. Completely concealed beneath a denim halter midi dress. "Different."

"With clothes on, you mean?"

His eyes went round and his cheeks went red. He peeked over his shoulder, and I remembered: I was sitting with a married man in an establishment *he* chose. There was no telling who else in the space knew him.

"This was a bad idea," I said, reaching for my bag. "I really think I should go."

He caught my hand. Just like the night he told me too much and I began my journey of shit decisions. "Please don't leave."

Now I was the one speechlessly staring.

He snatched his own hand back as though my skin had suddenly burned him. "Shit. Sorry. I didn't mean... I shouldn't've..."

"You good over there?"

He sighed and shook his head. "May I start over?"

All of a sudden, I was sitting with Aerosmith: a wild-haired, green-eyed kindergarten whirlwind I student-taught while working on my master's degree (and yes: that was his real name). Every time he got in trouble (which was often... kid had negative infinity impulse control), he'd be sent to me. And though he couldn't pronounce the *th* in my last name, he'd look up at me with his cute little sad face and say, "Can I have a do-over, Ms. Caruhvers?"

A crack formed in my wall. "Go ahead."

T sat up straighter. "First: thank you. Second: I know this whole meeting-in-regular-life thing is likely unconventional for a woman of your... professional ilk and acclaim—"

"I would hope a rendezvous in a coffee shop with a woman you've seen naked a dozen times despite not knowing her real name is 'unconventional' for you too, sweetheart."

"I— Okay, fair. Really fair, actually."

For a few seconds we just stared at each other.

Then he started laughing.

"What's so funny?"

"I mean, this ridiculous exchange is precisely why I couldn't resist asking you to meet in another setting," he said. "I know you're in character when dancing, but I could *feel*—even based on how you check me—that the real you is a person I need to know."

I couldn't *stand* it, but that sprinkling of sweet talk felt like an Alka-Seltzer *plopped* right into my veins. Especially since the only person around who knew the real me had apparently replaced me with Guapa. Well . . . when she actually showed up for work.

It was nice to feel important.

I sat back and settled in.

"To your point: unconventional is an understatement," I said. "I could lose my job over this. Also: Where even *are* we, beloved?" I gestured around. "You couldn't think of a rendezvous point somebody Black would actually visit?" I threw a sugar cube at him. There'd been two brown ones and two white ones on the saucer with my drink. (Fucking ridiculous.)

"Wow, I *really* like when you call me 'beloved.' "

Not sure what my face did in response to that, but it clearly sent a message.

"Not that I think you *mean* anything by it," he corrected. "It's just that terms of endearment are outside my realm of typical experiences with other human beings."

"Aren't you married?"

His face darkened. "Trust me when I say that doesn't mean a thing."

"Damn. Sorry for bringing it up."

"Don't be. You came." He smiled. "That's worth its weight in gold to me."

"Yeah, my being here doesn't have any measurable weight. So, very cute analogy, but know it's not actually a compliment."

He laughed again.

I liked it, making him laugh. Especially with clothes on. It made me feel *good*. Alive.

Like a person.

I was titillated and terrified simultaneously. Because I still didn't know anything about him . . . but was also wary of learning. It was confusing.

And him gazing at me like I'd invented latte art wasn't helping in the least.

"So, what's the deal?" I asked, discomfort taking over. "You got me here. What is it you wanna do with me?" I didn't realize how sexual the question sounded until it was hanging in the air, but he either didn't pick up on it or chose to ignore.

"I'll be honest with you, Lucky, I hadn't thought that far—"

"Felice." The word had cannonballed off my tongue before I realized it was forming. And there was no way to take it back.

T looked just as, if not *more*, surprised as I was. "That's a beautiful name," he said. "Means a lot that you shared it with me."

He really had no idea. "Well, now I need to know your middle name." I crossed my arms.

"Wait, so then you'll have my first, middle, *and* last name, but I only get one of three from you?"

"That is correct."

He laughed again, then opened his sport coat and pulled an obnoxiously thin wallet from the inner pocket. A driver's license appeared in front of me, and I leaned over to read it.

"You *would* be named for one of America's founding assholes," I said. "And a known slaveholding one at that."

"Couldn't despise it more, if you want the truth. Have to keep it hidden from *everyone* because of the industry I work in."

He wanted me to ask what he did for a living. I knew because they *all* did.

So, I did the opposite. "If you despise it, why not change it? It's a short visit to the courthouse and a fee, right?"

He shrugged. "Guess I always felt like I had bigger fish to fry. What about you, though? How'd you come up with the name Lucky? And what got you into *your* industry?"

Certainly wasn't ready to go *there* yet. "That's a whole novel. And I doubt you have all day." I patted the back of his hand on the table. "Let's stick to you."

"All right then," he said. "What is it you'd like to know?"

"Are you in a Black fraternity?"

He laughed. "You flatter me, but no. I didn't go to college."

Huh. "Okay. Well, tell me more about the frying fish keeping you from a name change."

So he did. He talked about his faltering marriage and wanting a baby and his wife not being who he thought she was—this was when I learned that he'd chosen the Real Americano because he owned a condo in the building above it for times he "needed to get away."

"I, uhhh . . . don't actually drink coffee."

He also talked about his job being stressful and really wanting to walk away but knowing he couldn't. "It'd be like flushing fifteen years of hard work down the toilet."

He talked, and I listened. About his childhood ("mega privileged"), his hopes ("that my wife changes her mind about a kid"), and his ultimate goal ("never having to work again").

By the time his phone rang—his assistant telling him he was late for a meeting—he seemed significantly lighter.

"Man, I *really* hate that I gotta jet so abruptly, but please take it as a compliment that I lost track of time," he told me as he prepped to leave. "It's been a while since I was able to speak freely like that, and I hope I didn't overload you."

"I'm a stripper, T. That dump was mild compared to some of the shit others have told me."

He smiled like it was Christmas. "You're even easier to talk to than I imagined, Felice."

It was that—the use of my given name—that shoved me up and over the summit of a hill I hadn't realized I was climbing. Because when he said it, he was gazing at me in a way that I *knew* meant he'd shifted to some nebulous space beyond platonic in his mind.

I needed to shut it down. Not harshly or in a way that would bruise his ego, but through a strategic dispensation of the truth: he was barking up the wrong tree.

However . . .

Though I had zero interest in fucking Thomas Jefferson McIntyre, there was no denying how good it felt to be treated like a *person*. Especially after the shit Micah's mean ass had put me through.

So, when he rose to his feet, I did too. "I need to get going as well. I'll walk you out."

When we got to the exit, and I reached for the door handle, he caught my hand (again) and told me I was never permitted to touch a door if he was around. I tucked my chin and swallowed my resistance. Interacting with men who insisted on abiding by archaic gender roles was one of my least favorite things on earth—fully capable of opening my own door, thank you very fucking much.

But I let it ride.

We got to my car first, and he opened the door for me. That was fine because it was expected. I did *not* expect him to hug me—far tighter than a friend would—and kiss me on the cheek before letting me get in, but still: I didn't flinch.

"Hit me later, yeah?" He shut the door and walked off without waiting for a response.

I could feel the aggravation tingling in my fingertips and scratching at the back of my throat, desperate to *do* something. Shout, shower, Hulk Smash, scrub his kiss off my face—but then my eyes dropped to my dashboard. There, tucked in the center—smack between the digital speedometer and the other circle that displayed some car shit I didn't understand—was a picture of me and the person I loved more than I could stand.

I was suddenly so enraged, I wanted to lay on the horn and scream. No matter how frequently it happened, being reminded that Micah didn't give a high-flying fuck about me hit like a punch to the throat every single time.

As the tears spilled over, I did scream (though the horn remained untouched). I grabbed the photo, balled it up, and tossed it over my shoulder.

Vision still blurred, I grabbed my little burner flip phone and tapped out a text message (which always took forever without a QWERTY keyboard):

> **Thanks again for the chat.**
> **Hate to admit it, but you're not so bad.** ☺
> **Just realized what day it is, so . . .**
> **guess I'll be seeing you at the club later?**

I snapped the thing shut without waiting for a reply and tossed it onto the passenger seat.

FRIDAY, MAY 30

Lyriq

I GRAB THE WHEEL at ten and two and squeeze with all my might. "Goddammit!" If I could, I'd rip the whole fucking steering column out and toss it onto the highway.

I drop my eyes to the pair of phones in my cup holders. While waiting for a response to either of the messages I sent with the *flip* on the right half an hour ago—neither T nor Jeff replied yesterday—the *smart* one on the left rang with a call from Bones.

Based on the way my stomach flipped itself inside out at the sight of his ridiculous diamond-encrusted grill on the screen, I shouldn't've answered. But of course I did anyway. (Intuition be damned!)

It was *not* a good call. And now I'm *not* in a good place.

My oncologist is going to shit.

The light turns green.

I was forty-seven minutes into the hour-long drive for a checkup when the call came in. "Hello?"

"We got another problem, Lyriq."

Bones was keeping his anger in check. I could hear it in his voice.

"Just got a call from the bank," he said. "They noticed a discrepancy in the deposit Clutch dropped in the overnight box yesterday. Now as *I'm* the person who does the nightly count and shift to the safe, and I'm incredibly diligent with *my* mathematics when it comes to *my* club and *my* ledger and *my* money, as I'm sure *you* can imagine, this call came as quite a shock to me."

I didn't reply.

"Even more shocking was the amount of the discrepancy. Do you know how much it was?"

(*Was that some sort of trick question?*) "Can't say that I do."

"It was ten bands, Lyriq. As in ten *thousand* dollars."

My palms went slick on the steering wheel. Why was this happening *now* of all times?

"Now, I know making weekly deposits instead of daily ones makes me an anomaly in this industry," Bones continued. "I know that. And I'll admit that going through a week's worth of security footage was a pain in my muthafuckin' ass. But you know what I found, Big Dawg?"

My pulse was off the charts by that point. "What'd you find?"

"Last Friday? When that girl was here because *you* talked me into letting her be a Bottle Boomer so she could 'get a feel for what the night crowd is like' as I believe you put it? She somehow wound up in my *locked* office—apparently while I was taking a shit—grabbed a stack of cash from a pile I'd already counted, and slipped right back on out. Any idea how that could've happened, Lyriq?"

I felt like I was underwater. It was *good* that I was flying down the highway because it forced me to keep my eyes open.

I did know how Charm got in the office. I'd *sent* her there—with *my* keys—to grab the clipboard I'd forgotten inside with that night's run of show.

Of course, I hadn't known Bones was in the middle of a count. And he wouldn't have told me. He knew I *never* wanted to know when he was counting.

Even the thought of bills running through a currency counting machine was enough to make my throat close in panic. It conjured horrible memories of the men who used to sell access to my body without compensating me fairly, then would make me watch as they calculated the proceeds.

"I really don't know, Bones," I lied.

"Well, until you figure it out, that money is on your tab," he replied. "Imma suggest that you don't come back up in here without it, you feel me?"

The line went dead.

I shake my head as I turn into the parking lot of the women's health center, and once I'm parked, it feels like the life drains out of me. Of course the day of *this* checkup is when I get news that the little twat who stopped showing up also stole a bunch of money. Of course. I almost don't wanna go in.

I let my head drop back and shut my eyes, and for the second time in three days, a series of images I've spent two years ignoring runs through my head on a loop—Felice dancing; Felice fighting; Felice losing . . .

Except this time there are an extra couple of frames: a folded wad of rubber-banded bills; Felice not responding; a hand grabbing the money; my own guilty face in the mirrored wall of the hallway once out of the room—

The song "Karma" blasts into the air like a gunshot as my phone rings again. I assigned it to the day-shift dancer who'd chosen it as a stage name.

No doubt the girl is calling out of work. It's the only reason they ever call.

"Fuck you, universe," I say, getting out of the car and leaving the phone ringing.

IT WILL NEVER cease to amaze me that a woman I regularly danced naked for—while her man sat right beside her—would wind up saving my life.

Literally.

Felice and I had been dancing together for about a month the first time Kia came into the club. And she was just different. I'd danced for women before, but it wasn't my favorite thing to do. They were always either too timid or too turnt to fully appreciate my hard work. Kia, though? Bitch locked onto me like she was drowning and I was the life preserver. Her attention made me feel powerful in a way I doubt I'll ever understand.

After that first time, on the third Thursday of every month, she would walk in on the arm of her husband—"I prefer to be led," she told me one time—and immediately request to see her "favorite beauty." Besides her constantly lavishing me with compliments about my "immaculate waist-to-hip ratio," "divinely crafted breasts," and "life-savingly lush thighs," we rarely talked while I did my thing.

But it was Kia, a mere two nights after I betrayed Felice more horribly than she would ever know (though I'm clearly paying for it now, thanks to Five-Finger-Discount Damaris), who made me stop dancing the moment my breasts were bare to point out an area of skin she suddenly "didn't like."

At first I wanted to tell the beautiful bitch to fuck all the way off. But then she reached into her twelve-thousand-dollar handbag and handed me a card. First and last one I ever got from a lady.

That's when she went from "Kia" to "Dr. Kia Chamblee, MD-ONC."

Within a few weeks, I would learn *from* Dr. Chamblee that I'd developed "very rare, though extremely aggressive" inflammatory breast cancer and would need to start chemotherapy, get a double mastectomy, and follow both with radiation therapy if I wanted to live to see my twenty-seventh birthday (which was only three months away).

Now, as I hop up onto the examination table in my paper gown, I marvel over just how much my life has changed. It's wild to think that these checkups have made *me* one of Dr. Chamblee's regulars. And even wilder: Kia still sees me topless every time we meet.

It's just that now, nothing in that region is nice to look at.

"Hey, Love Bug!" Dr. Chamblee comes in but stops dead when she sees me. "Wow, girl. You are *red*," she says, shutting the door. "What's going on?" She walks over and takes my chin in her hand to examine my eyes.

It makes me want to cry.

I snatch away instead.

"Ah, one of *those* days, I see. Let's get right to it, then." She turns to the little sink to wash her hands. "Lay on back," she says. "You know the drill."

I do as I'm told. It's not that I don't *want* to talk. Dr. Chamblee is one of the easiest people in the world to talk to. Probably helps that we met while I was working, so there's really nothing for me to hide. But for a cancer doctor—which she told me required "extensive schooling *and* proving oneself to white people over and over again according to standards their ancestors set believing that people like us would never be able to meet them"—to be *so* nonjudgmental? *And* treat me like a person worth saving and caring for? It was too much sometimes.

Also, what could I even say right now? Bones's call is sinking in: Charm stole a bunch of money and *absconded like a thief in the night* as I heard GRE-Prep Lush say once.

And I have to replace it. Which means draining the money I've been saving for—

"So, you ready to talk about reconstruction?" Dr. Chamblee says, opening my paper gown to examine my torso. "Last I checked, you'd found your plastic surgeon of choice, right?"

The questions hit me like a kick to my flat-ass chest and my eyes fill with tears. My "surgeon of choice" was the best of the best of the best . . . and didn't take my insurance.

I'd worked so damn hard to save that money.

As much as I appreciate my status as a *living legend* at the club, and as grateful as I am to be a salaried employee with health coverage and a 401(k), nobody really knows how much *less* money I make as a result of not being able to dance.

Also: I hardly let myself think, let alone *talk*, about what it REALLY felt like to lose my titties. When forced to do my *previous* job, it was the one thing I found I could control: a solid eight times out of ten, I managed to keep a shirt on. Once I transitioned to dancing, knowing so few "clients" had seen my bare breasts gave me just enough of a sense of bodily autonomy to keep me grounded.

But despite only having cancer in the left one (*Lauren*), Dr. Chamblee suggested that it would be safest to take the right one (*Rosalyn*) too.

Tears are flowing free now.

"Oh, honey." She steps away to grab a box of tissues. "Sit your beautiful ass up and let me hug you."

The moment her arms are around me, I unravel. Honestly, if not for the good doctor's own ample bosom to cry into, I'm sure the whole goddamn building would hear my sobs.

It just makes me cry harder.

Like, fine: I did my dirt. There was no denying that. But wasn't losing the one ... well, two parts of my body that made me feel like I belong to *me* punishment enough?

"It's gonna be okay," Dr. Chamblee says, rubbing circles on my back. "This shit sucks and it's hard and I know you've been to the pit of hell—"

Man, she has no fucking idea ...

"—but you *came back*, pretty girl." She takes me by the shoulders and looks me in the eye. "You went to hell, and you came *back*. You're *here*. It's only up now. Okay?"

I grab a few tissues, blow my nose, and wipe my face. Nod.

"Okay, then. Do you want to talk about reconstruction now?"

I shake my head no.

"That's what I figured. Well, as you know, there's no rush. We'll revisit whenever you're ready."

As the checkup goes on and she expresses enthusiasm over how "well" I seem to be doing, I can feel my fire reignite.

Because she's right: I have been to hell and back. And I am still here.

Have I made some mistakes? Of course. Even done some terribly shitty things? Also yes.

But who the hell hasn't?

It was one thing for Damaris to stop showing up to work. I could let that go because it happened all the time. Hell, just a couple of days ago, a (newer, but still) dancer walked out in the middle of her daytime set—topless and in a thong—because a guy in the crowd shouted something that reminded her of her late father.

But for a new employee to take a bunch of money and then *poof!* herself away ... leaving *me* liable? That's something I can't let slide.

Time to find the little bitch.

BEFORE

Lucky

IT'D BEEN SIX WEEKS since my coffee shop rendezvous with T. And despite his persistent requests to "meet and continue the conversation," I'd come to my senses and hadn't seen him outside of work again.

Not that we didn't communicate at all. He came to see me at work that night (and paid me double what he typically did per song—so I gave him three). And then the following afternoon, he texted to tell me he wanted to "shift all communication" to a different number. I saved it in my work phone under an alias so I could tell them apart.

But something just... never felt right. He acted more like a doting courtier than a buddy-ol-pal—lots of telling me I was on his mind and checking on me and asking if I needed anything—and I knew that making *any* space for engagement beyond the walls of the club would unquestionably give him the wrong idea.

But then came the golden kiwis.

I originally went to the Old Fourth Ward Farmers Market that day to re-up on fresh spices. (Very few people knew it, but I was one hell of a cook.) However, community farmers markets are a fucking trap. Hence the green popcorn (with *spirulina*, whatever the hell that was), fresh flowers, half dozen duck eggs, vegan pimento cheese (made from cashews, of all things), whipped shea body butter, and five-pack sampler of roll-on perfume oils. All inside the "handmade" raffia beach bag I bought to carry the shit I hadn't intended to buy.

I was drawn to the fruit stand by the mini watermelons on display. It'd been a while since I had watermelon, and seeing them made me realize how much I missed it. The mini ones were small enough to fit in my new bag, so I figured I'd grab a couple. (See? A trap.)

But when I saw the slender brunette—she was maybe twenty-two at most—doing the selling, I got self-conscious. Back in middle school, when my mama used to pack watermelon chunks in my lunch, a pretty brown-haired bitch just like the one selling the fruit had looked little brown me dead in the face one day and said, "You know that's slave food, right? Aren't you guys supposed to be *free* now or whatever?"

And though I made sure to bring watermelon chunks and eat them in her cunty, pink face every day after that for the rest of the year, when Mama set a heaping bowl of the stuff in front of me on the first day of summer, I'd totally lost my taste for it.

"Omg that *dress!*" fruit-stand girl said. I looked down. I was wearing an off-shoulder mustard sundress with puffed sleeves. "My lord, you are gorgeous!"

It caught me so off guard, all I could do was stare.

"Shit, sorry!" Her cheeks flushed pink. "I hope that wasn't out of line . . ."

"No, no, it's okay," I said, failing to resist the urge to make sure the girl's feelings weren't hurt. "I appreciate the compliment. Just . . . wasn't expecting it."

"Gotcha. Well, it's true." She shrugged.

When I again didn't respond (no clue what'd gotten into me), the girl cleared her throat. "I see your shopping bag there . . . might I interest you in some fruit? Most of it is grown on my family's farms, but I'd be lying if I said it all is."

That made me laugh. "I appreciate the honesty." My eyes flicked to the watermelons, then quickly away. "What, umm . . . do you recommend?"

"Well, if you're into sweet Georgia peaches, I handpicked both of those basketfuls just this morning." She pointed to the heaping piles. "However, if you'd prefer something a little more exotic, those delicious golden kiwis right in front of you were—"

"Flown in from New Zealand yesterday," came a voice from my right that made me feel like a bucket of ice water had been dumped on my head. A hand reached out and grabbed one of the oblong brown fruits, tossed it into the air, and caught it. "Hi, Felice," T said.

"Wait, do you two know each other?" from the girl.

For a beat, he just stared at me, eyes full of some hungry emotion I couldn't name, but knew I wanted no parts of.

Yet again, I was speechless.

"In a manner of speaking, yes." He turned to the girl and grinned. "Felice, this is my cousin Olivia. Recent graduate of Cornell who has decided to forego business school and instead sell fruit from our grandfather's orchards at farmers markets around the city."

"Not everybody loves money more than life, Tommy Boy," Olivia replied. "Also, *you* went through the trouble to import the kiwis."

I smiled in spite of myself. Olivia was a spunky one.

(Though hearing what she called him made me wonder if *Tommy* is linked to some sort of family trauma, and that's why he snapped on me at the club that one time.)

"Touché," from T. "Via, this is Felice. She's one of my therapeutic service providers."

"Oh my god, you're a *therapist*?"

Now I started at T. *Was this fool serious?*

"Jesus," Olivia continued. "There's no way I could talk to you about my problems. You're way too pretty."

"Via, pass me a knife and a spoon," T said. "She's gotta taste this." He turned to me. "I'm gonna presume you've never had a golden kiwi before?"

"Can't say I have." The presumption irritated me despite its accuracy. With all the "concern" he'd been showing for my well-being in our messages, I'd forgotten how arrogant he could be.

Also, what the fuck planet was I even on, standing here talking about kiwis (of all things) with a white man who'd had my whole ass in his face two nights prior? *And* his Ivy League–grad cousin??

"Well, you just wait." He sliced the fruit in half, exposing the genuinely golden interior, and shoved the spoon in one side. Then he held the whole thing out to me.

Which is when I noticed something I'd never seen before: his wedding ring.

I took the kiwi and dug in while two of the strangest white people I'd ever encountered watched on.

The first hunk slid onto my tongue and—

"Hey, TJ? Everything all right over there?"

The voice had come from behind us. A woman's.

"Welp," Olivia said. "Guess that's *your* cue . . ."

T took a deep breath, then looked over his shoulder and waved. "Be right there, honey!"

I didn't dare turn around.

"Ladies, the missus calls," T continued. "Via, you're crushing it as usual. Keep up the excellent work and call me if you need anything. And bag up a half dozen of those kiwis for Felice on me. I can tell she likes them."

He turned to me then. "And I'll see *you* at our next session."

"Here you go, beautiful!" Olivia passed me a brown paper bag as he walked off.

"Thank you, Olivia."

"It was lovely to meet you!" she said. "And kudos to you for being a therapist, girl. Especially if you work with men like my cousin."

I turned around then.

And almost dropped my bag.

T's wife wasn't the willowy, white runway model I'd created in my mind based on his complaints. *She says a baby will ruin her body... which is just selfish if you ask me.*

The woman he walked up to and kissed on the mouth wasn't willowy at all. She was tall and toned and perfectly proportioned (definitely a gym girly). Beautiful rack above a teensy waist above impeccable hips above exquisitely long legs. All on glorious display in a white sports bra and biker short set with bunched athletic socks and pristine white Jordan 1 Retro high-tops.

She was undeniably a work of art.

She also wasn't white.

In fact, the color of her skin was what really got under mine. It so reminded me of peanut butter—which I preferred to eat straight from the jar—my mouth watered.

"Don't forget there's more where those came from!" Olivia said.

I froze, feeling caught—the woman I was ogling was her cousin's wife, after all.

But she was gazing at me, a proverbial twinkle in her darker-than-T's-but-still-green eyes. "Come back whenever you'd like," she said. "Next batch is on me."

I SPENT THE rest of the day thinking less about the odd encounter, and more about the stunning woman. Largely because I was irritated that I hadn't gotten a good look at her face.

Body envy typically wasn't a *thing* for me. I'd worked hard and invested well in acquiring and maintaining the lovely shape of the one I lived in—there was a neon sign in my surgeon's office that perfectly articulated my physique philosophy: *Squats + Shifted Fat = An Ass Divine.*

But something about T's wife had wriggled its way down into my bone marrow. There was something so solid about the way she'd moved as she walked off on his arm with her head on his shoulder.

I thought about her all the way through my solo set. Imagined my own body as water coursing over hers, down over her perfectly sloped hills and into her deep valleys. It was a strange and unexpected experience, anchoring a person I hadn't actually met as my focal point for motion. There was just something about connecting T's complaints with an entity that *didn't* look like a Tory Burch–draped Malibu Barbie that made me feel things I could only express through dance.

It didn't help that Micah was in the building and clearly (to me at least) not feeling well. I'd caught the tail end of her shared set with Guapa and could tell from the sweat on her face and the visible tension in her muscles that she was fighting to power through it, and it aggravated me to no end that my instinctive response was worry. Because I didn't want to care anymore. It wasn't like Micah gave a shit if I did.

Yet still: once my set was over, I couldn't help but look for her. Make sure she was good. From a distance. It was a Wednesday night, and a relatively slow one at that, so moving through the floor was easy. But then . . .

"Yo, Lucky," came a voice from my left. "It's a customer waiting for you in Jade VIP."

That got my attention. Especially since it was Bones delivering the message. He rarely came out onto the floor when the place was jumping, and certainly not to play *Fetch the Dancer*. Also, the VIP rooms—there were four total, each named for the shade of green used in its interior design: emerald, mint, forest, and jade—were usually reserved for ultra-high-profile visitors. Most "regular" customers didn't even know they were back there.

"Say what now?"

"Jade VIP," Bones repeated. "And put some pep in that step, yeah? Keeping customers waiting isn't the Boom Town way." And then he stared at me until I got moving in the right direction.

My heart raced the whole way back. There was no place on earth I hated more than the Boom Town VIP rooms. I once overheard Bones describe them as a "microcosmic Vegas" to some big-deal music manager who was planning a visit for his newest client. "What happens in them stays in them, you feel me?" It'd been enough for the man to fork over the ten-thousand-dollar fee for the room itself.

And though all the dancers chosen for the group's enthrallment walked away with far more in tips than they would've on an average night, the things we'd had to do to get it . . .

I was totally fine with never stepping inside any of those dens of iniquity ever again. And because I had so many regulars, unless requested (which thankfully didn't happen often), I was rarely available when they were in use and usually able to avoid them.

I had to pull it together.

The rooms were on a long hallway that could only be accessed by two doors: one led out to the club's loading dock—this was typically how the VIP guests came into the building without anyone knowing they'd been there until after they'd left—and one inside the club, hidden behind a single panel of the green velvet curtains that lined the interior walls of the main show floor.

Said hallway was eerily quiet once the door closed behind me. Not that I'd seen many horror films in my life—why someone would watch something to scare themselves on purpose was beyond me—but looking down the tunnel of green (because of course this part of the club was lit neon shamrock like the rest of it) created the sensation of staring at an exit I'd never reach.

There were two rooms on each side, and Jade was second on the right. I forced my feet forward, even though the sound of my stilettos against the floor reverberated like gunshots. When I reached the door, I took a deep breath before opening it.

My eyes had to adjust to the lower light, but the décor inside this one was East Asian derivative and utterly tasteless: there were actual jade dragon sculptures in two corners that bracketed a full-wall mural of a sad attempt at a graffiti-style Chinese temple (in green-tone, of course).

At first I thought Bones had told me the wrong room: Jade was typically only used if the other three were occupied because some socially conscious rapper had come for a visit and expressed disdain for the décor (he apparently had a Chinese American wife).

There also didn't seem to be anyone inside. "Umm . . . hello?"

"Right behind you."

I spun around, ready to swing, and there was T's goofy ass. Laughing. And holding out one of two identical drinks. (Bourbon sours, surely.)

"Oh, absolutely fuck you," I said, shoving him before taking my drink out of his hand. "You trying to give me a damn heart attack?"

He blushed a little and, still smiling, lowered his chin. *Semi*-repentantly. "Sorry about that. And sorry about being in here." He gestured around the tacky room. "Just . . . don't need anybody seeing me tonight."

He looked me over and took a sip of his drink.

It gave me pause, his sudden concern about being spotted. Yes, it was odd to see him on a Wednesday—his regular visits happened on Tuesdays, Thursdays, and Saturdays.

But still.

"Drink up." He nodded at my glass.

As I took the first sip—indeed, a bourbon sour—a couple of other things came together. He'd surely paid an ungodly amount of money for the use of this space. Which meant he knew about it. Bones had a very strict policy about dancers *and* staff never mentioning or confirming the existence of the secret rooms . . . so who had told T they were here?

And speaking of Bones, T being *here* and me being summoned meant T had interacted directly with the GM.

I really didn't love it.

"Is . . . it a problem that you're here tonight?" I asked, taking another nervous gulp despite hating the drink. I needed to dull my edges. Mellow shit out a bit.

"Not exactly," Thomas replied. "Well, not a *new* one, I should say. Same shit, same toilet regarding my personal life."

"Okay . . ."

"It's just that Wednesdays are usually date night."

My pulse spiked at the thought of his wife. No shade to my colleagues, but the woman was far more attractive than any bitch in *this* building, me included. That he would come *here* instead of spending time with *her*—

"Seeing *you* at the Old Fourth Ward market today, though?" He shook his head. "*That* was a surprise I wasn't expecting—"

"That's kinda what a 'surprise' is, T. Something unexpected?" I took a larger swallow of the drink and winked.

"Yes, well, even more unexpected was the way my lovely wife fell out of her tree over your dress. She wouldn't stop talking about it."

"'Fell out of her tree'? That's a new one."

He shrugged and came closer. "All I know is that after running into you today, I needed to see you tonight."

The liquor on his breath made me nervous. I'd never seen him drunk before. "Is that so?"

"Without question." He took my hand. "I've missed you, Felice. My therapist made me accept the fact that you don't want to see me outside of this space anymore—"

"I thought *I* was your therapist," I cut in, needing to say something.

Thomas laughed. "Touché."

He talked to his therapist about me? What the hell did he say? "Your cousin is adorable, by the way."

"I think she's got a crush on you. Called to flood me with questions not five minutes after we parted ways."

"That didn't present a problem with your wife?"

"Ah, they don't really talk to each other. And even if they did, Via is nothing if not loyal to her favorite cousin." He grinned. "Besides, what's there to tell, hmm?" Another step closer. "As you just mentioned, you're my therapist."

I cleared my throat. All of this needed to end. And quickly.

"So, you ready for your dance, then?" I went and grabbed a high-backed chair from a corner to set it closer to the round stage in the center of the room. Like the stages on the main floor, it had a pole in the middle that disappeared into a hole in the ceiling. Where the left wall had the dragons and the mural, the other three were lined with thick green velvet curtains, just like out on the main floor. On the right side of the room, the curtains were flush against the wall. But at the back, they hid a section of the space that could be used—and frequently was when the room was occupied—as a bed.

I hoped to God T didn't know about that part.

I stepped onto the circular platform, grabbed its shiny, silver centerpiece, and commenced walking around it. "Pole or no pole?" I asked, pulling myself close to it and whipping around to face him. I snaked my body down into a squat with the pole between my shoulder blades.

"Why don't you want to see me anymore, Felice?"

Oh boy. "Respectfully, T: please don't call me that inside this building. You gonna sit down?"

He took the seat.

"Now, as I was saying..." I turned away from him, wrapped one leg around the pole, and arched backwards. He looked less threatening upside down. "Pole or no pole?"

"I'll be your pole."

He was getting on my nerves. I stepped down and leaned right into his mug. "We wanna be difficult tonight, I see—"

And he did something he'd never done before: he reached for my face.

I hated every millisecond of being stunned still as he ran a fingertip around my ear and along my jaw. And didn't stop. Over the center of my neck and throat and down my chest, right between my breasts. He hooked that finger into my bikini strap and tugged. "Oh, you have no idea, Felice."

I tried to speak, but no words would form. Which he seemed to take as some sort of silent assent. "God, your skin is soft," he continued, reaching for my thigh.

That unfroze me. I pushed his hand away and stood. "You know better than this, T. Whether we're out on that floor or here in this room, the rules of engagement are the same."

And I never figured out how to describe what happened next.

Maybe it was all too fast or too shocking or I blacked out. But after coming to with my (still-clothed) upper body on the platform, and my legs on the floor, G-string torn and missing a stiletto, whenever

I tried to recall the next who-knows-how-many minutes, all I could find were five sensory flashes: a vaguely familiar voice hissing *Do you have any idea how much I've paid you over the past four months?*; the uncomfortable scratch of a calloused palm against the thin skin of my throat; the sight of a white smoke detector on the ceiling; the putrid smell of masculine sweat mixed with designer cologne; and the taste of saliva in my mouth that wasn't mine.

The next morning, I woke up in my bed with an aching lower back and a vagina that felt like it'd been blowtorched. I had no idea how I'd gotten home.

But when I finally broke down, it wasn't because of what had happened. About that, no matter how hard I tried, I couldn't feel anything at all.

I cried because the face I saw when I closed my eyes wasn't T's.

It was Micah's.

FRIDAY, MAY 30 (PART TWO)

Lyriq

I CAN'T EVEN SAY THAT I *decide* to take a detour. It's more like I'm driving along, the brim of my floppy hat pulled low, with jazz pouring from the speakers at a volume typically reserved for trap music, and I notice I'm in an exit-only lane for I-85 South the moment it becomes too late for me to get out of it.

What's plaguing me now isn't what I witnessed in Jade VIP the night I saw Felice for the last time. It's that I was desperate enough to do what I did, *and* believe I'd get away with it.

I'd snuck into that suite because nobody ever used it. I was so wrung out from my set with Guapa—she wasn't half as good a dancer as Felice and we had no chemistry, so every second was work— I barely made it to the hidden bed before collapsing.

I hadn't been asleep for very long when I heard the voices, and at first I panicked. But when a peek through a gap in the curtains revealed Thomas McIntyre doing what he was doing to the only person on earth who I knew truly cared about me, my panic turned to shock, and then to rage.

But just as Thomas appeared to be finishing, I felt a bolt of pain through my left breast that was so intense, I gasped aloud.

Monster man stopped his maniac thrusting and looked up. He didn't investigate, but it seemed to knock some sense into him.

When he saw Felice beneath him, his eyes went wide. "Oh no..." He scrambled to his feet. "Oh no, oh no, oh no."

He rushed to pull his pants up. "*Shit!* What the fuck did I *do*? Felice?"

Felice didn't respond.

I covered my mouth and squeezed my eyes shut. The tears were flowing fast and hot, and I needed to keep quiet.

But I was in so much pain, it was hard to breathe.

I didn't move until after I heard the door groan open and click shut.

Felice also hadn't moved, so I assumed—hoped—she was unconscious. I'd been there before: left to fend for myself in a strange place after a strange encounter with a strange man. It wasn't fun, but Felice was tough. She'd survive it just like I did. She didn't have much of a choice—

There was another explosion of pain, and a wail burst out of my throat.

I crept out of the nook and moved as quietly as I could around the edge of the room. But just before I got to the door, I saw the wad of bills by Lucky's hip. My hand went to my sore breast. The skin was hot—as though a boob could spike a fever.

I was in trouble, and I knew it. Just as well as I knew the only reason I was there at all that night was because I was falling behind on bills. Between random bouts of sickness and debilitating fatigue, I'd missed so much work, I was on the verge of not being able to pay the mortgage on my condo.

I took a step closer to Felice. And another one. And another. If she was unconscious, she'd never know the money had been there.

Another step.

I could see her chest rising and falling with each breath.

I told myself she'd be perfectly fine once she woke up. She'd put the whole thing behind her and move on. Just like I'd had to do.

But then I got close enough to see her face. Her mouth was shut tight . . . but her eyes were wide open. My body couldn't figure out whether to scream or run.

"Luck?" I said. "Can you hear me?"

No response.

I looked at my friend. The first woman I'd ever loved. The person I was totally still in love with. She was the most beautiful human being I'd ever seen, Felice was. She had a smile that could light up any room; beautiful, natural hair (that stayed covered at work, but still); a banger of a body wrapped in skin that seemed to glow golden brown from the inside—

There was another searing breast pang.

But the money. I *needed* that money. I would be out of work for a while, I just knew it.

I got closer. "Leese?" I tried one last time, giving her shoulder a light shake.

Nothing.

So, I grabbed the wad of bills and left the room.

My exit looms up on the right.

Is everything in me screaming out to turn around? Hell yeah. When I moved out of Tink's four years ago, I swore on my dead mama I would never go back for any reason. But this is bigger than me now. Cuz that girl fucked all the way up when she fixed her grubby little unmanicured fingers to shit on my kindness so thoroughly.

Is Tink likely to be a *smidge* upset that I've seemingly misplaced the "baby cousin" she entrusted to my care? Zero question. Especially since I haven't paid back the money she fronted me six months ago when I had to take off work for three weeks because of a painful lump in my armpit. (Turned out to be a nasty cyst, but it had to be biopsied considering my "medical history" or whatever.)

But I gotta make some headway on this shit. I've worked too damn hard and come too far to allow some hard-up-for-money baby twat—who I got back on a pole to train, mind you—to fuck up my flow. In fact, the closer I get to my destination, and the faster my heart beats as a result, the more I remember about Before and what I've survived.

Compared to Before, the cancer thing was scary as shit, but not the worst thing ever. At least with cancer, whether I wound up dead or in remission, from the moment of diagnosis, I knew without question that there was an end in sight.

As I stop at a red light, I grab a napkin out of the glove box to wipe my eyes. (So much *crying* today. Ugh.) Before isn't something I let myself think much about because I've never seen the point. I'm not there anymore and I am never fucking going back.

Today, though? Maybe it's because I had a checkup and have yet to get my armor back on (it's impossible to "resist vulnerability," as Dr. Chamblee put it, when someone is examining your bare breasts—or lack thereof—for signs of a disease that could kill you). Or maybe it's the school-aged dudes selling bottles of water at the traffic light. (Felice used to always buy a couple bottles. "Better water than dope, so I can't knock the hustle.") Or maybe it's the girl leaned against the side of the gas station, her pink dress and warm brown skin mad out of place against the cream-colored stucco (I've certainly been her before) . . .

But as I turn onto Tink's street, I get flooded with memories.

So much of Before is a blur—I'm sure all the drugs and alcohol have something to do with that part. What I do know is that I needed money. So, a friend of mine who seemed to have plenty set me up on a "date" with a man at least a decade older than me.

He invited me to a party. When I got to the address—a newly built townhome in a run-down part of town—I was handed a different outfit at the front door and told to change. By the time I came out of the bathroom, there was a limo outside.

It was full of other women. My friend included.

Next thing I knew, we were all walking into a pink mansion. No clue where it was located because we had quite a bit of champagne on the way. But instead of walking into a party, I wound up beside my friend in what was essentially a lineup. She told me to follow her lead. When a guy—who I later found out had paid to be there—chose her to be his companion for the evening, she made it clear to him that she and I were a package deal.

And so it began.

There was another party invite the next weekend. And another a few days later for one midweek. Eventually I was doing party escorting four or five nights per week. Sometimes the attendees were in town for business conferences—*Work all day, play all night.* Sometimes the parties were for specific occasions: birthdays were big, second only to week-before-the-wedding bachelor bonanzas. And sometimes, they were after-parties full of celebrities (which were the worst of all: not only were those motherfuckers cheap as all hell, they acted like they were doing us a favor by letting them treat us like a collection of holes).

"Clients" were tall, short, fat, rail thin, clean, filthy, white, Black, Puerto Rican, Haitian, Asian, Pakistani, American, foreign, filthy rich, "in debt up to their eyeballs," attractive, hideous, athletic, disabled, well-fragranced, sewage-stank, young, old, and everything in between. Some played by the rules, where others "paid extra" to make their own.

Not that *I* or any of the other girls ever found that price difference in our pockets. There wasn't a planet in this universe or the next where the bossman would've permitted a "team member" to be paid directly. And as badly as I wanted to go independent, I knew if I tried it, he'd make me disappear.

Like he did the friend who introduced me to him.

There were trains, teabags, Eiffel towers, golden showers, fingers, thumbs, fists. There were bruises, stitches, black eyes, busted lips, soreness so intense I couldn't walk, a cracked rib, a tracheal contusion, ice baths, IVs. He kept a paramedic, a chiropractor, and an OB/GYN physician's assistant on payroll.

And then there was Tink.

My first time meeting her, I had to swallow a laugh. I'd picked up my hotel key and instructions per usual, but when I walked into the suite and saw the small woman, who looked to be about my age—though dressed like she shopped exclusively in men's big and tall stores—kicked back in a recliner with her hands clasped over her midsection, I thought it was a joke. So I looked over my shoulder at the door.

"Nah, you in the right place." She sat up in the chair and looked me over head to toe. "Do a little spin for me."

I did as I was told.

"Well, goddamn," she said. "At least they wasn't lyin' about you being a bad bitch."

By then I was facing her again. "I'm not good at cunnilingus," I blurted without thinking. (Which wasn't true. I was just . . . uncomfortable.)

Thankfully, she laughed. "Guess it's a good thing I am, then, huh?"

Except she never touched me. Instead, she got up, made me sit in the recliner, kicked it back, and told me to "chill" as she went to the suite's kitchenette. Of course, I couldn't relax at all cuz the shit felt weird, but when she came back, she brought a steaming cup of liquid on a saucer for me to drink.

Once I finished it, she led me to the bedroom and told me to strip down and get under the covers. Then she tossed a heavy blanket over me and said she'd be right back.

When I woke up, she was sitting in a chair across the room, fully clothed and reading a book. "How'd you sleep?" she asked without looking up.

I was too stunned to respond.

She went on: "The massage therapist is waiting for you in the living room. Let her know where you want her to focus."

During our third "encounter"—the moment I arrived to the five-star hotel, I was escorted to the spa—Tink told me the truth: as a part of her parole agreement, she worked with an organization that helped women who were interested get free from trafficking. "And I'm good at this shit," she said. "So long as my piss tests stay clean and I don't get caught in possession, they keep twelve off my back so I can run my other enterprises in peace."

And she offered me an out as well as a place to stay until I got back on my feet, but said I couldn't ask questions or complain about the accommodations.

I take a deep breath as the house looms up on the right, but I can't bring myself to look at it until I'm parked and out of the car. Once I feel the car door shut behind me, and I hear the little *beep!* that lets me know I've locked it, I breathe in deep, shut my eyes, and lift my head.

When I open them, I stop breathing.

Every entrance to the house—doors *and* windows—has been covered with thick metal barriers.

What the fuck?

My eyes are pulled to the wall mailbox beside the front door—

Tink insisted on keeping it hanging there as a decoy—and it reminds me of the other box. The *Dropbox*, Tink called it. It's on the side of the house, door camouflaged by the grungy siding. I'm scared as shit and feel ridiculous, but I decide to check it.

There's an unmarked envelope inside. I shove it into my pocket and run back to my car. Which surely looks suspicious, but I don't care.

After fleeing for a solid ten minutes, I pull into a QuikTrip to try and get my heart rate down, but every time I blink, I see those metal barricades over Tink's windows and doors. How long has the house been that way?

I reach for my phone to call Damaris. It'll be my first time trying since she stopped showing up.

When it goes straight to voicemail, I hang up and call again.

And again.

And again.

Nothing.

I take a deep breath and stare at my handbag. Felice's flip phone is inside, and on it is what I planned to investigate before I took my detour.

Feels dumb as hell to even bother, considering the present circumstances—I can't even find a girl who vanished six days ago, so there's no way I'll ever find Felice. Especially since I still haven't gotten responses to those messages I sent. But I need to accomplish *something*. Might lose what little remains of my sanity if I don't.

I reopen Lucky's text thread with Jeff. There was a monthslong break in their messaging, but the one that reestablished communication was from him. An address.

I plug it into my GPS, then pull my visor down to check my reflection. I look a goddamn mess—eyes read *I just smoked a blunt after not sleeping for three days,* nose is giving *leads the pulling of Santa's sleigh,* and though I don't know what leprosy looks like, the random red blotches that have overtaken my neck and upper chest feel like they might fit the description.

But whatever. I shove my shades onto my face and adjust my floppy hat.

Maybe one day I'll learn when to quit when I'm behind.

THE HOUSE IS deep charcoal, big and modern—lots of glass and sharp lines. It looks newer and stands out among all the white and cream (though equally large) houses around it. The driveway aligns with the cross street I used to enter the neighborhood, so I'm able to park in front of a different house a short distance back from the stop sign. And thank God for this *big-body Benz,* as Bones puts it. There's no question somebody would call the cops if I was sitting here in a Camry.

The spot gives me a great view of something I didn't expect to see (though it doesn't help me at all): a beautiful, light-skinned Black woman in the modern house's front yard—which has a big tree with a swing, and grass so green it doesn't seem natural—hanging out on a blanket with a baby in her lap.

She takes the little girl's hands and claps them together, and the baby laughs so hard, she topples backwards. Her chubby legs stick up in the air before they drop to the blanket.

I can't look away.

And it's not even the kid part. I never wanted those and have no interest in somebody *needing* me that much. No, thank you.

It's more that I didn't know shit like this was real. The house, the yard, the swing, the grass, this nice-ass neighborhood . . . I can almost guarantee that most of these people leave their front doors unlocked.

I've only ever seen this sort of thing in Lifetime movies about disgruntled white housewives who pretend to be happy but want the pool boy to rail them: so seeing a bitch who looks like *me* living a life like that?

I bet she has an *herb* garden and a perfect backyard with fruit trees and shit.

She looks in my direction. In fact, if the way her eyes are squinting is any indication, she's looking right at my car. Trying to see into it.

She won't be able to because my windshield is tinted, but still: that's no good. How the hell will I explain this if she comes over here? Or calls the cops? *Sorry about the loitering, it's just that my homegirl vanished without a trace while I was undergoing cancer treatment just over a year ago, and then this other girl disappeared, and a white man showed up, which made me feel like I needed to investigate the older disappearance. So I pulled out my homegirl's old phone and powered it on, and she was texting with some man named Jeff who sent her the address of the house* you *were in front of—cute baby by the way—so I had to roll by and see who lives there . . . Looks like it's you!*

If this *was* Jeff's house, I'm guessing he's moved since then.

The woman is getting to her feet. And scooping up the baby. And now shielding her eyes to try and get a better look . . . at me.

I can't drive off now: she'll get my tag number. And backing down the street would be suspect as hell.

She takes a step forward and I reach to put the car in gear, but just as I do, a massive, black, and vaguely familiar pickup truck—though this is Atlanta and the things are everywhere—appears from the left and turns into the driveway. That pulls her attention away from me, which totally gives me a window to get the fuck outta here . . .

But I need to see who's in the truck. I cannot leave without knowing if it's a Black man.

As the pickup's parked lights come on, the woman speed walks to the driver's side. She's gonna point out my car. I know she will.

And yet I still can't bring myself to drive off.

The truck door swings wide, but she moves into the open space, preventing the driver from getting out.

Thankfully, that doesn't last long: when the baby is pulled from the woman's arms and into the cab, the woman steps back with a mini stomp and locks her arms at her sides. Shit is fully giving *adult tantrum*.

As the driver climbs out holding the baby, homegirl does precisely what I'm expecting her to: she points at my car. (And loses hella cool points in the process . . . Sis done moved out here to the burbs and morphed from Katrina to Karen.)

The driver—definitely a man—shifts the baby to his opposite arm and shields his eyes as he looks in my direction.

I never really knew what people meant by "the seconds stretched into hours" until this very moment.

Because as Thomas McIntyre stares at my car, every moment of waiting to see what he'll do feels like its own hellish eternity. I know my windshield is tinted but . . . what if the light is hitting in the perfect way for him to see through? What the hell will I do if he figures out it's me?

Time ticks on . . . and on . . .

And on—

He waves a hand, clearly dismissing her concern. Feels a little harsh, but I'd be lying if I said I'm not relieved.

I don't pull off until the McIntyres are inside the house with the front door shut.

BEFORE

Lucky

NOT ONLY WAS THE sixth time not the charm, I seemed to have run out of pee.

Time to take a lap.

I exited the bathroom to pace my condo—a thing I did when I needed to ground myself but didn't feel like descending twenty-six stories to stand barefoot in the grass. I'd been listening to self-help audiobooks nonstop and decided to lean into a tip from the latest one: *focus on each of your five physical senses in turn, and then add a sixth: gratitude.* (How they decided *gratitude* was a sensory concept was beyond me, but what'd I have to lose?)

I popped an Altoid into my mouth, then *felt* my heel sink into the plush—freshly robo-vac'd!—cream cashmere rug. As my arch and toes followed suit, I shoved the mint to the roof of my mouth to fully *taste* the coolness of it all. I *smelled* snickerdoodles as I approached the kitchen—and *saw* the light-up fragrance diffuser plugged into the side of the island. *Heard* the gentle hum of the fridge before the crash of ice into the dispenser startled the shit out of me.

When I entered my bedroom, I looked at the detail of gold-flecked wallpaper, the inky black of the velvet chaise longue, and the sheer texture of the curtains that created the princess canopy bed of my dreams—which I was *thankful* for.

The sensation along the soles of my feet changed as I stepped from soft carpet to cold tile. There they all were, gaping up at me from the bathroom counter through six pairs of vertical-line eyes. Every pee stick glaringly positive.

I sighed and looked in the mirror. My stomach was hidden beneath an oversized T-shirt Micah had given me:

Are you Hungry, Angry, Lonely or Tired? **HALT** and Practice Self-Care!

This advice was dispensed by a mushroom. Which felt appropriate except . . . well, if the tests were accurate (and they had to be, right? There were six of them with the same result), I couldn't partake of any fun fungi for the time being.

I typically wasn't one to take the Lord's name in vain, but Jesus fucking Christ.

How was this happening again??

I grabbed the trash can from the floor and swept the half jury of pregnancy tests inside (*GUILTY AS CHARGED!*), removed the bag and tied it shut so not a single one of the damn things could get out, then walked back to the kitchen to add it to the leftovers I'd tossed into the big bin mere hours before. Felt like a different lifetime.

And then I just . . . stood there. Staring at my murky reflection in the television.

The most shocking thing wasn't that I'd gotten pregnant: I'm a human with two X chromosomes and a womb that worked the way I was told it would in middle school sex ed. From the time I started my cycle in fifth grade, pregnancy had always been on the potential outcome list when it came to heterosexual intercourse . . .

It was just that I hadn't had very much of *that* in my life. And certainly not in recent history.

The last time I'd had sex with a boy (only the second boy ever) had been sophomore year in college—a whole ten years prior. There'd been Molly involved.

This time, there hadn't been any drugs (that I knew of, at least). And though I knew who the father was without question or doubt—and that knowledge horrified some part of me I couldn't seem to access—I couldn't remember *how* I'd gotten pregnant. Like the act itself.

Was I aware that there'd been sex and that it hadn't been consensual? Absolutely. There wasn't a galaxy in any universe where I would've willingly *and* knowingly given Thomas Jefferson McIntyre—who was surely descended from slave-owning stock, as his name suggested—access to my personal pussy portal to the Pleasure Dimension.

But I also knew I couldn't prove it and had no evidence. When you added my profession to the mix, there was no world where anyone who could actually do anything would believe me. It'd been just over a month since the incident, but I remembered less now than when I'd first woken up—if "woken up" was even accurate. The last thing I had was T standing over me, looking feral.

And then it was morning. And I had a throbbing migraine and pain in that magic portal from the fieriest pit of hell.

It hit me hard as I fought to make out my facial features in the black of the TV screen. I was unequivocally alone. Who could I call to share the news with? Or even ask for advice? I was too embarrassed to call my mom because I wouldn't be able to lie to her about the circumstances. She wouldn't judge me, but she *would* shift all her energy into figuring out how to end T's life. Nobody needed that shit.

Also couldn't call the person I most wanted to talk to—even if Micah hadn't resoundingly iced me out of her life, she was clearly going through some shit of her own and didn't want me to know about it.

I hated even thinking about her. Which sucked because it was damn near impossible not to. She'd gotten down inside me. With her thick skin and her resilience and her practicality and how she shot shit straight. I missed her barking laugh and the fire in her eyes and how much it meant that she'd let me *see* her. Most of the places I spent time—my condo, my car, the club—were draped in memories of her naked body in motion.

It was part of the reason I was staring at the TV. Everywhere else—all kitchen countertops included—conjured memories of soft flesh and salty skin, erect nipples and quivering thighs, curled toes and bent knees. Her puckered portal that took *me* to another dimension. I missed Micah with every molecule. Missed her swaying curves and the sweet scent of her arousal. Her sultry voice and the taste of her pleasure and the way her skin would prickle with goose bumps at my touch.

I'd changed without her. And not for the better: Something inside me had died in her absence.

And now there was something new in there, coming alive.

My eyes fell to the couch. It was wide and deep and the color of full-bodied tempranillo. Which is what we'd been drinking the last time we started kissing on it before peeling off what little we had on and entangling our legs to bring our bodies together. We'd rocked against each other, slipping and sweating and throbbing until we co-climbed to a peak of shared ecstasy.

I really had to let her go.

My hand went to my stomach. I felt insane for even thinking it, but conception circumstances aside, perhaps a spark of new life was precisely what I needed.

Work that night felt like something out of a fever dream. I didn't want to be there, so I felt precisely zero rush from flinging my bare body around on a pole. It suddenly seemed so hollow. So ... devoid of any real meaning. Which mattered in a way that it hadn't before.

It was like the double lines in the windows of those pregnancy tests gave view to far more than an explanation for my absentee period. The thought of creating new life somehow cracked my mind open to the possibility that *my* life wanted to give me more than a few thousand dollars a night for supplying strangers with visual memories to masturbate to.

However, in the most ass-backwards dose of irony ever, I got the most requests for private dances I'd ever experienced. T hadn't returned to the club—nor had I heard from him—since the night he decided to rape me in that wormhole to hell that was Jade VIP—so all but two requests came from individuals I'd never danced for.

Every song was its own form of well-paid torture. Because without that spark of excitement at seeing a customer's pupils dilate when they caught that first glimpse of nipple ... I just felt like a hoe. And a silly one at that. Why was I pouring my time and energy into gratifying men I couldn't give two shits about?

The transactional nature of the whole enterprise dropped down the pole through the ceiling hole with the weight of a white Honda Accord. And despite just how much cash I was racking up—I left that night with just over five thousand dollars—I knew without question that I was ready to be done.

I just had no clue how the hell to get out. And that was the worst part of the night: all the questions swirling around in my brain like some unstoppable rebel force.

What would I do instead? Could I live off a kindergarten teacher's salary? What luxuries would I have to let go of? My manicures? Spa membership and monthly facials and yoni steams? I needed those yoni steams . . . Would I wind up walking around with busted feet? There was no way I could do that . . . And the whole "Who's the daddy?" thing . . . What would I do about that? Should I tell him it's his? He said he wanted a baby . . . but he has a whole wife! Not that that seemed to mean anything to him . . . And how would I tell him? It wasn't like he'd been back . . . Did I have to tell him at all? What if he got weird and possessive—

"Yo, you good?" came a man's voice. "Don't get me wrong, the titties are immaculate, but I asked for this dance so I could see it *all*, and I feel like you not really *here* right now."

He was my twenty-third private of the night.

I looked him over. He was handsome: tall, if the length of his legs was any indication; deep brown skin; clean-cut; casually but nicely dressed—plaid button-down, black skinny jeans, high-top sneakers. Well put together overall, and likely a successful guy and a perfect gentleman.

Just not in here. He'd come in here to let all that nice-guy shit fall away. In here he was a paying customer who'd come to purchase a specific service. He didn't care what I was dealing with. That I'd been raped and was now pregnant. That the woman I was in love with and wanted to give my everything to wouldn't even look at me. That my whole goddamn world had been flipped on its head, and that the bulk of my mental energy was going towards holding my shit together so I could do my job.

He didn't know any of those things, but even if he did, he wouldn't have cared. He was paying me so he wouldn't have to.

I knew then what I would do. And it was desperate.

But you know what they say about desperate times.

I dropped my chin and smiled at him. "Awww, come on, baby. Don't get impatient on me now." I slid my hand around the back of his neck and pulled myself in so he'd get a nice close-up of the immaculate titties he mentioned. Then I dropped my voice to the sultriest whisper I could muster. "Let me take my time."

On my way out, I had Clutch pour me a double of ninety-dollar-per-shot tequila, and then downed it in two gulps—my last liquor hurrah. Needed to soften my edges but steel my nerves at the same time.

Once in the car, I powered up my little flip phone.

It was 3:47 a.m. I wrote my message:

> Hey, so I've decided to get serious about a job switch. You know my educational background, so if you have leads, please let me know.

To my shock, the reply was instant.

> Seems rather sudden . . . Care to expound?

Before I could let myself think about what the hell I was doing, I tapped out my response:

> Just found out I'm pregnant.

I hit send and tossed my phone on the passenger seat. Then shut my eyes.

I was so goddamn tired.

The song "Peaches and Cream" blasted into the air, and my eyelids popped wide. Was he really *calling* me? At almost four in the morning?

I didn't answer.

He called again.

"Uhhhh . . . hello?"

"Just making sure I read that message correctly?" he said, groggy (and clearly half asleep).

"We can totally talk about this once the sun is up, T. Go back to bed—"

"Oh no, I'm up." He groaned as though literally getting up. "Trust me on that one."

Was he serious? "T—"

"I didn't know you were seeing anyone, Felice."

"What do you—?" I caught myself as it clicked: he was assuming someone else was the father.

A plume of rage unfurled behind my breastbone, and I shut my eyes. Took a deep breath. As fucked-up as it all was, I was wise enough to know that unleashing the flames of hell on his ass wouldn't help me right now. And help is what I needed more than anything. "I mean, I don't tell you *everything*."

"Who is he?"

"Excuse me?"

"The father," he said, voice hardening. "Who is he?"

"I'd like to keep that part to myself, if you don't mind."

"I can't assist you if you're going to block me out. So, I guess this conversation is moot. Goodnigh—"

My panic spiked. "His name is Micah. But I'd prefer not to say more."

"Micah . . ." he replied. "Sounds gay."

This whole thing was a mistake. "You know what, don't worry about it," I said. "There *was* a point when you told me I could reach out if I ever decided I wanted a change, but that offer was clearly conditional—"

"Look, I'm sorry. I reacted. I'm just . . . protective of you."

This flash of fury shot from my gut to my skull and was so intense, I sobered up for a second. *Protective? Was he fucking serious?* "That sure is an interesting thing for *you* to say—"

"Just let me talk for a sec, all right?"

I didn't respond. Heart was beating too fast.

"Brett just started a consulting business—"

"I'm sorry, who's Brett?"

"My wife. Her name is LaBrettney."

(That shut me right the fuck back up. Despite how much he talked about her, he'd never mentioned her name. If he had, I would've *known* she was a Black woman . . . Would that have changed his and my interactions?)

"As I was saying," he went on, "she just started a consultancy. Her background is in elementary education like you, and this thing she's doing is all about creating 'age-appropriate and culturally responsive socioemotional educational content,' whatever the hell that means."

"Okay . . ."

"She could use some structural and administrative assistance, and your master's thesis makes you the perfect candidate."

"Why do you know about my master's thesis?"

"Not relevant, but I'll oblige: I got curious and had a connect at Emory dig it up for me a couple months ago after you told me you'd completed it there."

"Jesus . . . stalker much?"

The line went cold, and for a moment, the fog cleared: I was talking to the man who'd violated me in the most vile way and I was now with child. *His* child. And he was acting as though nothing had happened between us.

"You interested or not, Felice?"

God, this was going to be a disaster. "I'd just need to learn a bit more about what the position entails, Thomas."

"You know I hate it when you call me that. Especially while you're working."

I breathed in deep. Everything in me wanted to set the entire ecosystem of this man's life ablaze. It just . . . wouldn't help me. "My apologies," I said, "T."

"That's also not the number you called."

Jesus Christ. "*Jeff*," I said, the irritation in my voice unmistakable. "If you wouldn't mind telling me a bit more, I'd appreciate it, Jeff."

"Thank you. I'm going to tell Brett you applied for a position at my company, but were overqualified, and that when I looked over your résumé, I thought she might want to talk to you."

"All right."

"I'll reach out tomorrow with the time and location for an interview with her. Don't overdress. She'll see right through it. Put on something like that sundress you were wearing at the farmers market. Just not that exact one, because she liked it—"

"Huh?"

"I told you that, remember? The first thing she said when I got back to her was, '*That woman at the fruit stand has the prettiest dress on.*'"

That sent a chill down both my arms. I didn't remember at all. "And you told me this when?"

"That same night. I came in to see you and . . . actually, never mind. It doesn't matter. Last thing, and then I'm going back to bed before she wakes up and realizes I'm gone."

Why the hell had he gotten out of bed in the first damn place? "I'm listening."

"Under no circumstances can she know what *else* you do or how you and I actually met."

I couldn't help but sigh. "I figured as much."

"It bore reiterating. Look for a message from me around ten a.m. Goodnight."

He hung up without waiting for a response.

SATURDAY, MAY 31

Lyriq

I READ THROUGH THE PAPER in my hand three times to make sure I'm not crazy.

But there the shit is, clear as day: Thomas Jefferson McIntyre listed as co-owner on the *deed* to the Boom Town building.

I squeeze my eyes shut, shake my head clear, and look at the paper again.

It's still there.

When I got home last night after making my Thomas/Jeff discovery, I started digging. I found a bunch of stuff that filled in some blanks about the creeper white man who keeps popping up in suspicious circumstances: a wedding announcement with photos (the woman I saw in the yard—LaBrettney Johnson-McIntyre—is definitely ol' boy's wife . . . which, *Really, sis??*); his name on an online business journal's *Recently Promoted* list when he made CEO; a short write-up about him buying that coffee shop; watermarked photos of him being honored at a Forbes 40 Under 40 event . . .

Every picture of his smug-ass face and quote about how great and "innovative" a businessman he is made me want to pistol-whip his ass and toss him off a building.

A search of the address I visited not only revealed *Johnson-McIntyre, LaBrettney Denise* as the deeded homeowner, but a list of every residential property in Thomas's name: there was a one-bedroom condo in Old Fourth Ward—same building as the café I went by; a house on Lake Lanier—of course he owns a house on a haunted-ass lake; and another house in a town called Carillon Beach, just outside Panama City.

A couple more clicks landed me on a record of his commercial real estate assets. That's where shit got wild. The café was on there. As was a recording studio in East Atlanta.

But when I saw . . .

Boom Town, Adult Entertainment Establishment, Atlanta, GA—Co-owner

It didn't quite register when I read it the first time.

I clicked the circle to reload the page at least fifteen times.

Obviously didn't sleep a damn wink with that shit burned on the insides of my eyelids, and it was bothering me so much, I couldn't even get myself off.

So, the minute I knew the club would be empty, I hopped in my car.

Even now, standing behind Bones's desk with the literal deed in my hand, I'm struggling to believe it's true.

"Fuck you doing in here?" comes a voice I'm not expecting. Bones is standing in the doorway looking as confused as a church girl on a stripper pole. Confusion that shifts to anger at the sight of the open file cabinet drawer and paper in my hand. "You going through my shit? Are you outcha fuckin' mind?"

Maybe it's the lack of sleep . . . or maybe my irritation over feeling so in the dark about everything. But when I open my mouth, something I doubt either of us is expecting flies out: "So, you just lettin' that white man take over your shit?"

"The hell you say to me?"

"I don't think I was unclear." Right now, I got enough fire raging inside me to match the heat coming in my direction instead of taking cover. "All the times you've called this place your 'life's work' and 'pride and joy' or whatever, and you sold part of it off to some random-ass white man?"

"You don't know what the fuck you talkin' 'bout, Lyriq. Do us both a favor and quit before you fall further behind—"

"How could you, Bones?"

"How could I *what*? You sound like a crazy person right now, and the fact that you up in *my* office going through *my* shit ain't helpin' your case."

"That man hurt Lucky!"

"You need to leave, Lyriq."

"Shit, he mighta done something to Charm too—"

"I said you need to leave." He's using the calm voice that I know from experience is a warning.

But I won't be made to feel like there's something wrong with *me*. I *know* all this shit is connected somehow.

They both had his business card and both disappeared. Felice was interacting with him outside of this place. Charm probably was too . . . right?

It's the only thing that makes sense. Maybe Charm told Tink some shit and she started investigating but didn't realize she was jumping in a shark tank while on her period and then *boom!* Next thing you know, the cops show up and raid the place.

It's all connected. I can't figure it out, but I *know* it's connected.

"You don't know what that man did to Lucky, Bones! I saw it with my own eyes—"

"Felice introduced me to him, you goofy bitch!"

I open my mouth to clap back . . . but then shut it. I'm not sure what I'm more stunned by: what he said or him saying her real name. He knows every dancer's, obviously, but I've never heard him actually use one.

"Ain't got shit to say now, huh?" Bones goes on. "*She* brought *him* to *me*. I don't even wanna tell you cuz you on some silly shit right now, but revenue got slim for this club when y'all stopped dancing together. You had your lil situation going on, and she randomly dropped her workdays to like three per week. And you know what happened, Lyriq? Niggas stopped showing up. The Lovely Ladies WERE Boom Town. And y'all just up and dipped on me, man."

Something that looks like hurt crosses Bones's face. (Not that I buy it . . . the only thing this man truly loves is money.)

"One night when you was out, I watched Luck work the room," he says. "Muthafuckas was *clamoring* for her attention. Even that lady you used to dance for . . . the one who husband would bring her up in here? Lucky got her ass too. And when I tell you your girl was *performing*?? Got damn." He shook his head. "I'm spinnin' just *thinking* about it."

"Lucky danced for Kia?" This isn't the most important part of what he said, and I *know* that. But the addition of something *else* to the list of things I didn't know has me ready to combust. Why hadn't Kia told me? How long had this gone on?

Had she liked Felice better than me?

"I hated firing her, man."

That gives me pause. "Whatchu mean *firing* her?"

"Precisely what the fuck I said."

"But that's *not* what you said before." My internal alarm is crowing like a damn rooster at sunrise. "You told me she stopped showing up. When I got back after my treatment, and I asked where she was, that's what you said." There's nothing I remember more clearly. *She no-call/no-showed a week ago*. With the most *couldn't-give-a-fuck* shrug I'd ever seen.

"Don't matter what I said back then." He waves the discrepancy away. "What I'm telling you *now* is that I fired her. It was obvious she ain't wanna work here no more for real, and it was easier for me to tell people y'all retired than for niggas to come up in here one night she was here and get excited but come back another night and she be absent. That shit kept happening, and it got on my nerves."

I don't respond.

"That dance she did for your lady friend wound up being one of her last," Bones says. "Her ass tried to sneak out after it. I watched her rush to the bathroom and caught her on the way to the back door. She claimed she'd gotten sick, so I let her leave, but that next afternoon, white boy showed up looking for me. Told me he was tryna 'get his feet wet' in the industry, whatever the hell *that* meant, and Lucky'd told him I might be looking for investors. Made me an offer I honestly couldn't refuse. Once I had that money, I didn't really need her ass anymore. So, I cut her loose." He shrugs and looks away.

I've been dealing with the grimy piece of shit long enough to recognize the tell: he's lying. Both overtly and by omission. I'm not completely sure which is what and how many parts of this story are true—there's always *some* truth layered in when he gets to weaving webs—but I know this story of Lucky's departure has been edited.

"He raped her, Bones," I say. "In Jade VIP."

He just stares at me.

"I saw that shit with my own eyes—"

"That's none of your business nor mine."

His empty-eyed glare triggers a ringing in my ears. Bossman's face superimposes Bones's for a sec, and I have to shake my head and blink to clear it.

"Come to think of it, none of this shit is any of *your* business. You really need to leave—"

"Charm was underage, Bones," I say then, despite not knowing for sure. I just need him to take *something* I'm saying seriously.

And despite the new look aimed at me—we've gone from barely suppressed rage to the type of shock that I know will give way to something explosive—I instantly feel lighter.

"Come again?"

"The boy said she was nineteen, right? He wasn't lying—"

"What the FUCK, Lyriq?" He takes a big stride closer, and I send up a silent prayer of thanks for the desk between us.

"I know, I know." I put the deed down and raise my hands in surrender. "I shouldn't have hired her. I owed her cousin a favor and—"

"You should really stop talking and leave."

I look Bones right in the eye. "You're not getting it, B. There's at least one person actively looking for this girl. Doesn't seem like anyone's gone to the police, and maybe no one will . . . But she's been gone a week now. If anyone gets serious about finding her—"

"I should really fuckin' kill you, Micah."

"Yeah, I hear that, but it might be best to try and find the girl first, don't you think?" I should stop. I know I should.

But I can't.

"Anybody find out she was working here, not only is this club cooked, you and your little business partner are going to jail. Might wanna consider asking him if he's seen her. I found his card in her stuff."

The smack comes so fast, my brain doesn't register that it happened until my palm—because my hand went up on instinct—feels the burst of heat coming off my cheek. That's when the sting sets in.

The crazed look in Bones's eyes makes the unspoken messages ring as loud as the bass in the walls on a Town Hall Tuesday: this is a person who *will* kill me.

And who knows something.

"What the hell happened to Felice, Bones? Were you in on it?"

He gets right in my face. "You better figure this out, Lyriq. YOU hired that girl. All this shit is on *you*," comes the reply. "I don't know where the bitch is or what she's doing, but I *do* know she stole from me. That shit is on *your* head."

Struggling to breathe now.

"If you don't want a groundhog delivering mail to a slot in your casket, Imma suggest you get it all sorted—and fast."

Everything goes black.

IF WAKING UP in a different place than I passed out isn't disorienting enough, when I realize where I am, my pulse surges so fast, I almost black out again. A pole stretches up into a hole in the ceiling above me, and all four walls are lit from top and bottom, turning the room an eerie shade of jade green.

I sit up, my eyes pulled to the curtain hiding the bed where I'd lain in silent terror, watching Thomas do what he did to Felice.

And now I'm crying. Hard.

A couple things hit me at once: First, before today, I really did have special favor with Bones. The other girls would point it out all the time, but I'd deny it because I couldn't see it from their perspective. I'd heard rumors of his cruelty—calling and getting dancers fired when they'd secured new jobs because they wanted to stop dancing, then refusing to hire them back; having their cars broken into while they were on the clock if there were rumors of paid rendezvous outside the club (*I employ dancers, not prostitutes.*); sending ledgers with a fabricated lists of "debts" dancers had to pay if they complained about treatment from clients . . .

But that hadn't been my experience with him. So, I never really believed them.

And the fact that I'm learning of this cruelty through experience means whatever favor I *did* have is gone. It's scary as fuck.

I wipe my eyes. Not only am I in the room where I last saw Felice, I came to in the exact spot where Thomas held her down. I look up at the ceiling in the corner. It's faint, but there's a small red light.

That son of a bitch knew all along.

Felice didn't "introduce" Bones and Thomas. She couldn't have: Access to the VIP hallway didn't get granted to just *anybody*. The men already knew each other. They had to.

So why did he lie?

I blink and there's Felice, open-eyed and frozen. It was my last time seeing her in person. And I'd just left her there.

I smack the stage with my fists and cry out. I couldn't see it back then—had too much of my own shit going on. Or maybe I just didn't want to. Was afraid to.

But I can see it now: Felice needed me. She needed me and I needed her, and we needed each other. But she wasn't there because I'd shut her out. Which meant I couldn't be there for her either.

Except . . . I *was* there. Like . . . literally. Right fucking there. Watching. Doing nothing.

I saw her lying in this spot, eyes on the ceiling. And I knew what would happen. I knew she'd "wake up," but that her memory would be fuzzy. I knew there'd be a hole I could slip into and that she'd have no recollection of my presence. I knew because I'd been where she was.

The shit was all too fucking familiar.

I look up at the camera again. Bones already knew that I'd been in here. Which means Bones also knows what I did. What I took.

It's not like I actually give a fuck about her. The words blare in my head like a wrong-answer buzzer on a damn game show. It's what I'd said the night Bones tried to bait me into revealing my feelings for Lucky by threatening to fire her.

And I know him. God, do I know him. His reason for putting me here might as well be a green neon sign on the wall: *Don't act like you care now.*

Except I do.

THE WOMAN FROM the front yard answers the door with the baby on her hip, and it shocks me so bad I just stand there with my mouth open. Maybe it's the lack of sleep (plus the slap and the blackout?), but no matter how many times I try to blink my vision clear, when I look at the little girl's face—no clue how old she is but certainly less than a year—all I see is Felice.

"Can I help you?" the woman says, pulling my gaze to hers. She's smiling—politely. But it doesn't reach her eyes.

"Oh. Yeah, sorry." I gotta pull it together. "Is Thomas here?"

Her (immaculately threaded) eyebrows tug together, and she hitches the baby up higher on her hip and squeezes her tighter. "No, he isn't."

"Any idea when he'll be back?" I can't help but look past her into the house. A house that Felice was probably inside of at some point. "HEY, THOMAS!" I take a step closer.

"Whoa, now—" A hand hits my chest.

But I keep yelling. What is there to lose? "YOU IN THERE, THOMAS? DON'T HIDE BEHIND YOUR PRETTY WIFE! TELL ME WHERE THE GIRL IS!"

The baby starts crying, and I stumble back. Because the woman—LaBrettney—just pushed me. Her face—which is just a smidge darker than mine—has reddened in warning. "Imma need you to get the fuck off my doorstep."

The baby cries harder.

I try to speak, but she holds a hand up. "I don't know who you are, but it'd be in your best interest to *never* come back here," she says, somehow still a picture of calm. "I'm not usually one to threaten the police on another Black person—especially not a Black woman. But you have crossed the line. Get gone and don't return."

She slams the door.

BEFORE

Lucky

SIXTEEN WEEKS. THAT'S HOW long I lasted before any customers seemed to notice there was something going on with me.

It started during a private dance—turns out that twenty-third guy I'd danced for the night I reached out to Thomas not only forgave my initial lack of attention, but by the time I was done with him, he'd decided he needed to start seeing me regularly. Even brought his girlfriend a few times.

His name was Brandon, and he was a day trader. He was also a little too observant. "What's going on with them hips, Mama?" he asked one night. I was bent over in his face. Shaking it with every ounce of energy I had in me.

Mama. If only he knew.

"Whatchu mean, love?" I dropped down into a squat while keeping the bounce going. And not even to be enticing. Because he was spot-on about my hips: they were killing me.

Had to give 'em a good stretch.

"Don't take this the wrong way, but you strugglin' a lil bit today, sweets. The sweat at that hairline, the tension in your quads, and the slower-than-normal twerk pace are a dead giveaway. You sure you good?"

(Did I mention Brandon was also a personal trainer who did *physique* competitions on the side?)

I turned around and kicked a leg up so one of my newest shoes—six-inch acrylic platforms with embedded LED lights that made them glow green (another attempt to draw attention away from how stiff my dancing had gotten)—was propped up on the back of the green velvet couch where he sat.

For a deeper stretch. But I did hope the face full of lady glory would shut him up.

It sorta worked. "Don't get me wrong," he said, staring straight at said glory and licking his lips. "I'm loving *everything* you doin' right now and certainly don't want you to stop. Just saying I can tell you tight."

I wound my hips to tease him with an even closer view (and to loosen that hip flexor). "Is that so?"

"I mean . . ."

Now I had him. I could feel it. A surge of adrenaline took over. Or maybe it was some other hormone. Pregnancy had a bunch of them shooting around all willy-nilly. Whatever it was, it made me feel like the Lucky who used to turn this bitch out six nights per week. "I, uhhh . . ."

I loved it when they got tongue-tied.

"I, uhh . . . I meant I could tell . . . got *damn*, girl."

I smiled and shifted to straddle him, but a bolt of pain shot down my left thigh, so I used the back of the couch to pull myself upright—took everything in me to not cry out.

Thankfully the song was ending. I stood up, grabbed my G-string from where I'd dropped it into his lap, and took my bikini top from over his shoulder. Started to dress.

"Just so you know, I meant I could tell your *joints* are tight," he said, sliding a folded wad of cash beneath my garter. "Not . . . well, you know."

"Mmhmm." I bent to look him right in the eye. "Well, you were right about the other thing too. I'm even tighter than them skinny jeans you got on."

He shut his eyes and let his head fall back. "You ain't even have to do me like that, Lucky."

"Until next time, then?" I sashayed away.

Obviously couldn't have alcohol to loosen up. Nor could I slather myself in Tiger Balm like I did at home. So, I snuck behind one of the stages to stretch for real. Committed to slow and sensual instead of vigorous.

And it worked: the next few dances were for newbies who'd never seen me headline, so none of them had expectations. Gave me free reign to move however I liked. Though when one guy—likely mid-to-late-fifties, short, stout, and brown-skinned, with perfectly groomed and solidly salt-and-pepper facial hair—exclaimed, "My god, what a wonderful Thursday!" as I removed my bottoms, my brain betrayed me with thoughts of T. Thursdays had been one of his regular nights.

I wouldn't even admit it to *me* at that point—felt too much like self-betrayal—but I missed the *old* T. The moderately polite and well-dressed white man I couldn't stand but also looked forward to seeing. He'd been so *different* back then. I would dance, and he would watch while telling me about shit in his life that had him stressed out: having to clean up messes at work that he hadn't made; having time he needed to do his job well usurped by workshops HR had made mandatory for all employees (he never told me what he did, and I had a personal policy not to look clients up online, but he seemed pretty high up in his company); issues with his wife...

I questioned *all* of it now. Especially the stuff about the wife—

"Goddawg, Imma have to get to this city more often," Teddy Grandpa proclaimed, chopping into my thoughts. "Them gals back home in Montgomery ain't got *nothin'* on you Georgia Peaches!"

I couldn't help it. I burst out laughing.

"My sincerest apologies for the interruption," came a new voice from the left. It was deep and rumbled like thunder. When I turned, I found myself looking into the eyes of the most beautiful, older Black man I'd ever seen in my life. He was tall and broad-shouldered, not quite as old as the man in front of me, but seasoned for sure. Under no circumstances was I *ever* supposed to let a different patron interrupt a private dance, but this guy commanded attention in a way that made it impossible to obey that rule.

I just gulped and stared at him, utterly knocked off my game.

"I'm so sorry, sir, and I'll reimburse you for every moment you're losing with this queen because of me," the man said to the grandpa before shifting back to me, "but my wife insisted that I deliver a message: she'd like to be your next audience-of-one. Or the one after that if there's someone else in line."

"Your *wife*?" The grandpa was flabbergasted.

"That's correct," the man replied. "Of all the date nights I plan, this one seems to be her favorite."

"Well, I'll be damned."

The other man chuckled. "I won't take up any more of your time," he said. "Miss, if you'd oblige my wife, I'd be eternally grateful. The couch in our home is lovely, but I'd prefer not to be banished to it. We'll be seated right over there."

He pointed somewhere behind me, and I turned to look. There, eyeballing me from across the floor was a woman so stunning, my mouth fell open (which was rather embarrassing).

Her husband gazed in her direction and smiled. "She's really something, isn't she? Hopefully you'll come meet her shortly." He tossed me a wink and walked away.

My gut twisted. Because I knew precisely who the woman was: back when she'd been speaking to me—while as high as the damn moon in this case—Micah mentioned a couple in their mid-forties who she "hate-loved" because their relationship "gives a little too much *unattainable goals.*" It'd been one of the few times she let me see beneath her crusty-ass exoskeleton.

This was surely them.

Which meant I had every reason to vanish after this song ended and send another dancer over with my apologies and a lie: *the request for private dances has been exceptionally high tonight.*

I knew all I'd be able to think about while dancing was Micah: Where was she? Had she said anything to this woman before leaving? Was the woman enjoying my dancing as much as she enjoyed Micah's? Was she thinking about Micah while watching me?

Why wasn't Micah here?

The song ended, and I patted the old man's cheek and began to re-dress, unable to resist a glance in the woman's direction.

Not only was she still staring at me, she crooked a finger and beckoned me over.

THE THING ABOUT LaBrettney McIntyre that kept catching me off guard: she was nothing like the gnatty old shrew Thomas described. I'd shown up for my interview at their home nervous as hell—she'd insisted that I come there since it was the place I'd be working alongside her. The house was big and modern and brick, painted the color of a well-sharpened No. 2 pencil point. *Now I get what Micah meant by "gives too much unattainable goals,"* I thought as I lifted my fist to knock on the front door.

My knuckles never made contact. The door flew open and there before me stood the goddess of a woman I'd seen in the park (in a coffee bean colored athleisure set this time instead of all white).

Her face was even more stunning up close: flawless (peanut) buttery skin, eyes the bright copper of a new penny, immaculate cheekbones, absurdly plump and pouty lips . . .

And the first thing she said to me? "Oh my god, you're a Black woman!"

Had no clue how to respond to that. So, I didn't.

"Damn, you're also fine as hell," she went on. (Definitely no clue what to do with *that*, but also couldn't deny I liked it.) "Totally inappropriate, I know . . . but humor me and do a slow three-sixty?"

Shocked—and flattered—I did as she asked. When I was facing her again, she was gazing at me like I'd just shown her something she'd never seen before.

Made me *real* self-conscious. I had no idea how to read her.

Within a few minutes, though, I was sitting at the McIntyres' reclaimed, raw-edged, and partially petrified wood dining table while LaBrettney bustled around the kitchen making coffee to go with the vegan pimento cheese and avocado sandwiches on warm pita bread. We clicked instantly, and right inside the house where Thomas Jefferson McIntyre laid his head to rest most nights, LaBrettney—Brett—and I became fast friends.

It was uncomfortable as shit at first considering my little womb occupant, but then our chemistry took over.

Was there some crackly tension between us as women who undeniably found each other attractive? Without question. But we never crossed the line. And she consulted me on everything—like flat-out refused to make any decisions for *her* business without running them by me first—and though it initially made me feel imposter-y when she'd refer to me as her "business partner" when pitching for consulting contracts, it became very clear over time that she meant it.

And even though T ("TJ" to Brett) never came up in our discussions—their marriage was the one thing she stayed mum on, which made things easier: most of the time, I could forget they belonged to each other—it went without saying that he could never find out how close we'd gotten. So, despite never having talked about it, we'd fall right into employer/employee mode any time he was around. He no longer came to the club, so for the first few months of working with Brett, I was more or less able to treat him as a nonentity.

Except an entity he was. And because of him, there was a new entity. And after dancing for Dr. Kia Chamblee in that sixteenth week, I could no longer pretend otherwise regarding either reality.

She'd requested two songs, and after reaching her and experiencing her energy, I couldn't help but oblige. She had one of the most striking faces I'd ever seen, and her fragrance made me think of sitting in front of a fire with a steaming mug of hot, buttered rum. The first song to come on was typical trap shit, and she hyped me up as I popped and clapped and shook it. I'd smiled the whole way through.

But then the second song hit different. It was slower. Deeper. Still bass-heavy and lyrically misogynistic, but a totally different vibe. She and I locked eyes, and she beckoned me closer, so I leaned in.

"This song was my request," she purred into my ear. Her voice against my skin made me tingle all over. And she ran a fingertip over my ear and then along my jawline to my chin—which felt mildly familiar, though I couldn't pinpoint why.

I also couldn't resist closing my eyes.

They popped back open when she gently kissed me on the lips. "Let's see what you can do, Beauty Queen."

Midway through the song, she asked if she could touch me. I said yes.

It was my second mistake (the first had been agreeing to dance for her at all). Because as she ran one of her astoundingly soft palms down my rib cage into the dip of my waist and then out over my hip and down my thigh, something inside me bloomed at her tenderness.

It took all I had to keep my knees from buckling.

I was so enraptured by this woman *I* was supposed to be entertaining, I didn't think anything of it when a quizzical look crossed her face as she stared at my breasts, then dropped her gaze to my midsection.

I was in her lap when the song ended, but before I could get up, she whispered something else in my ear: "How far along are you? About fifteen weeks?"

My whole body stiffened.

"Don't panic. It's not obvious," she continued. "I've been taking care of women's bodies for a long time."

I nodded. "Sixteen."

"Get a plan in place, okay? Everything in me wants to assist you, but hubby's sole stipulation for bringing me here is no contact with any of you chocolate Sirens outside this building. I've broken it once, but do my best to abide."

Micah crossed my mind at that moment, but I was too panicked about my *own* situation to engage with the thought of her. Despite what Dr. Chamblee said about it not being "obvious," the fact that there was now another human being who knew what I had going on—because I hadn't told a soul yet—intensified the gravity of the situation.

I felt like I weighed a thousand pounds. I saw the trio of stages with poles in my peripheral. I knew it was a mental thing, but the idea of getting my body up and around one of them made me feel like my heart would swan dive up outta my body if I opened my mouth.

I needed to vomit.

I shot up, grabbed my bikini, and tried to put it on as smoothly as possible while actively rushing towards the bathroom. My G-string was off-center, and I still had a boob hanging out when I slammed the stall door. But my best-kept secret rushed up my throat as I fell to my knees in front of the toilet bowl.

There was nothing left for me at Boom Town.

I had to get out. The question was: How? I was working for Brett part-time and had dropped my days in the club from six to three per week. And Brett paid well, but even at full-time, I'd need to figure out how to come up with what would amount to two nights' worth of dancing to make what I did at the club.

I could probably *keep* dancing for a bit . . . But when the pounds got to piling on and I started showing—

I retched again. And could feel the next round swirling.

Definitely wouldn't be returning to the floor that night.

It felt good to just . . . accept the truth. So good, a wave of peace crashed over me. Or hell: maybe it was the hormones. Either way, I certainly wasn't mad at that shit.

I grabbed some tissue to wipe my mouth, stood, and straightened my outfit. Told myself everything would be okay and made a plan: get to the dressing room and change, then sneak out the back door without being spotted. The following morning, I would call and explain that I'd gotten sick and had to leave, especially since I didn't know what was going on or if I was contagious. *You know how wild these stomach bugs can be*, I would say.

Easy peasy.

Except my plan unraveled the moment I exited the bathroom. Because Bones had seen me go in.

And was waiting for me.

I CHECKED MY reflection in the visor mirror before getting out of my car at the McIntyres' the following morning. I looked like the undead, but deader: my skin was ashen (despite the hundred-and-fifty-dollar moisturizer I slathered on like my life depended on it), the bags beneath my eyes were giving *vintage Louis Vuitton Keepall*, and the white parts around my pupils looked struck by craggy-red lightning.

My stomach churned.

But I had to keep it together. Obviously had some shit to figure out, but I still wasn't ready to tell Brett about the pregnancy. We never really talked about our personal lives, so I couldn't predict how she would respond. And I was able to work for her day in and day out because I could pretend all the things she didn't know just didn't exist.

But the baby was suddenly affirming its existence in the realest, most nauseating way. And despite everything I read about "morning sickness" being a first trimester thing, here I was, three weeks into the second one, shoving past my boss at one in the afternoon so I wouldn't puke all over her wildly overpriced yoga pants as soon as she opened the door.

She took the pregnancy news exceptionally well, Brett did. I was so overwhelmed when she chased me down to make sure I was okay, I wouldn't have been able to lie to her if I tried. And she'd gasped and jumped and *whooped* and bounced around like a big-ass kid who just learned she's going to Disney.

Which would've been fine had her husband not walked in.

"Everything all right in here?" he said.

Brett turned to him. "Felice is expecting, honey!" she said with a squeal.

He leaned against the open doorframe and crossed his arms. "Expecting what?"

My blood turned viscous, and I opened my mouth to speak, but—

"A *baby*, ya dummy!"

I felt Thomas's shifty eyes lock on me. "Well, who's the dad?"

"TJ! RUDE!" Brett grabbed the hand towel and snapped it at him. "That's none of our—"

"His name is Micah," I said, fighting to keep from rolling my eyes. Guess he had to make sure wifey heard him ask. "He and his husband wanted a child with one of their DNA—"

"Wait, so you're so some gay guys' surrogate?"

"Nah, I'm their baby mama," I said, looking him dead in the face. "We'll be coparenting."

"Ah," he said. "Well, congratulations, I guess."

Brett looked at her watch. "Oh shit, a client's calling. I left my phone in the other room . . ." And with that, she slipped past T and out of the small bathroom. "Hello? Hi, sorry, gimme just a sec. Currently talking to you on my watch . . ." she said as she bolted up the hallway.

Which left me there with *him*. And he was blocking the door. I already knew he could overpower me. (Hello? Pregnant with no recollection of how.) But I stood up anyway.

And too fast. My head swam.

"Whoa there," he said, catching my elbow when I wobbled. "You good?"

"I'm fine."

We met eyes again. I wanted to fucking scream. Because looking at his face from this angle—up—was a reminder that I used to look at it from a different one. And was paid well for it.

I tried to move past him, but he stopped me.

"I'm gonna ask you again: Are you good, Felice?"

I wasn't. At all. I was in trouble. Big, fat-ass trouble. Because in addition to my secret being out to the point where I no longer had control over it *and* suddenly puking my life away at random moments, I had Bones's displeasure at my chopped schedule spinning around my head.

"The club is struggling a bit without Lyriq and I headlining together," I told T. "Customers haven't taken to the new girls the way they took to us, and the number of nightly visitors has dropped." *Why* I was telling him, I wasn't sure. But it hung there in the air between us.

"Who told you that?" he asked.

"The owner. Who pretends he's just the GM."

Thomas nodded. "I'll take care of it." He stepped into the hallway.

"What? No." I followed him out. "There's nothing for you to '*take care of*'—"

But it was too late, and I knew it. So, I stopped.

Whatever he'd decided to do would be done. I doubted anyone knew that better than me.

So, I didn't bother chasing him down. It would've been a waste of my limited energy.

In fact, I didn't bother moving at all until I heard the front door shut behind him.

SUNDAY, JUNE 1

Lyriq

FUCK UP ALONG TWO AXES:

1. When Thomas McIntyre doesn't show up at the club the same day I show up at his house and leave my mildly psychotic message with his wife—and I am *ready* for that motherfucker, let me tell you—I relax just the tiniest bit. No, I don't *know* him, know him, but based on everything I've gathered, he seems like the type who would buck back unless (a) she didn't tell him I stopped by, or (b) he really does have something to hide and decides to keep his distance.
2. Then: Due to said *slight* relaxation, I'm less vigilant the following night.

Which I hate because I know better.

Despite that knowledge, when Karma goes down—while *exiting* the stage, no less—every ounce of my focus shifts to her. Club floor injuries can quickly morph into Expensive Lawsuits, and nobody has time for *that* shit.

When I get to her, three other dancers are crowded around like an unholy trinity of exiled angels. I shoo them off with a wave of my hand. "Get them fine asses back on the floor," I say, giving one a smack.

"I think I broke it," from Karma. She's in a heap at the bottom of the three stairs to the main stage, hand on her ankle. "I hate these fucking stilts we have to wear."

"And yet you typically wear them so well, Karma." I move her hand away so I can take a look. "What the hell happened?"

As she tells me about "getting dizzy" while on the pole, and I ask a line of questions designed to get her to admit she's at fault—*Did you drink enough water today? When's the last time you ate? What were you using to spot? How much alcohol did you have before your set?*

I'm so busy trying to absolve the club of any responsibility—yes, these bitches sign a waiver, but I've seen more than a few work their way around it—I don't notice a shadow has fallen over her (and therefore *me*) until she stops talking mid-sentence, and her mouth stays open.

I turn around. Bones is standing over me, hands tucked in pockets—which suggests *not a care in the world*, but means *I'm doing my damnedest not to throttle your ass*. His face is as blank as most of the patrons' would be if you asked them how their wives are doing.

And he isn't alone.

"Your company's been requested, Lyriq," he says, gesturing to Thomas McIntyre.

Who looks cool as a damn cucumber. "Long time no see." He smiles as he looks me over.

"You literally saw me when you came in here a week ago." I refuse to look at him. I hate that he managed to sneak up on me. Feels like getting beat at my own game. "We've got a bit of an emergency here, Bones. I think Karma might've—"

"It's an emergency I can take care of." The warning in Bones's voice hums as thickly as the reverb from the bass.

"Also, if I recall correctly, you still owe me a rain check from my first time ever coming in here," Thomas says. "I've come to collect."

And the bastard *winks* at me.

I stand then. Click my most demure smile in place and *bat, bat, bat* my lashes (which have been shedding like crazy and probably need a fill-in, but whatever). "Amazing you remember that. I'm flattered." I put a hand on my chest. Mostly for effect, but also because I can feel myself turning red with rage as I look into this man's monstrous green eyes. "I'm not sure how satisfying it would be, though: I haven't danced since I lost my pretty titties—you remember them, I'm sure. Cancer decided I needed humbling and took them away from me. I presume Bones mentioned that to you?"

Now I can't look at Bones. The fury wafting in my direction is so dense, I'd need a Michael Myers–style butcher knife to cut through it.

Thomas looks me over—I'm in a short, tight dress the color of ivy—and licks his lips. "Yeah, I'll definitely be fine. There's more than enough going on in other areas." Instantly makes me feel like a million spiders have decided to use my skin to get their ten-thousand steps in.

"Go ahead, Lyriq." Bones waves one of the bouncers over to come scoop Karma up off the floor. "I got this handled."

I open my mouth to resist, but—

"I appreciate how well you do your job, and I believe Mr. McIntyre will too."

The message is thinly veiled but clear as the VVS diamonds in the chain around Bones's neck: inside this club, I'm to do what I'm told because they're in charge.

Or at least they think they are.

I force a smile. "Where would you like to settle this . . . debt?"

Thomas doesn't smile back. In fact, his eyes do that thing where they narrow for moment so short, I would've missed it if I wasn't working so hard to maintain eye contact. "I have the perfect spot in mind."

The man is livid.

But so am I. Nearly a week of piecing together something I should've looked into a long time ago, plus some new shit I also gotta figure out. Both somehow involving this creep-ass white man who seems to think he owns as much of me as he does of this club.

Motherfucker's got another thing coming, though.

"After you," I say, stepping aside to let him lead.

I DO ALL right maintaining my gangster or whatever until I hear the door click shut, sealing us into hell. By the time I realized my error (Had I really just *followed* him like a damn puppy?), we were approaching the hidden door to VIP, and there was no turning back, because of course he would bring me here. He knows I know what he did to Felice in this room.

A rough hand closes around my forearm, and before I can process what's happening, I'm facing him, and he's got a finger in my face.

"I don't know who the fuck you think you are or what you're on, but let me bring us to an understanding," he growls. "If you ever *think* of visiting my home or going near my wife and daughter again—"

I knock his hand away and try to take a step back. "Let me guess: You'll kill me?"

"Oh, definitely not," he replies, dropping his voice and yanking me closer. Hurts like hell, but I refuse to flinch. That's what men like him look for: signs of weakness they can exploit. "That'd be letting you off way too easy," he says.

My panic spikes, but I don't respond.

"What I *will* do is shut this place down. Then I'll make sure every single person who winds up out of a job knows it's because of you. They'll rip you apart."

A knot forms in my throat, but I swallow it. "You can't do that. Bones would never allow—"

"Bones would never turn down a paycheck, sweetheart. What *I* say goes. Everything that happens with this club runs through me. *I* am judge, jury, and executioner—"

"I thought you said you wouldn't kill me."

"I won't have to," he says. "Your life can be over with you very much alive. Especially once I have you arrested for trafficking a minor."

Oh shit. So, she really *was* underage?

I lift my chin. "'Minor' means under eighteen, and I've certainly never 'trafficked' one—"

"The hiring age for this industry is twenty-one, Lyriq. Damaris was only nineteen. And as your signature is on her hiring paperwork—"

But I don't hear anything else.

Because even if Bones did give this demon a rundown of everything I said yesterday morning, the fact that he just used Charm's real name *and* mentioned her age in past tense is enough to make all my frustrations from the past week boil over. "You *raped* Lucky, you filthy son of a bitch!" I shout. "I *saw* you! I was right over there, and I saw the whole thing—"

"Weren't you ill and half passed out, Lyriq? How can you be sure of what you saw?" There's not a hint of remorse in his voice, but he does shove me back and let go of my wrist. "Felice was a sex worker who was paid well for her services."

"You think money gives you the right to fuck someone against their will?"

He rolls his eyes. "Against her will? Now I know you weren't seeing clearly. Maybe you were a little jealous—"

"*Excuse* me?"

Now he sighs and shakes his head. "You're projecting," he says. "Plain and simple. You never liked the idea that Felice—"

"Her stage name is *Lucky. You* don't deserve to call her anything else—"

"STOP INTERRUPTING ME, GODDAMMIT! You wanted what she had with me! The money, the time, the attention . . . I set that rain check with you, but *she's* the one who captivated me—"

"Your dick could hold the cure for cancer, and I still wouldn't let you fuck me."

Now *he's* the one who's speechless.

I step into *his* face. "It may not be obvious to anyone *else* around here, but I don't think it's a coincidence that the ones who do get your attention seem to go missing. Where's Charm, Thomas? You knock her up and get rid of her too? You know that daughter of yours sure looks a lot like Lucky."

Still nothing from him.

"And how many topless dances did you get from a girl too young to know Netflix used to mail DVDs, hmm? You prefer 'em fresh out of high school now? LaBrettney know she's married to a pedophile?"

Quicker than I can blink, my back's against a wall, and he's standing over me. This close, I can see the wildness in his eyes and smell liquor on his breath. I'm suddenly twenty-four again with some strange man demanding more from me than he paid for.

And it's hard to breathe.

A *ping!* chimes through the air, slicing the tension in two. His eyes narrow, but I'm ninety-eight percent sure that, this time, it doesn't have anything to do with me.

Still: I don't make a sound.

His phone *pings* again, and he leans so close that when he speaks, I can feel his spit on my sealed lips. How I manage not to puke all over his goofy-ass pink polo is beyond me. "Leave this alone, Ms. Johanssen," he says. (Shocking the shit out of me with the use of my given surname, as I'm sure he intended to.) "And I mean all of it. Past, present, and future. If you care anything about *anyone* here other than yourself, you'll not only wipe this entire encounter and anything else you think you witnessed in this room from your memory . . . you'll forget I even exist."

He's so close, he's practically kissing me.

"I do hope we understand each other," he whispers against my mouth. Then he turns to leave, pulling his phone from his pocket and checking the incoming messages.

The last thing I see before I drop this time is him disappearing through the door.

BEFORE

Lucky

AS WARM AND WELCOMING as the Walter Women's Wellness Center always was, and as much as I looked forward to my checkups as a result, on *this* particular day, I was ready to get out of there almost as soon as I walked in.

Maybe it was the bizarre reality of it all: I was at thirty-five weeks, my back ached, my breasts hurt, my feet were swollen, my nose had widened, and I'd developed a waddle. I avoided mirrors the way I'd done visibly drunk men back at the club. The sight of myself not looking like *myself* unnerved the shit out of me, and earlier that morning I'd discovered that my favorite Louboutin wedges no longer fit. And what was worse: it didn't actually matter since I couldn't see my feet anymore.

Or maybe my desire to flee had to do with the fact that my trek down the typically empty hallway to the OB department was suddenly littered with couples. Barring one pregnant lady/other lady pairing—and I'm pretty sure they were married—everywhere I looked, bulging-bellied women held on to the arms of the men that (I presumed) had impregnated them. The glints of light off diamond wedding rings felt like being jabbed in the pupils with hot needles—must've been nice to have a *real* partner-in-creation.

Most likely, though, my yearning to get the hell out of there—despite the ultrasound tech showing me my baby girl's face in 3D—had to do with getting a glimpse into the lobby of the oncology wing as a woman came out of it.

Said lobby was gorgeous, of course.

Despite what Dr. Chamblee said about not getting involved, when I got to the club the following night, Clutch handed me an envelope with a note that included the name and number of the center, as well as the doctor to request when setting up an appointment. Then my first time in the building, she'd come over to obstetrics to tell me hello. I'd commented on how *un*-doctor's-office-like the space was. Which was when I found out that she was a breast cancer survivor—"The irony of a cancer doctor getting cancer isn't lost on me . . ."—and she and that heavenly husband who brought her to the club had built this place from the ground up.

Definitely couldn't deny that the oncology lobby looked extra comfortable. But it was the glimpse I caught of a light-skinned woman in a wildly over-the-top, floppy-brimmed hat that hit me in a way I didn't want to acknowledge. I couldn't *really* see her because the doors were sliding shut, but she looked so much like Micah, I thought I might be going insane.

As soon as I heard, "Baby girl looks great. See you next week," from *my* doctor (also an immaculate Black woman), I got myself dressed and got the hell out of there.

I slowed down only when passing oncology again. Hoping the doors would open so I could see if the floppy-hatted woman was still there. I needed to know if it *was* Micah.

They stayed closed.

IT'S NOT THAT the condo wasn't nice . . . it was. *Really* nice, if you want the truth. I wound up moving into the place when I offhandedly mentioned to T that I'd found a renter for my own condo and would return to North Carolina to be near family until I could sell.

You'd've thought he knew it was his baby based on all the flabbergasted sputtering he did in response. *I mean, but you have support here . . . You're well established with your doctor, right? You really wanna start over somewhere this far along? And what about Brett? How's she supposed to manage without you? You really think it wise to do an out-of-state move in your condition? At least wait until after the baby arrives and we can meet her. Brett will be devastated if she can't be in the delivery room . . .*

A number of his points were valid. And I really didn't *want* to go. At least not right then. I knew I'd eventually have to—I'd managed my money well during my years as a dancer and had saved a solid amount . . . But it would only carry me so far. So, at twenty-nine weeks, when T showed me his condo above the coffee shop where we first connected outside work, and I heard him say all living expenses would be included? I moved in.

The furniture was gorgeous (I hated it, but Thomas and I had similar tastes in home décor). The neighborhood was fine, it was close to the Atlanta Beltline—easy access to a perfect walking path—and I had access to unlimited beverages and delicious café treats right downstairs.

And he really did mean *all* living expenses. Groceries included. I'd just put in an order with concierge, and bags would appear on the doorstep a couple hours later.

The hardest part was knowing I had to keep the whole arrangement from the woman I worked for and had grown quite fond of.

And speaking of LaBrettney, even the *car* was fine. It was a "gift" from her—she'd been none too thrilled the day I walked in a little sweatier than usual and she found out I took the bus because I'd sold my own car to cut back on expenses.

Of course she hadn't the slightest idea that I was fine with taking the bus because I was living in a condo her husband secretly owned, and the bus stop was twenty feet from the door to the building. If she'd known *that*, I doubt I would've arrived on the morning of my second bus commute and found a brand-new, top-of-the-line white Honda Accord sitting in the driveway with a giant red bow on the roof.

In a strange way, rejecting her gift while also hiding a bunch of shit from her—that I'd been a dancer, her husband was a cheater, and I was living like his mistress (without the sex because *gross*) *and* carrying his child . . . you know, the basics—felt infinitely shittier than graciously accepting it.

I named the car Casper.

And all of it was fine. *Nice* even: him taking care of me in one direction, her taking care of me in another . . .

I just hated that nothing I had was actually *mine*. A truth I got reminded of every time I walked into the condo, turned off the alarm, and heard *Welcome home, Thomas!* in the voice of some AI bitch. And though the car—which was distinctly *not* my G-Wagon but did what it needed to do—was registered to me, my name wasn't on the title tucked into the glove box with the owner's manual. Thomas's was.

I hadn't earned any of it, so I didn't have ownership. And with my barely recognizable face, elephant feet, and what felt like an alien spawn writhing around inside me whenever she felt froggy, my body no longer felt like it belonged to me either.

It was like being fifteen all over again.

I hated being reminded of that time in my life. Hated it. It had all been so fucking cliché. I was a week into my first job working concessions at the local movie theater when a group of boys strutted in like they owned the place. And the leader of the pack—Derrick was his name—wound up at my register.

It wouldn't be until a few years later, after I joined the Genders and Sexualities Alliance at my all-girls college, that I'd learn from the other lezzies about the concept of *That One*: the singular, unexpected guy who gets a gay girl's motor running. Derrick had been that for me. He was tall and brown and cut and just so damn fine. I'd known I liked girls since I was six and couldn't imagine a future when I wasn't married to my best girl friend, but the way Derrick looked at me when he stepped up to the counter... like he was seeing a sky full of stars for the first time?

Nobody had ever looked at me like that before.

It tripped me all the way up. Didn't help that I'd finally worked up the courage to ask that "best friend" since we were six if we could be more—hers were the first tongue, nipples, labia, and clit I'd ever had in my mouth. She'd shot me down with what felt like a twelve-gauge at close range. "I am *not* gay, Felice." It had hurt so much, I low-key didn't want to be gay anymore either.

So, when this beautiful boy gazed at me the way he did and then got tongue-tied when I asked for his order, I was a goner. When he came back in the middle of his movie and told me he was struggling to pay attention because he hadn't asked for my number, I bought that shit hook, line and sinker.

We went to different schools, but he was a senior and had a car, so we saw each other pretty regularly. And to my surprise, he turned out not to be the playboy type I'd braced myself for: he was a star, three-sport athlete at his school—football, basketball, and golf—but a virgin who took care of me and protected me and doted on me. He'd have flowers delivered to me at school, would take me to and from work, and always made sure I'd eaten. There was even a time I had really bad cramps and he showed up at my school midday with a hot water bottle. Just walked right on in during a class change and found me.

When he told me he loved me after a few months of hanging out, I knew he was telling the truth.

The first time we had penis-in-vagina sex, he was everything straight girls dreamed of (according to the smutty romance novels I read back then, at least): he touched me like I was made of flower petals, looked me in the eye, and consistently asked if I was okay. Didn't last long, of course, but we did it again a few hours later.

And it was after that second time that I knew I wanted to break up. Because despite all the passion and intensity and requisite heavy breathing, humming, and occasional moaning I was doing? The actual sex did nothing for me. In fact, when he moved my bra aside to lick and then suck my nipple, all I could think about was the way my ex–best friend's nips felt when they hardened against my own tongue. I had to fight the cringe as he trailed kisses over my stomach, and the moment he put his face between my legs and went to work, my mind went straight to how much better *she* was at it. And though his body looked amazing, sweat-sheened and thrusting in perfect rhythm, every time I blinked, I saw my most favorite mental image: that of her "magic city," as we called it, lowering to fill my waiting mouth.

I eventually just shut my eyes and reached down to get myself off to what was happening in my imagination while he was doing his thing. Which he took to mean that I was enjoying him so much, I couldn't help but touch myself. (Men, am I right?)

I managed to avoid being alone with him for a couple weeks after we did the deed and used the time to plot my exit. But then I missed my period. Took me an additional week to get past feeling like a walking PSA, but I eventually typed out a text on my little brick Nokia: I think I might be pregnant.

We made plans to get together on a Thursday night. I rehearsed my *I'd really like to break up, so if I am pregnant, I don't plan to stay that way* speech a thousand times. But it never happened. Not five minutes from my house, he took his eyes off the road to smile at me as we approached a green light, and didn't notice the SUV barreling towards the intersection from our left. A perfect T-bone. Killed him on impact.

My injuries were minor in comparison—a broken finger, bruised ribs, and a mild concussion from my head smacking into the passenger window. But when I regained consciousness at the hospital, the doctor fixed me in a blue-eyed stare and confirmed the implications of my gone-ghost period.

Everything happened superfast after that. On the morning of Derrick's funeral a week and a half later, I was in the middle of a U-Haul bench seat between my parents, en route to our new home just outside Durham, North Carolina. When offered the option to terminate the pregnancy and carry on with my regular teenage life like nothing happened, I didn't take it. I honestly just . . . couldn't. Not after Derrick's life had ended so abruptly. So, we went with plan B: move to another city, arrange for an at-birth adoption, and homeschool until the baby came.

Physically, the pregnancy had gone just fine: I didn't have a single complication and never even got morning sickness. Emotionally, though? It was like I'd been dropped from the top of the Tower of Terror and couldn't stop falling. My dad did his best to be supportive, but the rounder my belly got, the further he drifted from me. And my mom was my biggest cheerleader as she'd always been—it was over the course of those thirty-nine weeks that I learned the true meaning of *unconditional love*—but it was all too much. My body had changed, I had no friends, and I never left the new house. Combine all that with my embarrassment over being fifteen and gay, but pregnant, AND my grief over the death of the first person to make me feel like there was more to me than I realized, and by the time I reached twenty weeks, I wanted nothing more than for *everything* to just stop.

Thing was: every time I reached the brink and seriously considered ending it all, I would dream about Derrick. He'd been such a *good* guy and had so much promise. So much going for him— accolades on accolades, football scholarship to Morehouse (his dream school) secured, the apple of the eye of all who met him. And he'd genuinely loved me. Allowing his legacy to live on in the DNA of our shared child felt like the least I could do.

I never held the baby. Never laid eyes on the baby, even. Despite the danger involved, I opted to be put under for the entire birthing process. And my parents thankfully consented. They knew as well as I did how things had to go for *me* to be okay. So, one minute, I was counting down from ten, and the next, I was waking up with an empty midsection.

To this day, I have no idea if that baby was a boy or a girl. Intuition told me *girl*, but I never found out for sure. Couldn't risk getting attached. And the minute I broke back through to light after a monthslong, steeply uphill trek through major postpartum depression, I vowed to never sleep with another man again.

Yet somehow, here the fuck I was almost twenty years later, knocked up, alone, and sobbing like a toddler with a booboo on a fifteen-thousand-dollar couch in a living space that didn't belong to me. And I couldn't figure out why. Why was I there? What kept me from terminating, especially considering the circumstances? Why had I heard *this* baby's heartbeat and known I would keep her? I journaled about it for months but never came up with concrete answers.

I knew this little girl would be all mine, and a part of me couldn't wait . . . But there were so many questions I couldn't answer. Would the baby look like him? Would my little girl see him and recognize him and connect with him and want to be held by him? Was I wrong for not telling him the truth? And what about LaBrettney? What would *she* say?

I shut my eyes as the tears continued to fall, and an image of the woman in the floppy hat materialized like a hologram.

Without giving it too much thought—honestly didn't have the capacity for *thinking* much at that point—I grabbed my phone and called Micah. I was ready to tell her everything: assault, pregnancy, missing her, wanting her, needing her, not giving a fuck at all about how things went before . . .

She didn't answer.

If she had, things might've gone differently.

Like, not to point fingers or whatever, but the only reason I did what I did next—and what I'm pretty sure sealed my fate—is because Micah hadn't answered my call at a moment that I desperately needed her to. I could feel the dark place from before tugging at me because of how alone I felt.

So, I called the only person who knew precisely *where* I was and why. A person who happened to be downstairs discussing a purchase and remodel plan for the flailing coffee shop where we'd first crossed the line by meeting outside of Boom Town.

"I'll be up in ten minutes," he said.

And I knew. I *knew* the moment the door shut behind him on his way out after our brief conversation that I was in deep shit.

If someone had asked *how* I knew, I wouldn't have been able to say . . . maybe it was pure intuition. But something about T's response to my confession—that (1) "Micah" wasn't actually a guy, (2) I hadn't been with *any* guys in over a decade, and (3) the baby making my midsection stick out like I'd swallowed a watermelon seed was therefore his—made my palms feel like I'd dipped them in lukewarm water.

Because he didn't really respond at all. Despite my vaguely dramatic truth-puke all over the spotless glass table between us, he didn't move. Almost like he'd frozen in time. Pretty sure he even stopped blinking. His face still held a *concerned and actively listening* expression, but it was like the light had gone out of his eyes. No one could've convinced me they hadn't shifted from light green to dark.

"Umm . . . Thomas?" I said after an eerily long silence.

He blinked a few times and then his eyebrows lifted. "Hmm?"

"Did . . . you hear what I said?"

"About?"

"Umm . . . the baby?"

His eyes narrowed.

"And how . . . it's yours?"

"Huh?" And then he shook his head (like he was coming back into his body?). "Right. No. Of course." Nodding then. "Makes perfect sense. I'll, umm . . ." He looked at his watch . . . "Hey, what time is it?" . . . and stood. "Shit, I gotta run." He made a beeline for the door.

"Umm . . ." (I didn't know what the fuck else to say.)

Once his hand was on the knob, he turned and finally looked at me for real. "Everything is going to be fine, okay? Like *perfectly* fine," he said. "I'll get a trust fund set up tomorrow, and we can discuss logistics and all that. You're still moving, yeah?"

"Definitely." Whatever uncertainty I'd had about returning to North Carolina *poofed* away like a little cloud of truck exhaust.

"Yeah, I think that's a great idea," he said. "Be close to family and everything. You and I will need to come up with terms so we understand our *roles* and all that, but I'll make sure the kid is taken care of—"

"That is *not* why I told you, T—"

"I know, I know, you're 'not that type of woman,' blah blah." (With air quotes and everything.) "Just letting you know that if the kid truly *is* mine, I'll make sure it never wants for anything. We'll talk later, all right?"

And he walked out.

As soon as the door was shut, I called Micah again. I had no clue how to process any of what had just happened. Like what had he meant, "if" the kid truly was his? Had he not heard what the fuck I'd said?

Again, she didn't answer.

I sucked in a deep breath and let it out as slowly as I could. It felt like my worst nightmare was hurtling towards its climax. Which meant it would end soon.

Because *I* would end soon. I could feel it as powerfully as the baby's sudden kick.

So, I went to lie down.

"Sorry, sweet pea," I said cradling my tummy. "I gave it my best."

As I drifted off to sleep, I could swear I heard my own mama weeping.

MONDAY, JUNE 2

Lyriq

Need to know you're all right . . .

Read 2:23 p.m.

I LOOK UP INTO THE hopeful face of Dejuan, the dumbass boy who refuses to believe the girl he (stupidly) fell for would disappear without a trace and not tell him. I happened to be out on the floor tonight when he strode in like some damn crusader on a mission to convert lost souls by any means necessary.

"You . . . sent her a text," I say.

"Yeah, and it was *read* at 2:23 p.m. You can see it right there—"

He points to the screen, but I swat his hand away. "I'm not blind, sweetheart," I say, more perturbed than I'm ready to admit.

I'd settled into this particular mystery going unsolved considering my lack of leads *and* the open threat to my life as I knew it. So, the boy showing up yet again—this time with his phone stuck out like he discovered something important—is really fuckin' up my flow.

"She left you on read." *Which I'm sure stings because you clearly think you're in love with her*, I don't add.

He's clearly going through it. "Right!"

I just stare at him.

"Don't you get it? If it's read, it means she *saw* it."

"Okay..."

"This is the first message to pop up as read since Friday before last."

I really wish he would just drop— "Wait..." I say as the revelation registers. "Really?"

"Yeah. Scroll through."

As much as I want to say no and tell him he should give this up because the girl is long gone now and obviously not that into him if she hasn't even been checking his messages, I do as he says. Shit, at least she doesn't have him blocked: none of the messages I've sent over the past week have even shown as delivered.

This kid, though, Dejuan... he's been texting her two to three times per day since she turned up missing. Ten days total. And all just... check-ins.

> **Saw you didn't come home last night. You good?**
>
> **Me again... not trying to be a nuisance. Just checking on you...**
>
> **Really hope you're okay, Damaris. Could you please let me know?**
>
> **Didn't want anything. Just hope you're safe...**

And on and on.

It hits me in a way I'm not expecting, all the genuine concern without being pushy. It was how Felice had been with me when I started having breast pains and began to pull away. Never aggressive. Just genuinely concerned. Which I hadn't been able to appreciate at the time. But to see it from a *man*—

"I'm telling you, Miss Lyriq: something is wrong."

"Maybe she's just in a hard place and doesn't want to talk to you." I continue to read through the messages he's sent her. "Or anyone else for that matter." *I've been there*, I don't say, even though a part of me wants to.

A memory drops into my head like Guapa's signature trick where she backflips while holding on to the pole and lands on the floor in an admittedly impressive middle split, thighs and ass bouncing on impact: a little less than a year ago, I had a god-awful radiation session at the women's center that left my skin red, itchy, and on the verge of blistering. I was lying on my back in bed, topless and crying, when my phone rang. It was Felice.

I didn't answer.

Nor did I answer when she called a second time an hour or so later. I just . . . couldn't.

"That's the thing, though, Miss Lyriq—"

"You really gotta drop the 'Miss,' kid."

"Nah, my mama would kill me. Anyway, what I'm saying is she told me a *lot* of stuff. Like stuff she's never told anyone—"

But his voice fades from my consciousness. I'm still scrolling through his phone, and the day before Charm stopped responding, she'd sent him a message:

> Don't show these to anyone cuz
> it would get me in trouble and
> I need to keep this job . . . but
> look how cute she is!

Attached were two images of Damaris, cheek-to-cheek with a fat-faced (and yes: cute as hell) baby girl.

The same baby girl who was propped on Thomas McIntyre's wife's hip when she'd answered the door two days ago.

> Damn, that's wild.
> Look like she could be yours.

Whoa now, don't curse me!
I definitely don't want kids.
Feels like having a baby sister,
though. I always wanted one of
those, but my parents weren't
with it.

> Lol, glad you're getting to
> live your dream then!
> How old is she?

A little over ten months.

"Miss Lyriq? You all right?"

"Whose baby is this?" I say, holding the phone up.

"Oh shit, you weren't supposed to see those!" He grabs the phone from my hand. "Damn," he says, shaking his head. "She's gonna kill me. I wasn't think—"

"Sweetheart, I need to know whose baby it is."

"I mean, I can't give you a *name* cuz I don't have one," he replies. "But she was working for one of my homegirls from high school, Via, whose family runs a fruit stand at the farmers market a few days per week. Apparently Via's older cousin, a guy, saw Damar—I mean

Charm, excuse me—and offered her a job as a part-time nanny. Shit was mad suspect to *me*... Some random older dude is like *Hey, you're good at selling fruit, come take care of my kid*? And you're just like, '*Bet!*'? With no questions asked?" He shakes his head. "This is why I think something's up, Miss Lyriq."

The *Miss* grates again, but I bite my tongue.

"She was... kind of oblivious to potential danger? Anyway, she obviously took the job. But you're not supposed to know that."

"And this friend of yours... what's her last name?"

"McIntyre. And her name is Olivia. But I already checked to see if she or her cousin seen or heard from D, and she said no."

"And you believe her?"

"No reason not to, really. I've known Via forever, feels like. We had a little short-lived co-crush situation in, like, tenth grade, but my mama has never been down with me dating white girls, so it didn't go anywhere. Can't imagine why she would lie to me about seeing Damaris. Especially as I'm the person who connected the two of them."

"Connected them for what?"

He looks around the club and bites his lip.

"I don't have all night, honey. You gonna tell me, or nah?"

He sighs and drops his chin. "Look, you really not 'posed to be hearing *any* of this from me, but Damaris didn't really love working here. She been dancin' her whole life, but doing it in *this* context was making her hate her passion—"

"I need relevant facts, not a biography."

"My bad. Anyway, like I was saying, she ain't really like it here. Only reason I found out this is where she worked is because she canceled on a date one afternoon, so I went to check on her and found her crying in her bathroom. Some nasty old man apparently told her she reminded him of his granddaughter while she was dancing topless, and that shit creeped her out. She also told me about some big-bellied white man who said he wanted to see her 'nappy nigger twat.'" His jaw clenches. "That was the night she asked if I knew of anybody who was hiring. I called Via cuz her family is rich as hell and super well-connected, so I figured if anyone would have a lead, she would."

"And you said this Via person claims she hasn't seen or heard from Charm?"

"From Damaris, but yeah. Via don't know nothin' about 'Charm,' and D made me swear I would keep it that way."

I nod. "And you never saw this other cousin she was working for? The guy?"

"Nah, I didn't. Which I'm kinda glad about cuz I'm not sure what I would do if I knew what he looked like and saw him on the street—"

There's a commotion near the entrance, and we both turn to see what's going on.

"Whoa, is that Lil Aylie?" he says.

"Excuse me, who?"

"Lil Aylie!" He looks down at me wide-eyed.

Shit. I totally see what a girl like Damaris would see in a guy like this. He seems so . . . untainted.

"He's like the biggest up-and-coming rapper there is right now. Had a track go viral because of a social media trend, and now it's a massive hit and he just signed his first deal with a major record label. That's totally him!"

Which *him* the kid is referring to, I'm not sure, as about six all came in at once. Five younger-looking Black guys—who are all casually dressed but wearing very sparkly diamond chains—and a mid-thirties white man.

One I recognize but really don't want to see, considering everything Dejuan just told me.

Wherever Damaris was (is?), someone read at least one of her messages today.

Had it been her? Or the green-eyed demon who just walked in as a part of some young rapper's entourage?

It takes everything in me not to point Thomas McIntyre out and tell the kid: "*That's* him."

BEFORE

LaBrettney

THE CONDO HAD BEEN scrubbed inside out, upside down, forwards, backwards, high and low. I knew because I'd stopped by there on my way home to make sure.

My eyes fell to the pair of white gloves on the coffee table in our oversized living room. Lately TJ had taken to complaining that our home "feels far too expansive for just the two of us. Especially if we aren't having children."

The size of our home making him uncomfortable is the reason I'd refused to sell it. The house had been a "wedding gift" to me—mine was the sole name on the deed. It seemed extravagant and romantic to the friends and colleagues he was trying to impress, but I knew better: there's little worse than a love-bombing motherfucker with too much money.

But he'd been at home with me plenty as of late. Hadn't occurred to him that if he moved Felice into his precious little Midtown condo, he'd have to sleep in our house where he belonged. No more multi-night "business trips."

In a way, I was thankful to Felice for becoming my husband's latest obsession. His sick need to root himself into the soil of random women's lives had finally tripped him up: in giving his secret sanctuary to Felice, he no longer had a go-to setting for his extramarital activities.

Not that he had a clue I knew any of this. He was still under the delusion that I didn't know the condo existed. Also didn't know I knew about the coffee shop. And the stake he bought in that club a few months ago.

But I knew everything.

Anyway, the gloves: I'd gone into the condo with them on after the concierge called to let me know the cleaning crew TJ hired had left the building. (Thomas Jefferson McIntyre was nothing if not predictable.) I'd checked behind them to make *sure* everything was clean—I knew *he* wasn't going to do it, and there needed to be no trace of Felice whatsoever. There'd been one locked drawer in the china cabinet that I couldn't find a key to, but as I was pretty sure TJ had been the one to lock it, I tried not to worry too much about it.

The place was spotless. *Truly* spotless. All traces of her ever having been there, erased. The linens had been burned, the furniture wiped down, the carpet shampooed where necessary, and everything twice disinfected. Looked like he'd also had them replace all the toilet seats, area rugs, and kitchen utensils.

I'd be lying if I said it hadn't hurt to walk in and know she'd been living in his secret million-dollar condo.

After I learned he'd moved her in—concierge spilled the beans when I called to ask if there was someone in the apartment after he'd spent six consecutive nights at home—I left her at the house where she was helping me with a project and went to see what she'd done with the place. (And to pay the concierge what I owed him for the information.) Felice only stayed there for a handful of months, but bits of her had been deposited in ways that made her presence there knowable. Candles spread about, some with the wooden stems from burned incense sticks poking up out of them haphazardly (which I'm sure made TJ's flesh crawl); coconut oil and apple cider vinegar in the pantry (for her hair, though I'm sure he had no clue); a cast-iron pan with a layer of black crud caked at the bottom sitting in the oven (that surely got *immediately* tossed out when the cleaners saw it); a U-shaped body pillow she must've snuggled up with every night...

All of it was gone. Now the place was back to looking like it could be the building's model home. Sterile and lifeless. Like chicken with no seasoning.

I pulled my eyes away from the gloves and looked out the window.

I hated that any of this was even necessary. That he'd gotten himself into another damn mess and then decided *I* needed to fix it yet again. But when he'd come home the night Felice told him the baby was his? My god, he'd been a wreck. He went on and on and on about *How could she even SUGGEST such a thing?* and *Didn't she know how much he had at stake?* And *Why couldn't Felice SEE that?* And *The very idea(!) of one Thomas J. McIntyre siring a child with an EXOTIC DANCER (of all things)?* (The "extramarital" part didn't seem to register, but why would it?) It would've been *career suicide!*

I watched as his car turned into the driveway and disappeared along the side of the house. Then started to count. If the door between the mudroom and kitchen didn't open within sixteen seconds, I'd know he was lingering in the garage. Which he only did when something was wrong—

Said door creaked open—"Babe?"—then creaked again before clicking shut. Part of me wanted him to get the hinges oiled, but doing so would've make it difficult to hear his comings and goings, so I left it alone.

He made it inside in thirteen seconds.

"I'm in the living room," I called back.

Twenty-four seconds later, he came in, shrugged out of his blazer to toss it over the back of the couch, and took a seat in the chair furthest from me—which I tried not to think too much of. We met eyes, and I grinned and nodded to acknowledge his presence, then shifted my gaze back out the front window. It hooked onto the lowest branch of our hundred-year-old oak tree. Another thing he didn't know I knew: he'd had it assessed for a rope swing shortly after Felice shared the news of her pregnancy with us.

The one thing I didn't know was how long *he* knew she was pregnant before she told me.

I hadn't asked for details the night he came home talking about how she needed *to be disposed of.* (Like she was some piece of trash waiting to be thrown out? He obviously wanted her at some point . . .)

"Well?" he asked, attempting to draw my attention. I knew what he wanted to know, and also knew he wanted me to look him in the eye when I told him.

So I decided not to. Just reached into my handbag, pulled something that looked like a blackened mophead out of it, and tossed it in his direction.

It landed on the couch beside him.

A ponytail. Bound at the top with a black elastic band with at least a couple hundred thin box braids hanging loose.

A wave of green washed over his face, and his Adam's apple bobbed.

I had to fight to keep from smiling. It felt good to make him squirm.

"So, it's done, then?"

I nodded. "All done."

"And no one will . . ." *look for her,* he wanted to say. But the words wouldn't come out. For a hair of a second, he almost looked remorseful.

But then he shook his head. "You're sure—"

"Everything has been taken care of, my love," I said then, halting his thoughts before they could spin beyond his grip.

He looked at me and fell in love again. It wouldn't last long, no. But long enough for him to do something ridiculous like whisk me away on some lavish vacation tomorrow. TJ had never genuinely loved anyone. I don't think he was capable. But his loyalty (not the sexual type, obviously, but something a little deeper) was worth more than my five-carat diamond engagement ring. When I was the apple of TJ's eye, I could do no wrong. He'd believe anything I said and would do whatever I wanted him to. Except keep his dick in his pants, of course.

Just needed to seal the deal.

"There's one other thing," I said, reaching into my handbag again.

This time, I pulled out a blue folder, then stood and walked over to kneel in front of him. "I know this will seem sudden." I gently placed a hand on his knee. "I didn't bring it up before now because there was too much going on, and I needed to get some answers on my own first." I took a deep breath and dropped my chin.

His leg stiffened beneath my palm. He was uncomfortable.

Good.

When I looked up at him, I was crying. I knew there were black streaks running down my cheeks and that it would intensify his discomfort.

And I was right: he looked away.

I wiped my face, nose included, with the hand from his knee, and then put it back. He couldn't help it: he flinched.

I didn't move it. "I noticed how moved you were by Felice's pregnancy, TJ."

His eyes went wide.

"You've been asking me for a child for some time now, and I'll admit it: I've been afraid. But I went to see a doctor—"

"A doctor? What kind of doctor?"

"One who specializes in . . . fertility issues," I replied. I almost had him. "Which I found out I unfortunately do have."

His fists clenched on the armrests, but I didn't break eye contact.

"There's another route, though," I said, giving his knee a squeeze. I pushed up on my knees and leaned forward, my face now lit like the homes on our street at Christmastime. "So, I took it."

"Huh?"

I opened the folder and placed it on his lap. Inside was an info packet . . . and a sonogram image.

"What is this?"

"That's our baby." I pointed to the grayscale, though shockingly detailed, image of a fully formed face. It had a tiny fist tucked up under its chin as though deep in thought. "And *that*"—now I pointed to the sheet of paper—"is all we need to know about our baby's birth mother."

According to the info sheet I showed him, the mom was sixteen, Black/white biracial, and located in North Carolina, and this was her first pregnancy.

"It'll be four months or so until I can bring her home," I went on. "Something about some law there. But she's *ours*, babe. Can you believe it?"

He didn't respond.

Not then, and not later that day.

Or the next day.

Or the next week.

Or the next month.

He didn't say a word as I flipped one of our guest bedrooms into an excessively frilly nursery space, or as box after box after box of baby shit arrived on our doorstep.

When I left town for a week and came back with the most adorable little caramel-skinned baby girl either of us had ever laid eyes on, he still couldn't believe it. Not when the baby looked into his eyes, or when he placed his index finger against her palm and she wrapped her tiny hand around it.

When he finally broke free of the spell the baby had him under, there were tears streaming down his face.

"She's really ours?" he said, looking into my eyes.

I nodded. "She is."

He brushed the baby's cheek with the back of his finger. "What's her name?"

"You tell me."

He looked up again, stunned.

"She's ours." And I put my hand on *his* cheek. "But you should be the one to name her."

He took in the baby's features . . . her big brown eyes and button nose, café latte skin tone and itty-bitty lips. She was so much more perfect and familiar than he would ever realize.

I had him. And I knew he'd be #TeamBrett for a while after all I'd done.

"Felicity," he said. "Her name is Felicity."

PART TWO

A REAL CHARMER

Tuesday, May 27

Dear Lady Luck,

First, to address the obvious: yes, it is strange and feels mildly disrespectful to be writing in a journal that belonged to someone else. But after finding and reading this book of thoughts that belonged to you—especially considering where I am and what I have going on—I felt inspired to record what's happening to me and how I feel about it. Same way you did.

My name is Damaris Wilburn, and I am nineteen years old. Which, as I've come to realize over the past eleven months is a very transformational age.

Right now, I'm in trouble. I'm not sure how much or how deep, but I made a decision four days ago that I think has put my life in danger. I stole some money from this . . . place I was working at. Part of the reason I feel okay about addressing these journal entries to you is because, if I understand the mentions in your entries of "dancing for him" in connection to a "club," you had a job similar to the one I got when I moved to Atlanta.

I couldn't really tell how you felt about doing it—you'd stopped by the time you started writing, so all mentions are very matter of fact—but I'll tell you what I haven't told anybody: I REALLY fucking hated it.

I won't get into why because I'd rather not think about it too much—we'll just say some of the men were garbage bags shaped like human beings and how so many of them managed to have wives was beyond me. But from the first time an older, not-Black man (he was some sort of Middle Eastern) called me a racial slur while touching me and drooling over how young I looked ("Have you had your sweet sixteen yet, young lady?"), I knew I wouldn't last long. I thought I could handle it, but it was a stretch too far from my upbringing.

Then I encountered One who was different. One who seemed to be able to really SEE me. There was a lot I didn't know about him at first—he was just a guy who came in on his lunch shift one day saying he'd "heard there was a new talent on the Boom Town day shift and needed to see what the fuss was about." In fact, the first time I saw him, I was up on the spinning pole, and the sight of him so caught me off guard, I lost my spot, got dizzy, and had to come down to recenter. It was like seeing a ghost.

Todd Vickery.

All I'll say about Todd right now is that he forced me to grow up. In many ways, he's the reason I wound up on that pole in the first place. And even though once I was back on the ground I could see that the man who'd come closer was very much not the asshole I left in North Carolina, something about this new guy's face and hair and eyes and the way he carried himself—like nothing on earth could ever stop him from getting exactly what he wanted—lit something up inside me.

Initially, dancing for Thomas felt like a strange but sweet revenge: there I was, purposefully enticing a green-eyed bastard who looked like Todd, but very much wasn't—which meant Todd didn't own me or my body anymore. I'd taken me back and could do with my "vessel" as I pleased.

I felt powerful, holding sway over Thomas the way I got to every Monday, Wednesday, and Friday afternoon from 12:30 to 1:30 p.m. And he'll never know it because I would never tell him, but I made more from him during those three hours than most other girls made in five full daytime shifts.

That I wound up seeing him outside the club was some sort of serendipity. I never used the number on the card he gave me. I never used any of the numbers (though I did keep the cards to remind me of my powers, so to speak). My third week working for Via at the farmers market, I was unboxing golden kiwis, and there he was. Just as shocked and speechless as I was.

Later, I would wonder why I'd failed to connect the McIntyre on the business card with Via's last name. But the encounter he and I had that day changed everything. The next time he came into the club, he wouldn't let me dance for him. Just pulled me into a corner and broke down. Told me the reason he'd taken to me is because I reminded him of an old friend of his named Felice. She'd passed away, but he said that when he saw me move, it was like she was suddenly alive there in front of him again. (It's not an uncommon thing for me, people telling me I remind them of someone else, but this time was kind of creepy when I think about it now. At the time, though, it made me feel . . . special.)

However, when he saw me with Via, "something shifted in me," he said. "I realized how beautiful you are and how much life you have ahead of you, and I think you should transition out of this industry."

It was music to my ears, honestly. I felt like someone finally realized that *I*, a person, was inside the body they were gawking at. Which is when he told me he had a daughter and that his wife was getting back into her career, and they could use some help. He didn't want me to stop dancing immediately—nor did I want to . . . yes, I hated it, but the money was really good, and our bartender took care of me every shift to make it easier—but I started taking care of the little girl a few mornings per week.

And everything was fine. Great, even. I'd rented a little apartment beneath a friend's house, and with the money from the nanny job, fruit stand, and club, I was working enough to be able to start saving up for school . . .

But then last week something terrible happened.

I have this older cousin named Tink. Mind you: I didn't know she was my older cousin until about seven months ago, but that's neither here nor there now.

Unfortunately, one of Tink's "girls" set her up. Based on what China, one of the more recent house residents, told me, Tink "caped the bottom bitch of one of the city's most notorious pimps, and he got so mad, he sent in a plant to hide drugs on the property, then called in a raid."

(Couldn't make this stuff up if I tried.)

Tink was on parole, so they arrested her on the spot and set a $150,000 bail, but the cops cleaned the place out and confiscated all the cash she had in the house. So, there was no money to bond her out.

Which is where I messed up. I'd only managed to save $5,973. So, when the woman who'd hired and trained me—I only know her as Lyriq—asked me to come be a bottle girl for the night shift, I said yes, even though I knew the tips wouldn't be as good. And when she asked me to grab something out of the office and handed me a key, I said yes again.

And when I got in there and saw all that money...
I couldn't help it: I grabbed a single banded stack and stuck it in my fanny pack. When I got home, I combined it with the money I'd saved, hid it somewhere safe, wrote a note in code about where to find it, and delivered that note to a spot only Tink and the girls would know about.

But as soon as that letter was out of my hands, it hit me what I'd done.

And I got scared.

Couldn't bring myself to go back to my apartment (Because what if someone came looking for me??), so I turned off my phone and I slept in my car (which was kind of a loaner, but more on that later). I don't dance on Saturday or Sunday, though I did go to my farmers market job. And that worked in my favor because Via could tell something was off with me. I lied and told her Dejuan and I were in a fight and I needed a place to crash for a couple nights. Her couch is lovely.

Yesterday morning I went to take care of Felicity, as I've done every Monday for the past four weeks. And we went to the park as we always do. Which is where I saw one of the girls who was living at Tink's. She was there taking care of a little white girl. And she told me things were bad. That none of the girls dared go near the house for fear that their traffickers now know where it is. Apparently, one of the girls went back there to grab some of her stuff, and though she couldn't get in—place got boarded up a couple days after the raid—someone was staking the place out and saw her. The last message the girl sent to the group chat just said, **He found me. Erasing this phone and tossing it. Y'all be safe.**

Slept in my car again last night.

Then this morning, things took yet another turn. On Tuesdays, I typically work 10 to 12 for the McIntyres before heading to my afternoon shift at the club, but I was running a few minutes late. When I got to the house, though, it initially seemed like no one was there: I walked in and went straight to Felicity's room to get her up from her nap and take her to the kitchen for a morning snack as I always do, but her crib was empty. I was standing there, staring at the blush-colored sheet on the little mattress, when I heard laughter.

The door to one of the other bedrooms was cracked, and I'd just raised my fist to knock when a pair of muffled voices floated out into the hallway. One of them was Ms. LaBrettney's, for sure, but the other one . . . Not to jump to conclusions, but it definitely wasn't Thomas in there with her.

I didn't know what else to do, so I went downstairs and sat on the couch. Didn't know where Felicity was or if she was even there, but I also didn't want to just leave, because I really need the job. Not sure how much time passed, but eventually Ms. LaBrettney came out in a bathrobe, looking like she was walking on air. I felt bad about how abruptly the sight of me yanked her back down to earth.

Long story short, she'd texted AND left a voicemail letting me know she didn't need me to come today, but I'd missed both because my phone was off. And in the most bizarre twist of all, the moment I got back in the car, I turned my phone on, and not two minutes later Thomas called. Which is how I wound up here in this really nice apartment. Definitely the fanciest place I've ever stayed, though the coffee shop on the ground floor is under construction.

When Thomas (who I cannot call "Mr" anything, despite referring to his wife that way. FAR too weird considering he's seen me naked) called, he sounded more stressed than I would've expected, but when I told him that some shit had gone down with my cousin (true) and I'd missed work because I was trying to find a new place to live (lie), he shared his location and told me to come there.

Here.

I'll admit that I was nervous—never been truly alone with him before and I had no idea how things would go. He definitely acted a little strange when he opened the door—like far more concerned than seemed warranted? Maybe I was selling myself short, but I did my best to take my boss/trainer's advice and keep the "transactional" nature of my encounters with the guys I danced for top of mind, even if they shared really personal details of their lives with me. "Harsh as fuck, I know, but these niggas do NOT care about you. Never ever get that shit twisted."

Anyway, he's letting me crash here for the time being, but also insisted that I go back to work at the club tomorrow if I want to (1) "Stay here until you find a new place," and (2) "Continue as Felicity's nanny." That second part seemed unfair—I'm an excellent caretaker and see no reason for what I do or don't do at the club to have any bearing on my other job—and I have no idea how I'm going to handle things come tomorrow, but I'll cross that bridge when I get to it.

Just like you had to do with a number of things.

All in all, I'm glad I found this journal of yours. I got bored and started looking in drawers as I sometimes do when I'm in new spaces. And though almost all of them were empty—shout-out to the silverware drawer for not being a disappointment—the discovery of a locked one in the china cabinet got my wheels turning. Quick insert, wiggle and twist *with a bobby pin, and there sat this beautiful, leatherbound notebook. My guess is that the cabinet itself is some sort of high-priced antique, and Thomas bought it for the look and never bothered to check the drawers. Or maybe he did, but didn't have a key to the locked one, so he let it go.*

Either way, very grateful I found it. Gonna read through it again. And probably again.

Because as thankful as I am to be sleeping in a bed tonight, too many things don't feel right.

Wednesday, May 28

I think I might've messed up.

I do this thing sometimes where my curiosity will get the best of me, and I'll either ask the wrong question or one question too many. And I'll know it's happened because the person I'm talking to's demeanor will shift in a really noticeable way.

Sort of how you said Jeff's did after you told him the truth about your baby being his.

I've read your final journal entry probably twenty times now. It's so . . . compelling, I guess would be the word. It's clear you were afraid for your life and the life of your unborn child, but there was also this sense of, like . . . calm acceptance of whatever was coming? It kind of read like a cliff-hanger ending in a novel. Almost like none of it was real. (I've had a few moments when I've wondered if maybe it wasn't, and you're some mysterious storytelling fairy who leaves handwritten tales locked in china cabinets and chests of drawers for only the most intrepid of seekers to find. Can you tell I read a lot of books?)

Anyway, I've done my best to not speculate about what happened to you after you stopped writing, but after today, my curiosity got to bubbling. Which is where my mistake came in.

I did wind up turning my phone back off yesterday after using the GPS to get myself to this "condo" (how it's different from an apartment, I don't know, but whatever). But just before he left, Thomas said "8 a.m. tomorrow, yeah?" To which I dumbly replied, "Does she actually need me tomorrow?" and he got this really confused look on his face. "Of course she does. Why would you say that?"

Despite having had a secret relationship of my own in the past, it didn't occur to me that he wouldn't know his wife got rid of their kid and told the sitter not to come so she could have her side piece over. Don't remember what I said to play it off, but it was apparently satisfactory: he didn't say anything else about it, and I let it drop from my mind (to the point where I didn't even mention it in my journal entry yesterday).

So, I showed up today like I was supposed to, and man, was it awkward. One minute, Ms. LaBrettney was overly nice. Like, she noticed I was wearing the same shirt I wore on Monday (and also would've had on yesterday if I hadn't managed to snag some things I'm sure Via won't even notice are gone from her overflowing closet) and asked if I wanted "to do a little online shopping when Lissy goes down for her nap?" Also randomly offered to put gas in the car her husband gave me to use (see? a loaner).

But she would also hit me with questions like, "Hey, you didn't see anything out of place when you were here yesterday, did you?" Or, "Any idea exactly how long you were here yesterday? Or precisely what time you arrived? I want to make sure you're compensated for your time."

It was actually kind of fun giving answers that I knew would set her on edge. Like, "No, but I did hear some laughter coming from your room. You must've been watching something really funny!" And "Precisely, no, but I stood in Felicity's room looking confused for a while." And not even because I'm judging her for having an affair. It's more like . . . knowing this thing she knows I COULD know—and could destroy her with if I was that type of person—makes me feel powerful. Similar to how you described the feeling of dancing.

We didn't wind up online shopping during Felicity's nap, but there was a point when I was scrolling on my phone and my skin started to prickle. When I looked up, Ms. LaBrettney was staring at me. And she didn't look away when I met her eyes. "Is . . . everything okay?" I asked.

"Yeah, everything's fine." She still didn't look away. "You just remind me so much of a friend of mine. Like, sometimes I'll look up and see her instead of you."

"Oh. Got it."

I went back to my scrolling, but she was still staring. So, to try and break the ice, I said, "What's her name?"

"Most people just called her Lucky."

A bell went off in my head, but I tried to ignore it. This woman who is cheating on her husband having a friend people call "Lucky," and the existence of a journal written by a woman who refers to herself as "Lady Luck" locked away in said husband's condo could totally be a (very trippy) coincidence.

But it ate at me all day.

So, when Thomas showed up here this evening, that curiosity I've been trying to keep at bay took over.

The moment he walked in, I could tell he was agitated.

Which made me nervous—I've had enough negative experiences with agitated white boys to last three lifetimes. I remember this one time, Todd and I had plans to get together one evening, and so I sent him some nudes during the day. You know: give him a little preview of what he'd be getting later.

I had no idea he was in a meeting.

I could tell he was pissed the moment I got into his car, but I didn't know it was at ME until we got inside his apartment, and he detonated. "Have you lost your MIND, Damaris? I literally dropped my phone when I opened those pictures, and it landed on the floor FACE UP. Are you trying to get me fired?"

The accusation stung because I'd been nothing but the "goodest girl," as he used to call me. Both during sex ("My god, you are the goodest girl," he would say while holding me by the hair and thrusting up into my throat . . . always made me thankful that my brief bout with bulimia in ninth grade destroyed my gag reflex); and during services at our church ("There's that goodest girl!" said in greeting with a good ol' side hug as I'd walk into the sanctuary for youth group on Wednesdays).

Thomas, as it turned out, was mad because I hadn't been at the club when he showed up at the regular time today. He made a comment about "routine" and "keeping up appearances" and claimed that me not being there when he came looking for me was "embarrassing" for him.

I was surprised by how angry it made ME . . . and how much it stung. Here I thought he was different from the other assholes I met in that place, but now he was trying to make my absence from a job that was eating my soul about him and his image? "'Keeping up appearances,' huh?" I wanted to scream at him. "Is that what this is really about?"

Of course I didn't actually say that. If he kicked me out, I wouldn't have anywhere to go.

But then he smacked a nail in the coffin: "You likely don't have a job there anymore since you've decided not to show up three days in a row. Which means I also have to let you go."

"Let me go? What do you mean?"

"I mean we will no longer be employing you to care for our daughter."

I was speechless.

"We had an agreement that you would keep your other job for a while, Damaris. The optics of you caring for my child—"

"What 'optics'? Nobody even knows I work for you."

"But they'll find out," he said then. "They always do—"

"Who is 'they'?"

He shook his head. "It doesn't matter now. What's done is done."

And I recognized that response. The irrationality of some unnamed emotion in the driver's seat mixed with the power to make things that cause discomfort disappear. White dude signature. "Did something happen at work today?" I asked then, done playing scapegoat.

It was apparently the wrong question: he looked like I'd just told him his dog died. "Why would you ask that?"

(Clearly something HAD happened at work today.)

"Honestly, just curious," I said.

"Nothing you need to be concerned with," came the reply. "You need to figure out where you're going to stay."

That's the moment my reality hit me: I'd gone from three jobs to probably none (I doubted he would let Via keep me employed at the fruit stand) after giving away my savings AND the money I stole, I couldn't go back to my apartment, and I was being kicked out of the one place I knew I was safe because no one other than the man in front of me, his wife included, knew I was here.

There was no way I'd survive.

"I'm really sorry, Thomas," I said, turning on the waterworks. "I know I messed up, but . . . I need your help, okay? You don't understand how awful that place is, and once you gave me an out, I just . . . I couldn't go back there."

And though my tears were initially as fake as the ID I'd used to get hired, as that man stared at me, eyes wide—and the same color as Todd's—the sobs became very real.

And it (sort of) worked. Next thing I knew, I was sitting on the couch, and he was passing me a box of tissues.

"Look, I hear what you're saying," he said, still standing and strung as tight as a violin string. "And I'll help you as much as I can, but only for a short time. I don't mind you staying here for a few more days, but if you do, you have to lay low. I can't have you connected to me in any traceable way since you disappeared from that club." He ran a hand across the back of his neck. "It, uhhh . . . wouldn't be a good look for me."

Ms. LaBrettney's voice rang through my head again. Her mention of her friend "Lucky" became a whole fire alarm.

I gulped. "I understand."

And things probably would have been fine if I had left it at that. Or if he hadn't randomly locked on to the china cabinet and decided to go over to it.

He pulled open the top drawer. "Huh," he said. "I could've sworn this was locked." He puzzled over it for a few seconds before turning to me, brows furrowed. "Have you—?"

I shook my head. "I grew up with a china cabinet in the house, and my parents would've murdered me if I ever touched it." It was actually my grandma's, and I only visited her house three times in my life before she died. *"To this day, I never go near those things."*

He pulled the drawer open, then closed it. Open; closed. *"Interesting."*

"Where . . . did you get yours?"

He turned to me and smiled. "It was my grandma's. A wedding gift. Been in my family for seventy years."

And that did it. "Hey, can I ask you something random?"

He turned and shoved his hands in his pockets. "Sure."

"When I was at your house today, Ms. LaBrettney told me I reminded her of one of her friends. Lucky, I think she said the lady's name is? Do you know her?"

A flash of panic crossed his face so fast, if I hadn't been watching for it, I wouldn't have noticed.

He also took a beat too long to reply . . . AND cleared his throat. "I don't think I do," he said. "LaBrettney has quite a few friends that I've never had the pleasure of meeting."

I nodded. "Got it."

"Why'd you ask?"

(Why I wasn't expecting that question is beyond me.)

I shrugged. "I guess just wondering if you see it too," I said. "I was adopted, so I've never been around anybody who looks like me. Guess sometimes I wonder what it would be like."

He was gone, though. His body was there—standing very still and looking straight at me. But his eyes were empty and glazed over.

Just like you said Jeff's were.

He left a couple minutes later. Said concierge would leave some groceries on the doorstep within the hour and reiterated that no one could know I'm staying here.

And I agreed. Because what else was I supposed to do?

But now I can't stop wondering: What the hell happened to you?

Thursday, May 29

For nothing is hidden that will not be made manifest, nor is anything secret that will not be known and come to light.
—Luke 8:17

I saw Lyriq today.

I was reading and drinking tea in the cushy chair by the window when a white Mercedes pulled to the stop sign opposite the entrance to the parking garage. Didn't think anything of it initially, especially since the windows were tinted too dark to see inside.

But then the car didn't move.

So, I watched. Within probably a minute—though it definitely felt like longer—a guy came out of the building and crossed the street, and the driver of the Mercedes rolled down the window to talk to him.

It's taken me about six hours to fully accept that it was her. Because I really didn't want it to be. But after the bizarre line of questioning I just got from Thomas, I can no longer deny the truth: I messed up big. And I really need to figure out how the hell I'm going to fix it.

Because I HAVE to fix it this time. I know because that

verse of scripture I wrote at the top of the page is spinning around my head like it's on that 360 Jumbotron screen at the stadium where Dejuan took me to an Atlanta United game.

It's a verse I'll never ever, ever forget. I can still feel my mother's hot breath and spit against the side of my face as she whispered each word into my ear before telling me I needed "to be out of this house for good by the time Grandaddy strikes twelve." Grandaddy being the grandfather clock she inherited from her actual granddaddy—who you would think had been reincarnated AS the clock, considering the way she fawned over it.

A few hours prior, Marion and Marque Wilburn—my parents—had learned that their only daughter was "in possession of audacity at satanic proportions." And yes, I'd made a series of increasingly poor decisions, culminating with one that my parents (and God, if you let them tell it) perceived as unforgiveable.

But I've never gotten to tell my side of the story. And since I've read yours more times than I can count, I know you're the right person to tell it to.

I met Todd when I was in eighth grade and he was a high school senior. I was the only child of intensely Evangelical, middle-aged parents who'd conceived over and over and over again, and never had a child come to term. And they were unyieldingly devout and overprotective, but also super old-school. It was almost like they did everything they could to "train up the child in the way that (s)he should go," without any intention of allowing me to leave. Marion and Marque allowed for precisely zero "foolishness." Everything from my posture to the As on my report cards was expected to be straight. They didn't believe in babysitters, so I went everywhere they went and spent most of my time around adults.

I say all that to say I was very mature for my age. Even started my period early: at ten. And by the time I hit thirteen, I was hourglass-shaped with a big ol' booty and C-cups.

After a local news story broke about a sex scandal at my parents' home church involving a deacon, his deaconess wife, and a much younger college student they'd taken in for a summer semester, they decided God was telling them it was time for a change (after twenty-five years, mind you). So on Christmas of my eighth-grade year, we visited the shiny "new" church they'd avoided like the plague for a decade.

After a month of Sundays, the lead pastor approached us after service one day. I used to zone out hardcore back then—there are only so many times a girl can take the same "series" of "messages" about myriad Christian virtues before it all sounds like that teacher from Charlie Brown (one of the few cartoons I was allowed to watch as a kid). So, I didn't hear much of their conversation. But my ears perked up when the man, a youngish Black guy, said something about their congregation's philosophy regarding "the importance of peer relationships in a young Christian's Walk of Faith." And I was floored when he mentioned their youth group, and Marque and Marion told him I would be at the next meeting.

Todd was not the first person I noticed when I got there. That honor went to a gorgeous and goofy, hot cocoa–skinned boy named Malachi. He was fourteen and six feet tall, with bright brown eyes and dimples and thick lips and a mouth full of braces. I fought tooth and nail not to look at him.

Apparently not very successfully. Because at the end of the third meeting, one of the small group leaders—you guessed it: Todd—called me out as I was leaving the sanctuary. "Damaris, right?"

"Yes, that's correct."

"You enjoying Two-Twelve so far?"

"I am, thank you." *(Marion and Marque would've been so proud of the way I was handling myself while speaking to this "figure of authority.")* "Everyone has been very welcoming."

"Glad to hear it," *he replied.* "We call it that because that's the temperature when water boils, and we all want to be on fire for Jesus . . . But I was starting to wonder if the only person you can see is Malachi." *And he smirked.*

He did stuff like that a lot in those early years, Todd did. Gentle teasing. Smirking. He'd even wink at me from the stage when addressing the whole youth group. It didn't occur to me that he was flirting because I had no clue what flirting was. But I did know that as time went on, I liked how powerful and sexy his attention made me feel.

Things openly shifted between us at a Fourth of July bonfire just before I turned sixteen. He'd just finished his second year at Peace, a Christian university not fifteen minutes from our church, and I was headed into my junior year of high school. To this day I have no idea what was going on in his life, but when he sat down beside me, the first words out of his mouth were: "What's something in our faith that doesn't make sense to you, Damaris?"

What he couldn't have known: by that point, I'd been masturbating to thoughts of him after every youth group meeting for a solid six months. And I'm not sure if it was the beauty of the blaze or the warmth of the night or the flickering of fireflies in the distance or the fact that I could feel the hair on his legs brushing against my bare thigh, but I told him the truth: "I guess I struggle with the idea that God would put us in bodies that react to certain things if he didn't want us to enjoy them. Especially if everything he made is supposedly good."

For a second, he didn't respond, and I thought I'd said too much. But then he sighed. "That's really profound, Damaris." And he turned and hit me with those green eyes. Whether it was a reflection from the flames in front of us or something internal, I'll never know for sure, but there was fire dancing inside them. "I couldn't agree more."

We kissed for the first time that night.

For a while that's all it was: stolen moments of making out. He was more reserved than I expected a twenty-year-old man to be. It took me removing my own shirt and bra in the back seat of his car and guiding his mouth to my nipple after youth group one night—I was a beautifully perky D-cup by then—for it to click for him that I wanted to do more than kiss.

And when we got caught the first time, it wasn't as serious as it could've been. The lead youth pastor was a woman named Bethany who'd had her first kid at fifteen, and even though we both probably should've been kicked out based on what happened—we slipped away during the annual New Year's Eve lock-in, and she found us in the staff bathroom making out with his hand up my shirt—she instead pulled me aside, told me she understood what I was going through, and implored me to choose a different path.

Yes, she did tell my parents a massively downplayed version of the story: "There have been some minor flirtations that need to be reined in to prevent the development of temptations that will be difficult to resist." And yes, Todd and I got quietly separated at services (which was easy to subvert *once Bethany got fired for being "too progressive"), and my parents prohibited any communication outside the building.*

But all in all, it's more than safe to say that those "consequences" didn't teach me the lesson I needed to learn.

Him either, apparently: by the end of the summer before my senior year, we were fucking like rabbits anytime the opportunity presented itself.

Was it "wrong"? By every Evangelical moral standard, absolutely. But most of that—the sex outside of marriage and the deceit required to do it as frequently as we did and the illegal nature of the age difference—didn't bother me as much as it should've, considering my "faith." And despite him frequently expressing his reservations, he also frequently expressed his inability to resist my "lips, nips, or hips." Nine times out of ten, he was putty in my hands.

But shortly after he completed his bachelor's degree— right before I finally turned eighteen and we could be free— he was offered an assistant pastor position at our church.

And it was all downhill from there.

Right after Thomas left tonight—it's become a routine, it seems, him popping in to check on me since my phone is still off (now, at HIS request)—I reread the entry where you were trying to figure out why you'd decided to keep Jeff's baby despite the circumstances of conception. Because after seeing Lyriq outside this afternoon and then having Thomas show up and randomly insist that I share with him "any information about all past and present romantic partners" (like, excuse me, what??), I haven't been able to stop thinking about the decision *I* made and how I wound up in Atlanta in the first place.

Long story short: despite Todd completely flipping the

script and going all "I'm a pastor now, Damaris," and bugging out at random times, he and I continued to hook up in secret. A couple of months after my nineteenth birthday, I missed my period. I was in denial about what it meant for a couple weeks before I randomly overheard a couple girls on my tiny community college campus talking about how ridiculous North Carolina abortion laws are.

It hit me that I would have to make a decision in less than eight weeks if I wanted any sort of "choice" in the matter. (Even though for the first couple of weeks that get counted, there isn't even a baby in there yet? Make it make sense.) Then I went on a DNA and ancestry kick. Marion and Marque had shared precisely nothing with me about my birth parents other than the one slipup where they told an out-of-town guest at our old church, "Oh, you're from Atlanta? Our daughter probably has people there . . . it's where her birth mother is from," while I was within earshot.

But spitting in a tube and secretly mailing it off proved valuable: one of the tests revealed a potential relative in Atlanta. Latasha Jenkins was the name in the DNA database, but the first time she and I connected over the phone, she insisted that I call her what everyone else does: Tink.

Now I obviously didn't know this woman from Cain, and I knew everything she was telling me could've been a lie—my parents have been warning me about internet scammers since the moment their chosen private school for me assigned me a personal iPad in fourth grade. But I also couldn't imagine why Tink WOULD lie, or what harm could come from engaging with her. It wasn't like I had any money to send if she'd started requesting some.

She told me of a favorite older cousin who lost his life

shortly after finding out he'd gotten a girl pregnant—which the family only learned because the police did a sweep of his phone and found a short text from a number saved as "My Girl." When the family tried to contact her, the number had been disconnected.

Whether or not there was anything about the girl in the police report, Tink didn't know. And his parents—who I guess would be my biological grandparents, though it feels odd to think about—had both died within the past five years, so it wasn't possible to ask them. Since he hadn't introduced the girl to anyone he was close to, his little cousin included (Tink still seemed a bit offended by that), there was no one living who even knew the girl's name.

"But when I got that initial message from you, it gave me this tingling sensation in my stomach. And your age is spot-on. You gotta be Junior's long-lost kid!"

It sounded just ridiculous enough to be possible, so I leaned into it.

I didn't expect to ever have to take her up on the "If you ever need anything, you know where to find me. Please don't hesitate to reach out."

But at nine weeks, I told Todd I was pregnant.

And he asked me whose baby it was.

I terminated two days before the twelve-week cutoff.

Unfortunately, one of my mother's more rabble-rousy church friends just so happened to be staking the clinic out to plan an anti-abortion protest. Thus, my life took a turn that I never would've expected and wasn't the least bit ready for.

You decided to keep your baby—said it was "maybe a second chance to get it right." I can't go back and un-end my pregnancy (not that I would even want to as I know I made the right decision), but somehow, some way, I'm going to try and make amends for stealing that money.

I just can't help but wonder, though: Did you actually get that second chance?

For nothing is hidden that will not be made manifest, nor is anything secret that will not be known and come to light.
—*Luke 8:17*

Friday, May 30

I dreamed about Dejuan last night. I'm almost sure it's because Thomas was asking me about my love life, and I deliberately didn't mention him. But when I woke up with my hand tingling like he was holding it and instantly felt like crying when I realized he wasn't, it hit me that I've been scared to talk to you—or anyone else—about him.

The first time I met him, I thought he might be a murderer. The finest murderer I'd ever seen, for sure, but a murderer, nonetheless. Getting back and forth between Tink's and Boom Town involved a one-train + three-bus journey, and that night, I'd left the club late and wound up missing the final bus.

Was I scared shitless when a Dodge Charger that had flown by suddenly stopped and backed up? Absolutely. Seemed like something a murderer would do. But there was precisely nowhere for me to run or hide. So, I said a quick prayer, repenting of all my sins, and rededicated my life to Jesus. Just in case.

Once the car got back to me, the passenger window rolled down, revealing a red glow inside. The driver leaned over, and I swear my heart stopped, as cliché and ridiculous as that probably sounds. He was a gorgeous boy with flawless skin the color of Nutella and locs long enough to be pulled up into a big bun on top of his head. Diamond studs sparkled in his earlobes, and he had a smaller, matching one in his left nostril. I couldn't have spoken if I tried.

"I know people don't really do this anymore, but you clearly not from around here if you walking through this neighborhood at night. Can I offer you a ride?"

I didn't respond. (Because was he serious?)

"My name is Dejuan Taylor, and I promise all I care about is you reaching your destination safely."

We had a long beat of eye contact. There was nothing overtly "special" about Dejuan's eyes—they were a regular dark brown, and honestly a little sleepy-looking. But despite how ridiculous I felt about it, with him staring at me like that, I felt like I'd been sucked into a black hole and was in free fall.

Next thing I knew, I was fastening my seat belt as he shut the door. (He'd gotten out and come around to open it for me.)

On the ride to Tink's—six minutes in Dejuan's car that would've taken me another forty-two by foot—Dejuan told me he was twenty and a sociology major at Georgia State, but halfway through a year off to help his mom rehab after a car crash that killed his dad.

There was just something about him. He was a big guy—like, tall and muscular—but softer-spoken than I would've expected. Maybe it was his gentleness or maybe the tone of his voice. But within just a couple of minutes of being beside him, the tension that had been locked up in all my muscles felt like it had melted down into the red leather bucket seat.

And then we pulled up in front of Tink's. As usual, there was a small collection of mostly dudes posted up on the porch with my cousin at the center. Likely talking shit and smoking weed while shooting dice and laughing.

It made me smile. (Looking back, my time at Tink's was the safest I'd ever felt. Like in my whole life.)

"This is where you live?" he said.

I wasn't sure how to take the question. There was surprise in his voice, for sure, but I couldn't tell if there was also judgment. "Yeah, it is," I replied, unbuckling my seat belt and reaching for the door handle. "For now, at least."

"You looking for something different?" He turned to meet my eyes again, and I froze. "I'm only asking because we just finished renovating the basement apartment at my mom's spot. I planned to post an ad for a tenant in a few days, but I mean . . ." He shrugged and stuck his bottom lip out.

I wanted to bite it.

"It's not super big or overly luxurious or anything, but the space would be yours," he said. "Location is pretty top-notch too."

"Where is it?" I asked, suddenly fixated on his mouth in a way that creeped ME out.

"Lindridge. You heard of it?"

I had, in fact, heard of Lindridge. It was one train stop away from where I got off to go to Boom Town. "I have."

"Ey, where you from, anyway?"

"Is it really THAT obvious I'm not from here?"

He snorted. "Ain't an Atlanta bone in your body, baby girl."

I went hot all over. Which hadn't happened in a while. "Oh, whatever." I crossed my arms and turned away from him. Which made him laugh.

"Well, if you're interested, and you're free at any point tomorrow, I can come scoop you and take you to check it out," he said. "I care more about knowing there's somebody decent living in my mama's house than I do about money, so the rent can be negotiated."

I looked back at him then. Part of me hated how easily he'd knocked me off my guard, and as we stared at each other, something Clutch said to me at the club earlier popped into my head: "Sweet Pea, sometimes you really be giving if 'I've-never-been-shown-kindness' was a person."

Dejuan blinked, and I noticed how long his eyelashes were.

"You seem like decent peoples, at least," he said with a smirk. (These boys and their damn SMIRKING!) "Definitely brave *peoples* if you were planning to walk all the way here from the Bluff."

"The Bluff?"

"That's where I picked you up," he replied. "And now I know *you* not from around here. It was a nice neighborhood when my mama was coming up, but now it's the land of crackheads and prostitutes—"

"Sex workers."

He opened his mouth to respond, but then closed it.

I let my gaze drift out the windshield. "A woman can use her body in whatever way she pleases to make a living," I said. "And you shouldn't judge."

His eyebrows had risen then. Feels strange to write, but he seemed impressed. "You a lil different, ain't you?"

I flushed again.

"Point made, though. I'll update my software." He tapped his temple.

"You can pick me up at 8 a.m. tomorrow, but I need to be back here by 2," I said.

"Daaaamn, you tryna kick it witcha boy for six whole hours? How'd I manage to earn *that*?"

"Oh my god, that's not what I meant." I put my face in my hands.

He laughed again, and when I peeked through my hands, he was gazing at me like joy had been my invention.

I did wind up taking the apartment—for less than half of what he and his mom could've been getting for it based on the area. And with him literally seventeen stairs away most of the time, we got pretty close—there were movie nights and flowers on my doorstep and invitations to meals with him and his mom... who is also super sweet. There were picnics and soccer games and roller-skating, and smoking weed while staring up at the sky from the roof of the house. Deep conversations and crying on his shoulder and falling asleep in his arms. He was so good to me.

Which is something I haven't wanted to admit, even to myself. As much as I craved, and therefore couldn't resist leaning into, Dejuan's kindness, I also didn't feel like I deserved it. Like who the hell was I that this absolute dream of a guy had decided to devote so much time and attention to me? And more importantly: How long would it be before he realized I wasn't worth it?

In a weird way, I think dreaming about him last night shook me awake. Ever since I took that stupid money—and, like an idiot, hid it in a place that could put him in danger—I've been trying to pretend like he doesn't exist.

But he does. And I'm pretty sure I'm in love with him. Something I didn't think was possible after what Todd did to me.

And now I'm afraid, Lady Luck. I'm afraid that something bad will happen to him. And that it'll be because of me. Thomas randomly asking me about any "romantic attachments" on the same day Lyriq shows up outside the building where I'm hiding can't be a coincidence... Can it?

I want to call him, but also don't think I should... right now, there's no real proof that he and I had anything going on, but if someone from the club were to go to the address in my paperwork (really hate that I changed it from Tink's), and they learned that he'd spoken to or received a message from me recently . . .

No. It's too dangerous for all parties involved.

Even if I'm reaching, and it IS a coincidence, I gotta figure out how I'm gonna get out of here. There are too many unknowns for me to just walk out. Thomas told me to stay put . . . Is he monitoring me somehow? Are there hidden cameras in this place? Concierge surely knows someone is up here, even just based on the frequent food deliveries when Thomas isn't in the building . . . Did he tell them to let him know if I try to leave?

Then what if I manage to get out, and Lyriq has someone waiting for me?

Is this restitution? Was my mother right every time she quoted Romans 6:23? *For the wages of sin is death* . . .

Is someone going to die, Lady Luck?

Again?

Because the more time goes on and the stranger things get, the more I believe that's what happened to you.

Friday, May 30

Thomas just left after putting me through what felt like an interrogation, and if I'm being totally honest, it scared the shit out of me.

Around 3 p.m., I turned my phone on to send him an SOS message. "I think there's some stuff going on with my cousin, and I need to get out of the state."

He said he understood and would come by as soon as he

could, but to "try and relax for now" and make sure to turn my phone back off so no one could "trace my location."

All sounded very logical.

But something obviously happened between then and when he got here.

"Did you contact anyone else today?" The door hadn't even closed behind him.

I was sitting on the couch, reading an article called "Who Gets to Be Afraid in America?" in an old issue of The Atlantic—the only reading material he had in the place (well, other than this journal). And I froze.

The wildness in his eyes was terrifying.

"Hello? Earth to Damaris?"

I couldn't do anything but blink.

But then he came over and grabbed my upper arm. Pulled me to my feet. The magazine hitting the floor sounded like a death knell, and my heart roared in my ears. "Can you not hear me talking to you?"

I shook my head, fast and furious. "No." The tears were building and would spill over any second. "No, I didn't talk to anyone else today," I said. "I turned my phone off just like you told me to. I swear."

He stared into my eyes for a few long seconds, then let me go. "Have a seat."

I did as I was told.

For the next few minutes, he bustled around the apartment, opening and shutting cabinets and drawers and running his hand over the edges of doorframes. He disappeared into the bedroom, and I stopped breathing. I hide your journal in the zipper pocket at the bottom of a duffel bag I took from Via's. I think it was designed for shoes.

It's been a long time since I prayed for real, but I poured every ounce of my being into a plea that he wouldn't find it.

I've never been as thankful as the moment he came back out empty-handed.

Relief didn't last, though.

"I need to know exactly who you are. NO bullshit," he said as he sat down in one of the chairs opposite me. I was thankful for the coffee table between us, though deep down I knew it wouldn't do me any good if he decided to hurt me.

"Where is this coming from?" I said. "I'll obviously answer, but this change in demeanor—"

"You have precisely zero room or right to ask me anything right now, Damaris. Is that your real name?"

I sighed. "Yes. Damaris Marie Wilburn."

"How old are you?"

"I'll be twenty in a little over a month."

"How'd you get a job at Boom Town? You're underage and need a permit."

Lyriq's face popped into my head. I knew nothing about my hiring beyond auditioning and getting a job offer from her. Didn't feel wise to tell him that, though. "I had a fake ID."

"And your permit?"

"Was forged."

He narrowed his eyes but then seemed to accept my answer. "Where are you from?"

"Cary, North Carolina."

"Where are your parents?"

"Cary, North Carolina."

"Why are you here?"

"Because you told me not to leave."

"Don't be a smart-ass."

"I promise I'm not." I crossed my fingers. "That's literally why I'm here."

"I mean in Georgia. Why did you come here?"

I couldn't help it: my chin dropped. "There was nothing left for me in North Carolina."

"Do your parents know where you are?"

I snorted. "As if they would care."

"What'd you do to make them stop caring?"

"What makes you think I did something?" Eyes on his then. The asshole.

He just stared back.

I looked away. "They aren't even my real parents," I said. "I was adopted as a baby."

Alarm flashed across his face. (Which was weird as shit?) "But you have family here? You mentioned a cousin . . ."

"On my birth dad's side, yes. We connected through one of those DNA ancestry test sites."

"So, you've met your birth dad—"

"My birth dad is dead. Died before I was born."

"And your birth mom?"

"No one knows who she is. For all I know, she's dead too."

That shut him up for a minute.

"Tell me about this cousin," he eventually said.

"What about her?"

"Ah, so it's a girl."

"A woman, but yes."

"And does she have a name?"

I almost tossed out another smart-ass response but decided against it. "Latasha Jenkins."

"Does she drive a white Mercedes?"

"Huh?"

He shook his head. "Never mind. What's going on with this cousin?"

"What do you mean?"

It was the wrong thing to say despite being genuine: I WATCHED the fires of hell flare in his eyes.

"You sent me an SOS text at three this afternoon saying you needed to get out of town because you thought there was some stuff going on with your cousin."

Right. "Her house got raided."

"How do you know that?"

I lowered my eyes. "A friend told me, and I went and saw for myself last week."

"So, you've known this for a while but didn't mention it. Noted. What were the police looking for?"

"I have no idea."

He leaned forward then. Put his elbows on his knees.

It made my heart beat faster.

"You do drugs?" he asked.

"Never even tried any." Other than smoking green with Dejuan. But he didn't need to know that.

"Got a criminal record?"

"Nope."

"*Should* you have a criminal record, Damaris?"

And I hesitated. I did. Just for a hair of a second. "I don't think I understand the question."

He crossed his arms.

"I guess maybe I should? Could I get a criminal record for having a fake ID and a forged permit?"

And I tried to make my Beautiful-Little-Clueless-Girl act convincing. It'd worked a thousand times before: teachers, pastors, Todd . . .

Thomas, though, got up and crossed the room. Sat on the couch right beside me so his left side was pressed against my right one, and I was wedged against the arm. "I'm only going to say the following once, so I need you to listen closely. Understand?"

I took a deep breath. "Yes."

"I know that exactly one week ago, you stole a significant sum of money from your place of employment."

The tears came hot and fast this time, but I didn't move.

"As the person who's been housing, feeding, and keeping you safe, I am now complicit in your crime despite not knowing you'd committed one when you lied to my face about why you'd missed work."

I shut my eyes and swallowed a sob threatening to break loose.

"I have no intention of turning you in because, as of right now, that wouldn't be in my best interests. At the end of the day, you are a young Black woman, I'm a white man fifteen years your senior, and the world doesn't work the way it used to. There are zero possible outcomes where I escape being cast as the villain.

"As such, from here forward, you will do precisely as I say if you know what's good for you. I'll get you out of town because what's best for me is for you to disappear. If you deviate in any way from my directives, I will throw you to the wolves actively thirsting for your blood and face the unfair blowback head-on.

"I will return tomorrow with specific instructions, but for now, you are to stay inside this condo with your cell phone powered off. Do not turn it on or attempt to contact anyone outside these walls before my return. Myself included. Stay away from the windows and leave the front door double-bolted. No exceptions."

He paused, then turned to me and waited until I met his eyes. "I presume we understand each other, Damaris?"

The sound of my name from his mouth made me want to puke. "Yes, sir."

"Good." He stood. "Now go wash your face. Your crocodile tears make you look weak."

I went and did as he said, and when I returned to the living area he was gone . . .

But nothing about that was a relief.

Because he took my cell phone.

Saturday, May 31

He was different again when he came in today—less Big Bad Wolf of Wall Street, more frazzled White Rabbit in Wonderland—but I'm trying not to think too much about it. He did seem vaguely perturbed to find me still in bed at 4 p.m. . . . I didn't miss the disgust that washed over his face when I answered the door in dingy, makeshift pajamas, hair uncombed, face unwashed, and teeth unbrushed. But I couldn't have cared less.

After mumbling something like "I don't know how I ever thought you could hold a candle to her" (I'm telling you, he looked like he was about to short-circuit), he handed me a legal pad and a pen and made me write down his "instructions":

At 8 a.m. sharp tomorrow morning, I'm to take everything I own, which all needs to fit in a single duffel bag, and head down to the lobby, using the left elevator ONLY. Once I step off, I'm to fall in line right behind the concierge, who will be waiting to lead me behind the welcome desk to a staff-only set of stairs that'll spit me out on P2 of the building's parking deck. The white Accord I've been driving will be in the first space I see, unlocked and with the keys inside. I'm to get straight in, opening the driver door and the driver door only, and place my bag on the passenger seat. I'm to fasten my seat belt (rolled my eyes at that part) and proceed down one level to the exit, choosing the kiosk furthest from the attendant, and using the paid ticket that'll be sitting on the dashboard to get out.

Then I'm to drive to a paid parking lot that's already been programmed into the car's built-in nav system. ("You'll know it's the right one because it'll be across the street from a place called the Purple Unicorn," he told me.) He'll be waiting for me there in his truck.

"You got it?" he asked.

I took a few extra beats before answering, just because I could tell he was in a rush. "When do I get my phone back?" I asked. "Not sure it's a great idea for me to drive somewhere I've never been before without it."

The hellfire flashed green in his eyes. "If you'll refer to the very clear and detailed instructions you just wrote down, you'll see where I mentioned that the navigation system in the car you'll be driving will be preprogrammed with your destination. I will remind you that per the terms of our agreement yesterday, your job is to follow directions without questions or deviations. Now, I'll ask you again: Are we clear on the directives for tomorrow?"

I bit down on my tongue to keep the next snide thing from leaping off it. "Yeah, we're clear."

"*Wonderful.*" *He made a beeline for the door.*

And I don't know what came over me, Lady Luck, but I couldn't just let him leave like that. My mother used to do this thing where she'd randomly be super warm towards me—looking me in the eye and touching my cheek and asking how I was doing—and then she would tell me that she'd "like to have a conversation later."

But said "conversations" always wound up being unilateral, thinly veiled critiques about something she'd "noticed," followed by not-at-all veiled "correctives" I was expected to follow to the letter. The only time I was permitted to speak was in response to her favorite question: "Are we clear?"

The moment I said "Yes, Mama," she would nod once and take her leave. Move on to the next item on her to-do list.

And no matter how many times it had happened exactly like that before, the moment she was gone, I would cry. The hole in me that was desperate for her love, still empty and throbbing.

Lyriq's car outside a couple days ago popped into my mind. Had she been the one to tell him about the money?

"You haven't seen or heard from Lyriq, have you?" *I said as his hand wrapped around the doorknob.*

He froze. Which was . . . interesting.

"The dance manager at the club, I mean. I noticed she was here the other day—"

His head whipped around. I had no clue how to read the look on his face. It kind of looked like he was glitching. Or like . . . a bunch of different emotions were fighting to show themselves at the same time?

"Come again?"

"Her car was outside," *I said.* "She sat at the stop sign across the street for a while."

"Which day was this?"

"Thursday, I believe. Though they're all starting to run together."

"Hmm."

And that was it. Without another word, he pulled the door open and strode off into the hall.

I wanted to look out the window. Watch for his truck so I'd know he was gone.

But then I remembered I'm not allowed to.

I really can't wait to get out of here.

Fifteen hours to go.

Saturday, May 31 (June 1?)

It's seven minutes past midnight, and I am really, really scared.

Someone was just here.

I woke up maybe twenty minutes ago because I thought I heard a door close. Laid there frozen with my eyes wide open, hoping it'd been a dream.

As soon they drifted back shut, I did hear a noise. Like a loud thump.

Followed by a loudly whispered, "Shit!"

I slid out of bed as quietly as I could and crawled over to the wall behind the bedroom door. Figured if whoever was out there came in here, I'd be able to slip out behind them.

Said door was cracked. There was only one whispery voice—a woman who sounded a little like Ms. LaBrettney (though couldn't have been because Thomas said she didn't know about this place, didn't he?). But based on what the lady was saying, I think she was on the phone with someone.

What I know for sure is she was searching for something.

She made mention of the concierge—"I forgot how seriously the new guy takes his job. With the old one, I'd just slip him some cash and that would be that, but this teacher's pet ass wanted to fucking call to let him know I'm here! Had to make some shit up about a 'special surprise' and hit the guy with a wink AND five-hundred damn dollars for him to let me pass. And that was WITH a key." Then she asked, "Now where the hell is this thing?" And started opening and closing drawers and cabinets.

Just like Thomas had done the day he interrogated me.

"I'm not seeing it," the woman said. "Which drawer is it again? None of them are locked . . ."

Open, close. Open, close. Open, close . . .

"I'm telling you: there's nothing here. What'd you say it looks like again? Could it be somewhere else?"

Then: "I mean, we both knew this was a long shot. It's been, what, a year since you were last here?"

Then: "Yes, all the furniture is arranged the same way. You know how he is—no, it's not in the china cabinet. None of those drawers were locked. Is it in the bedroom, maybe?"

I crept to my feet and pressed my back against the wall.

"You sure?" Her footsteps got closer, and I raised my hands, ready to push the door into her as soon as it swung open.

The footsteps stopped. "I mean, you said it, not me. But I know it's important to you, so . . . You're positive it's not in the bedroom?"

Then: "Yeah, I hear you. Okay."

The footsteps began to recede.

"Aborting mission . . . Nah, don't worry about it, babe. It was worth a shot."

Her voice got quieter.

"Do wish this building had a back door, though. Glad I'm pretty, but not looking forward to fake flirting with the damn concierge—"

And I heard the door close behind her.

Which is the moment I realized I'd forgotten one of Thomas's "directives": leave the front door double-bolted.

Of course, my brain exploded with questions: Was this the reason for it? Did he know someone would come in? How many people have access to this place?

After not hearing anything for a solid minute, I went and clicked the second lock into place. Now I'm hiding in the closet.

I don't know what the hell is going on, but I'm ready for all this to be over. Really hate that Thomas is my only hope for getting out of this, but here we are.

God, I'm not sure if you're listening, but if you are: please let everything go according to plan tomorrow. If I have to be here any longer, I might lose my mind.

Sunday, June 1

I have no idea where I am, and I'm pretty sure that's how Thomas wants it to be. I followed his instructions to the letter this morning and took the cup of coffee he handed me when I got into his truck—"It's a new Geisha roast from Panama. Just got it in yesterday, and it's ground fresh and French-pressed for each cup. Should be a real hit when the shop reopens. Drink up."

So, I did. (Really hate coffee, by the way.)

Next thing I knew, he was shaking me awake. It'd been two hours.

"Let's go," he said, opening his door.

I exited the truck and looked around. We were in a three-car garage, parked in the space furthest from the entrance to what I presumed was a house. The other two were empty.

I grabbed my duffel from the back seat and followed him to the door . . . then almost tripped over my own feet once we crossed the threshold. We'd entered the kitchen, but you could see straight through the living room, which had two-story, floor-to-ceiling windows. The wall of glass gave a view to a backyard of lush greenery that gently sloped down a short hill to a small dock and expanse of water that stretched all the way to the horizon. With the sky clear and the sun high, the surface sparkled like it was draped in sequined fabric.

"I'll take it you've never seen Lake Lanier before?" He was standing with his hands in his pockets, watching me.

"Can't say I have," I returned my gaze to the glittering lake. "Only been in Atlanta since February."

"Well, welcome to life outside the city."

I didn't respond, but he kept going. "That lake provides flood protection, electricity, and water for millions of people, but it's also the second-deadliest man-made lake in the country. A thriving Black town was set on fire and overrun by a white mob in 1912 after two of the residents were accused of raping and killing a white girl. Whole town was flooded over when the dam was built to create this reservoir, and legend has it that the town's ghosts are still angry, so they pull people under."

I turned back to him. "Why are you telling me this?"

"No real reason. Just something I think about every time I look out these windows. Can't help but wonder how things in the past going differently would have changed the present."

It felt like the temperature in the room had dropped thirty degrees.

"Umm, how long will we be here?"

He looked at his watch. "As soon as I'm done showing you around, I'm headed back to the city. Got some business to take care of."

"And what about me?" It was a task to keep the panic out of my voice.

"Fridge and pantry are both stocked—had groceries delivered yesterday—so you should be fine until I return in a few days—"

"A few DAYS?!"

His face went stony. "Correct me if I'm wrong, but you have nowhere else to go and, as this cousin of yours is indisposed, no one else to turn to. Getting to spend a few days in a fully stocked luxury lake house where the people who want your pretty head on a platter can't find you is a goddamn gift."

I didn't respond to that.

"You can show yourself around." He made his way to the door. "Ungrateful little cunt." The door swung open and then slammed shut.

And he was gone.

For who knows how long, I just stood there, staring at the doorknob. Movement in my peripheral snapped me out of it. A pair of jet skis out on the water with two riders apiece.

I'd ridden one of those with Todd during a youth group retreat back home on Lake Jordan. We'd stopped to have sex on some random dock—tried to pull it off on the jet ski, but that didn't go as anticipated—before rejoining the group. "Damaris got us lost!" he told everyone when we pulled up to the rendezvous point eleven minutes late.

I was seventeen.

Thomas said this lake makes him wonder how something being different in the past would alter the present.

I couldn't help thinking about that too.

I took a deep breath and accepted my fate. It wasn't like he was wrong: if you're gonna be in witness protection, it might as well be in the Hamptons (not that I'd been there or knew what they were like, but this other dancer, Marvel, always talked about how nice it was there).

When I went to grab my duffel from where I'd dropped it beside the sprawling kitchen island, I noticed a leather pouch on the countertop that I don't think had been there before (though maybe it was, and I hadn't noticed it). I was afraid to touch it at first, but my curiosity won out. Which, looking back, was the best/worst thing that could've happened:

Best because my phone was inside. I could not have been more thrilled . . .

Until I saw the envelope.

It had my name on it. Which should've been a warning sign (but of course I didn't heed it).

There was a card inside.

It read:

Damaris,

Welcome to the lake. The home you're in was completed six months ago after a lengthy rebuild following a fire that destroyed the sixty-year-old cabin my grandfather built. He was one of the engineers who designed the dam that created the lake you see out the window.

As you may have noticed, there are no electronic screens of any sort anywhere in the space—no televisions, tablets, computers, etc. I've returned your phone, but know that it will be useless: the battery is nearly dead, you have no means of replenishing it, and even if you did, there's zero cell service inside the house.

I shall return at my earliest convenience.

Do make yourself at home.

Sincerely,
Your delighted host

I read through it three times, panic rising as my eyes ran over each word. Then I checked the door to the garage.

Locked.

I found a side door off the kitchen.

Locked.

Front door. Locked.

Sliding glass door in the master bedroom. Locked.

Door that I presume leads to the basement (where I'm guessing there's an exit). Locked.

Locked.

Locked.

Everything is locked. Either remotely or from the outside.

There's no getting out.

The only thing holding me together right now is rereading your words and writing to you. Though even that is beginning to falter: you mentioned both feeling "stuck" and being "trapped," but I'm 99% sure you didn't mean like this.

Now I can't stop thinking about exactly where I went so wrong. Stealing the money, obviously, but I wouldn't have done that if I hadn't been working at that stupid strip club. Which I wouldn't have needed to do if I'd never come to Atlanta. And I wouldn't have come to Atlanta if I hadn't . . .

There's really no bottom to this, is there?

The one thing it's impossible for me to figure out is if you had regrets. Because your journal entries just . . . stop.

Still have no idea what that means, but I wonder if my last one is coming too.

Monday, June 2

I didn't plan to write to you today . . . honestly didn't see the point since I've been fully convinced that I'm going to die here (does **Black girl all alone in the woods along a haunted lake with no means of contacting anyone** not sound like the plot of some gruesome horror film?).

But then some weird shit happened, and now I'm writing to you in a bathtub.

All started maybe an hour ago. I went down to the kitchen from the bedroom to get some water (which was an act of desperation: hadn't eaten or drunk anything since arriving at this place after being drugged with a cup of coffee, of all things), and I saw my phone on the island where I left it after reading Thomas's psycho "welcome card" and fleeing upstairs to find a bed to crawl into.

So, I picked it up (the phone, I mean) and walked over to the windows. Definitely can't see the lake as "beautiful," considering the story Thomas told me about it, but it was hard to take my eyes off it. Just glittering water hiding untold treachery as far as the eye could see.

At some point while standing there, gazing out at liquid death, I must've turned my phone on subconsciously. And I don't think I ever would've realized it if it hadn't pinged.

I froze when it did. That ping was the first sound I'd heard outside of my own quiet weeping in over twenty-four hours, and the last thing I wanted to do was get my hopes up about it. Especially since I wasn't sure it had happened for real. Being hyper-isolated like this can really mess with your head.

I took a deep breath and braced myself before gently turning my hand at my side and glancing down at the screen (feels a hair melodramatic looking back, but whatever).

It was 2:22 p.m.—which was jarring in itself, as I realized I hadn't seen a clock anywhere in the house and had no idea how much time was passing—and there was a single notification: "Dejuan Don Juan," as I have him saved, had just sent me a new message.

Stunned—had Thomas been lying about the lack of cell service in the house, solely to deter me from turning the thing on?—I opened it.

Need to know you're all right . . .

It was the latest in a string of similar messages from him, dating all the way back to the night I took that stupid money. In some of the others, he mentions "missing our movie nights" and "wishing I could see your smiling face right now," but the two that jolt me awake both say he "went by that place of employment we never talk about."

Trying not to panic over the fact that they haven't seen you either.

He'd been looking for me. Someone—other than the people I stole from—was actually looking for me.

And hasn't given up.

I sprang into action. No, not all right at all. Being held against my will. Sharing location. PLEASE SEND HELP!

Except the location wouldn't load . . . And the message wouldn't send.

I stuck the damn thing in the air, trying to recapture whatever signal had broken through. Got close to every window and went upstairs to try in each of the four bedrooms.

Not Delivered appeared in red beneath my message.

I tapped to try again as I rushed back down the stairs. The blue location dot sat adrift in a square of blank gray, but the progress bar at the top of the screen got so close to the end, I could almost taste it . . .

Not Delivered

I tapped to try one more time and returned to the spot by the window. Held the phone high in the air . . .

A voice filled the room: "I believe I told you that your phone wouldn't work," *Thomas said. I looked all around but couldn't find any cameras or speakers. I suddenly felt like I was in a fishbowl made of one-way mirrored glass.* "That house is made of reinforced concrete, and there are signal scramblers embedded in the walls."

"Why have you trapped me here?" *I shouted.* "Where are the cameras?"

"Regarding the latter, it would be deeply unwise for me to disclose their exact locations, but know that I can see you in every room—"

"So, you watched me shower this morning? And take a poop?"

"The cameras are there for security, not surveillance. Especially not the violative kind. You have full privacy in the bathrooms."

I made a mental note of that, but didn't reply.

"As to your first question, you are not 'trapped,' as you so crassly put it. You're being kept safe—"

"By locking me in with no means of escape?"

"By locking others out with no means of entry," he corrected. "Which I would hope you'd be grateful for."

"What's the point in 'locking others out' if no one even knows where I am?"

"Can't have you wandering off the premises in some misguided attempt to flee, now, can we? As I mentioned, that lake is mighty deadly. And you don't seem the type to possess wilderness survival skills—"

"So you are, in fact, keeping me in."

"Okay, I'll bite. When you put it that way, sure: I'm keeping you in. For your own good."

I was too pissed to respond that time.

"I'll arrive tomorrow at noon to check on you."

"Will I get to leave then?" I was asking sarcastically, as I'd already presumed the answer would be no, but . . .

"Potentially. Working on transport to get you across the Alabama state line, and therefore out of my hair for good. You'll be on your own then. Just waiting on final confirmation."

And there it was: a glimmer of hope.

One I had to chronicle from this empty tub.

I just pray it's not like the rays of sunlight bouncing off that lake. Glimmers so deceptively beautiful, they lure people in and drown them.

Tuesday, June 3

It's 11:11.

I won't make a wish—still haven't gotten over my pastor telling me the practice was "demonic" and would land me in hell when I tried to make what I thought would be an extra special one on my 11th birthday (which was on July 11th)—but I'm so nervous, I can't sit still.

I have no idea what's about to happen. Thomas is likely en route here if he's planning to arrive by noon, and what comes next for me is as big a mystery as what came next for you.

So, I guess this is me saying goodbye? Not sure I would've gotten through any of this if I hadn't had your words and your story to keep me grounded in a way. Make me feel a little less alone in what has been the most bizarre experience of my life. I'm going to put this journal in the bottom of my bag as I've done since I first found it, and hopefully I'll make it out of this alive and I'll be able to read back through this thing and marvel.

If not, it's been real.

Oh shit, he's calling my name. Looks like he got here early??

Pray for me, Lady Luck. Whoever, wherever you are.

PART THREE

BLACK AIR FORCE 1S

TUESDAY, JUNE 3

8:32 p.m.

IT'S THE BLOW TO the nape of the neck that finally does it.

Damaris will never know it, but the shock of pain that jolts her sympathetic nervous system back online happens when the car makes an erratic U-turn, and her body gets thrown to the right, shoving the back of her head up against a metal protrusion holding a netted pouch in place.

Said pouch currently contains a first aid kit. But she doesn't know that because when her eyes pop open, she can't see a thing.

She shuts them again. Breathes in deep and scans her body from head to toe to try and keep from freaking the fuck out. Her hands are tied behind her back. There's a familiar fragrance in the space around her, but it's hard to pinpoint what it is . . . especially since she has no idea where the hell she is or how she got there.

She's curled on her side with something soft and vaguely furry beneath her . . . which is when she realizes she's naked.

Panic rises.

Another breath, deeper this time. And another. There are two prominent sounds: a low rumble, and a medium-toned purr that varies in intensity. A bump tosses her body up into something hard with a loud *whump*, and a burst of pain shoots down her arm from her left shoulder, but she clenches her jaw to keep from crying out. Exactly why she needs to keep quiet, she's not sure yet . . . but she feels the weight of that imperative as deeply as the ache in her bones from her body being in such an awkward position for who knows how long. Either way, it's a good thing she doesn't make a sound: her silence is the only reason she's able to hear the faint jingle near her feet.

With her eyes still shut, she shifts her legs and tries using her toes to figure out what's in the cramped space with her. There's fabric. Rough to the touch, but a gentle push with the ball of her foot makes the object collapse just the slightest bit. Further movement reveals more fabric, but in a line that attaches to a hard piece of plastic with rounded edges. Then her big toe hits something small and cool. Metal.

There's the jingle again.

She rubs her toe against the object again, and it clicks: a zipper. Which could mean that the longer piece of fabric is—

She recognizes the smell now. A few weeks ago she'd opened the door to the basement apartment she was living in and found a gift sitting on the doorstep. It was from Dejuan. A bottle of hand-mixed perfume oil his mom had made just for her.

A pang shoots through her chest that has nothing to do with her current predicament. He'd been *so* good to her. And that oil . . . she'd put it . . .

Her bag. That's what's at her feet. And the last time she saw *that* she'd been . . . at that creepy-ass lake house. It was on the floor beside the door to the garage. Placed there so she could just grab it and go once *he* arrived to "get (her) out of town."

And arrive *he* did. Half an hour before *he* said *he* would.

But they hadn't left immediately as she'd expected.

Instead, *he* made her something warm to drink and told her to go lie down for a bit, as they had a long ride ahead and would need to leave closer to evening. That gave her pause because she wasn't the least bit tired . . .

But then the next thing she knew, she was waking up in the bed she'd slept in for the couple of nights she'd been at the lake house. And *he* was sitting in a chair at the foot of the bed. Watching her.

She sat up slowly and rubbed her eyes. A low buzz of panic started up between her ears, but she refused to let it show. "Is it time to go now?" she'd said—

There's a screech of tires, and her body is forced back against something hard and covered in rough fabric. By now she's figured out she's in the trunk of a car. And if the fuzzy sensation beneath her is any indication, she knows precisely what car she's in: the white, faux-fur rug had been in the trunk when Ms. LaBrettney handed her the keys to the white Accord.

The car is moving in reverse now—

It stops again, abruptly turns, and resumes forward motion. Her stomach heaves . . .

And everything comes flooding back.

He tried to kill her.

She asked if it was time to go, and he nodded . . . but then he said he needed to tell her some things first. The minute he mentioned the name *Felice*, she knew she was in far deeper shit than she would've dared to imagine. There was talk of a *vague infatuation* and *marital ups and downs* and *a night of lost control* . . . and *pregnancy* . . . and *panic* . . . and *powerlessness* . . . and *a problem that had to be solved* . . .

Which was when things took a turn.

Because when he pulled a pillow from behind the chair and stood to approach her, she did what she always did when she knew her life was in danger: she froze.

By the time he reached her, she was lying on her back, arms at her sides, staring at the ceiling. As though her physical being was just . . . consenting to the whole ordeal.

She'd shut her eyes as the pillow came down, and though her body thrashed a bit at first (*Had it changed its mind?*), she eventually saw a bright, white spot with blurred edges and dove into it. Over the course of the fall, everything faded to a silent, blissful black.

Felt very different from the black she was just . . . resurrected into.

In a cruelly ironic way, it makes sense that she's still alive. From what she's seen, people who are fine with dying—who don't go looking for it necessarily, but would be totally fine if death came knocking—rarely passed quickly. Also, *he*'d been so unhinged, it wouldn't surprise her one bit to learn that though he'd kept the pillow tight over her face for about a minute after she went limp, when he tossed it aside and set to work trying to figure out what to do with her body, he failed to check for a pulse (which she very much still had). Also didn't notice she was breathing (in that deeeeeeeep sleep kinda way) while he removed her clothes—

There's another swift whip to the right, and the sound from beneath her changes . . . like they're no longer on a paved road.

Her body kicks into high alert then. Because once he figures out she's not dead—

The car screeches to a halt, and she hears the click of changing gears.

All motion stops and the engine cuts off.

She squeezes her eyes shut even tighter, fucking enraged now. *What was the point in surviving the first murder attempt if she's still going to die?*

She really doesn't want to die now. It'd be such a waste!

A car door creaks open.

As quietly as she can, she feels around for something sharp or heavy. Can't move her body too much, or it'll be very clear she's not dead the moment he opens the trunk. If that really is her duffel bag at her feet, there are colored pencils in there that she could probably stab him in the neck with . . . but she can't exactly reach them.

The car shifts to the left before correcting, and then the door slams shut.

She hears footsteps.

So, she forces her entire body to relax and holds her breath. If she can just get herself to pass out again before he reaches the trunk—

TUESDAY, JUNE 3

Lyriq

WHEN I LOOK BACK on this night, I'll see a number of things I would've done differently if I hadn't been in such a rush.

Like the shoes. My Air Force 1s are sturdy for sure... but they're also bulky as shit. And low-top. Definitely not great for hiking through the woods. I've stepped on little rocks and roots and shit and rolled my ankle three times already.

Cargo pants are a plus—that side pocket above the knee was just wide and deep enough to hold the stretch of coiled rope—but I would've chosen a different wig. *No wig at all* didn't seem wise— the last thing I needed was for someone to recognize me... but this one's itchy as fuck and annoying the shit out of me. For one, it's too long. The aim was *slightly unhinged hiking white girl*, but the waist-length Russian blond is a tad overkill. I keep having to shove the "wispy bang," as the lady at the wig shop put it, out of my eyes, and the messy bun thing I pulled the rest of the hair up into on top of my head keeps snagging on twigs and shit.

And then there's the shovel. It's heavy. Can't drag it because it makes too much damn noise—and I'm certainly not trying to startle any woodland creatures into action. Honestly don't know why I brought the shovel . . . Okay, that's a lie, I totally do, but what the hell I look like out here *digging*?

I tap my phone screen to check the map. I *should* be at least halfway to my destination now. I'm not real big on *geography* or whatever, so it took me a while to realize the off-looking numbers in one of the messages "Jeff" sent to Lucky's phone back when he was still trying to convince her to meet up with him after the coffee shop encounter were coordinates.

It's occurred to me more times than I care to count that I might be headed to the place where she—

I just know *he* killed her, though. Or more likely had her killed. Can't imagine him doing the dirty work himself. Might ruin his manicure.

Something skitters across the path in front of me, and I jump and cover my mouth to keep from screaming aloud.

My ass is really out here in the woods!

It's gotta be done, Micah, says a voice in my head. *This is the only way to make things right.*

I push forward.

FRIDAY, JUNE 6

LADY JOSEPHINE STANDS IN the little cove a few feet up from the edge of the water. Her tent is gone, of course: wasn't no way she could sleep near where she found a whole dead body.

The cops. That's why she's here. And also why she didn't have as much liquid courage in her system as she typically would by this point in the day. She'd talked to the cops when they came for the body in the wee hours of this morning, and then they'd found her this afternoon and brought her back here so they could ask her more questions or whatever.

She bites her lip.

She was a little bit drunk, sure. But she'd answered every question they asked as truthfully as she could remember. Fine, fine: sometimes her memory got a wee bit choppy, and she failed to recall things just right. But she remembers what they were asking about quite well, thank you very damn much.

It's the other night—the one she thinks might be connected to the body somehow? Well, she didn't tell them about *that* night.

Should she have? Maybe she should've . . .

Then again, why would she? What the hell had they ever done for her besides harass and shame her and yell at her and take her sign away when she was only trying to raise a little money to eat? To drink, too, sure, but dammit, getting folks to care enough to even roll their windows down at those overpasses was hard work.

Besides, Lady Josephine's still not entirely sure that *other* night happened at all, let alone the way she remembers it. If she is recalling correctly, it was two nights prior to last night. She doesn't have a clue exactly where and how she'd passed out, but she woke up when she heard what sounded like a mighty struggle. There were two tones of grunting and heavy breathing mixed with the sound of sticks breaking underfoot and a swear word here and there. ("You little bitch!" was the phrase she heard most clearly, and she thinks it was in a man's voice. She really hated that.)

Then there was a **thunk** combined with an **OOOF**, and then a thud like something heavy hitting the ground.

THUNK . . . THUNK . . . THUNK . . . THUNK . . .

SPLAT.

More heavy breathing . . . but Lady Josephine was pretty sure it was only from one set of lungs that time.

She just lay there, staring up at the sky.

Then came the grunting. ***Grunt* . . .**

Grunt . . .

Grunt . . .

Grunt . . .

SPLASH!

She sat up. So, she was near the river then.

She made her way to her feet and looked around. She could see the surface of the water through the trees.

As she stumbled through the brush, shadows loomed up in ways that made it tricky to figure out where to put her feet. At one point, she tripped and almost hit her face on a rock, rolled to her back, and heaved a sigh of relief that she hadn't. Damn thing already looked like it was covered in blood.

She got back to standing and continued forward.

Or at least she thought it was forward. It was really more . . . sideways. Closer and closer to the river. Which seemed louder than she'd ever heard it before.

When she tripped again, she fell out of the tree line, and her knees landed in damp, red Georgia clay. She took a deep breath and again counted her blessings: a few feet further, and she would've tumbled into the water (which she'd wind up doing a couple nights later).

Someone cussed nearby.

She turned to her left, and there, a short distance away, was a person backlit by the moon. (*Is it an alien?* said a voice in her not-right mind.) Can't recall what the person's face looked like because Lady Josephine's eyes hooked onto a dark stain on the person's shirt and stuck there. Largely because the alien was holding the hem out and staring down at it. "Shit!" they whisper-shouted. "Shit, shit, fucking, shit, fuck, fuck, FUCK!"

"Do you need a new shirt?" Lady Josephine called out.

The person turned, startled. The slight shift in positioning revealed dark stains on their hands as well. It all had a red tint to it.

"You can have one of mine . . ." Lady Josephine was a little scared for sure, but she knew from years of surviving out here that sometimes the easiest way to avoid becoming prey was to make some sort of offering. Kinda like church.

And anyway, the offer was genuine. She always wore three shirts. Always. She pulled off the top layer, and then the middle one—it would be the cleanest of the three. "Take this one."

For a moment, the individual didn't move. Then its head cocked to the right. "You'd do that for me?" (Lady Josephine can't remember the tone of the voice, only that it didn't sound like an alien.)

She shrugged. "Sure, I would."

"How come?"

She had to think about that one for a moment. "Guess I was raised not to be a bystander."

"Huh," came the reply. "That's . . . admirable." The person looked out across the river for a breath, then turned back. "What's your name?"

Lady Josephine lifted her chin. "I'm Josephine."

"Well it's lovely you to meet you Ms. Josephine—"

"Lady."

"Hmm?"

"It's Lady Josephine."

The person nodded. "Yes, ma'am. My apologies, Lady Josephine. I think I'll take you up on that offer. I would love a new shirt."

Well, it ain't exactly new, began Lady Josephine's mind, but the person was speaking again.

"—burn this one," is all Lady Josephine caught.

"Come again?"

"I said the only thing is if I take that one, you gotta burn this one."

Lady Josephine didn't reply to that.

"You have somewhere you can do that? Not sure what your living situation is—"

"I can burn it, no problem," Lady Josephine cut in. It was damn near eighty degrees even in the nighttime, but a little campfire could be nice.

"All right, then," the person said, pulling the shirt off. "I'll fold it so you don't get blood on your hands."

Lady Josephine snapped to attention then. "Was that 'blood' you said?"

The person nodded. "Yes, it was. That's why it's gotta be burned."

Lady Josephine stared at it and tried to swallow her panic.

"I'm still gonna give it to you, though," the person went on, coming closer. "I can tell you're the type of person who won't go back on your word. And now that you know what's on it, I'm 100% sure you'll do what you said and burn it—"

"You can stop right there!" Lady Josephine blurted a bit more forcefully than she intended to. The person was absolutely right. "I'll toss you this shirt and you can leave that one on the ground right there. I'll keep my word."

The individual set the folded shirt on the ground. "Deal."

Lady Josephine didn't remember the shirt exchange, nor parting from the stranger, nor finding her way to her new camp. But she does know the fire smelled strange and burned with odd colors that night.

Now she walks to the water's edge and pulls her pants down. She angles her body and squats so her pee flows towards the spot in the water where she found the body. A last farewell.

"I'm sorry," she says aloud to the lapping water, unable to stop her tears. She couldn't have told those cops all that. They wouldn't have believed her.

"Wasn't nothin' more I could do."

THURSDAY, JUNE 5

Anchor 1: *Good evening, and welcome to Channel Two Action News at Eleven. Tonight: an alarming rise in missing persons cases has much of the city on edge...*

Anchor 2: *That's right, Vita. And in our top story: a woman got quite the shock early this evening when she discovered an as-yet-unidentified body in the Chattahoochee River near her campsite. Bernard Ray is on the scene with more details.*

Bernard: *On a typical night, Josephine Jones sleeps in a tent just inside the tree line above this Chattahoochee River cove. Last night, however, was anything but typical...*

Josephine: *It was just the strangest thing. I was looking for my camp—easy to get lost around here when it's dark out. I slipped and fell into the water a bit upstream, and that piece of rock jutting right over there? That's the only reason I made it out. I was sitting right* *here, trying to calm my nerves, when I noticed a thing in the water that shouldn't've been there. At first, it just looked like fabric . . . but then the water shifted and out popped a human hand! Scariest thing I've ever seen. And Lady Josephine has seen a whole lot.*

Anchor 2: *Not much is known about the body thus far, but a full investigation is underway.*

Anchor 1: *Counted among the missing persons cases are a ten-year-old Boy Scout who is said to have vanished during an overnight camping trip, a trio of Georgia State University undergraduates who departed on a planned vacation to Mexico but never returned, a rising record label executive said to have vanished en route to the airport, and a young woman whose boyfriend claims she fled his car while they were in traffic and disappeared into the woods.*

Anchor 2: *We've also received reports of an unidentified body surfacing inside a barrel in a Florida swamp, and one of a woman's remains turning up in the trunk of an impounded car at the Tennessee state line.*

Anchor 1: *Man, it's a little scary out there.*

Anchor 2: *Couldn't have said it better myself.*

Anchor 1: *More on these stories as they continue to develop.*

PART FOUR

MAGICALLY DELICIOUS

MONDAY, JUNE 9

Lucky

LaBRETTNEY STANDS, STEAMING MUG of black pekoe cupped between her hands, gazing out a picture window at the north Georgia mountains. She loved coming to this cabin. "Far away from all the hustle and bustle and scream of the city. And traffic. And light pollution. Like did you *know* there were this many stars in the sky?" she asked the first time she brought me here.

"It's so pretty up here in the summertime," she says now.

I don't respond, but it's fine: she's not looking for me to. Just needs to hear her own voice saying something she really believes. Which happens sometimes: much of the world she chose for herself eight years ago when she said yes to Thomas's proposal didn't align with her being.

He didn't align either, but it took her a while to see it.

They had never aligned . . . *will* never align.

Why she'd married him in the first place, she didn't know. "I thought I was in love," she told me through tears on our third night here. "I'd heard things here and there, but he'd never hurt *me*, so

I didn't think much of it. But there's something wrong with him, Felice."

Was I surprised when she called me in a panic on the last day of May (I'll never forget it) and said we needed to get out of town? "I think he hurt someone else . . . we need to go *now* before things get ugly."

Definitely surprised. But I was also relieved.

It'd been a long time coming.

We've been in the mountains for nine days now. The news has been on nonstop. I hate it—would love to just be here in peace—but she's desperate to know what happened to the girl. Damaris. *I figure if he hurt her* (she meant *killed* but could never bring herself to say it) *it'll eventually pop up on the news, right? And I need to know, Felice.*

There's no arguing with her when she gets in that space.

Five days in, there was breaking news about an unhoused woman finding a body in the Chattahoochee River, as well as mention of a woman's body turning up in a trunk.

Neither has been publicly identified yet. So, the TV stays on.

She hasn't heard a word from *him* in six days, but whether or not that bothers her, she won't say.

What she *has* said: "I hate that I can't put it past the man I married to have killed that sweet girl." I'll never tell her, but it irritated me that she still seemed to want to believe there was good in him somewhere . . . especially considering what she knew he'd done to me—and then asked her to do. But the entire ordeal had been a lot, so I let it ride. She *did* know "from the moment I laid eyes on Damaris" that she was another one of her husband's hand-selected forbidden fruits that he'd become obsessed with and wanted to keep close. That had been the case with me, but I did my best not to feel any way about it.

And speaking of *me*, Brett also said she would "never be able to forget the day he came into the house, eyes wide and wild and wicked.

Like a caged animal plotting its way free." It scared the shit out of her. "She's gotta go," he said (referring to *me*). "She's trying to end my career. I should've known better . . . She's lying, Brett. She wants to ruin us. *Us!* Can you believe that? We've taken her in and given her purpose, and she's going to destroy us if we don't do something about it."

He didn't realize how much Brett had already pieced together. That had been T's fatal flaw: he was so convinced of his own superiority, he'd underestimate people to the point of making careless mistakes. Like the night he was so immersed in something on his phone, when Brett asked if he had any evening plans, he accidentally told her the truth: *I'll probably catch some of the game and then swing by Boom Town. You?*

Brett, powerfully calm and intelligent woman that she is, swallowed down the *"What's 'Boom Town'?"* that had formed on her tongue and instead said: *I've got a couple of presentations to finish.*

And the moment the table had been cleared, Brett disappeared into her office and looked Boom Town up on the internet. Was she stunned to see her brilliant, week-old assistant on the homepage of a "gentlemen's lounge" website—especially after clicking on her photo and being taken to a video of said assistant bent over in a G-string with her ass cheeks clapping and her nipples slipping from her teeny-weeny-bikini? Absolutely.

But a little turned on too.

Brett said she'd watched that video "so many times, I lost count." It woke something up in her. Helped her make sense of the heat she'd feel all over whenever I was around.

As the clouds pass and the sky blazes blue again, Brett smiles near the window. She also claims she'd known the attraction between us was mutual "from jump." In fact, if not for *my* restraint—and the pregnancy and litany of secrets that came with it—Brett says she would've tried to lure me into bed much sooner. She'd certainly given it her best shot: wearing low-cut tops with no bra, and short shorts with no underwear whenever Thomas was out of town (Brett relished the moments she'd notice me noticing her body); touching my bare skin as frequently as possible; constantly complimenting me—*you're so damn smart, Felice . . . My god, you have a killer body . . . Sorry I'm staring, you're hard to look away from . . .* making it a point to stand unnecessarily close. ("You smell really good," I said to her one day while staring at her lips. I spilled about the pregnancy the day after.)

We'd grown so much closer than Thomas would ever know. So, on the day he busted in claiming I was trying to "ruin" him, Brett knew that not a word of what was spilling from his toxic-ass mouth was true.

So, she'd helped him form a plan. One that involved her—good ol' ever-loyal Brett—making the problem disappear (which she'd apparently done before, but I didn't wanna know anything about it) and not telling him a thing. *I'm sorry you'll have to keep it all to yourself,* she told me he'd said. *But it's imperative that I maintain plausible deniability. You understand this, yes?*

What Brett *understood* was that her husband was an idiot. And a coward. Not only could he not handle actually *doing* the thing he wanted done with me, he couldn't stomach even knowing about it. Which meant he would never investigate.

The ponytail she tossed on the couch beside him had been cut off a wig . . . and had proven a theory right and won her a bet: I've never in my life worn box braids, but Brett was certain Thomas would swallow the ruse hook, line and sinker. Because he never paid any real attention to anyone.

There'd been a few times that Brett noticed him eyeing Felicity with curiosity—except for her much lighter skin tone, the baby girl had stolen my entire face. But Brett knew that even if all the evidence was right there for him to put two and two together—the uncanny resemblance, the baby's age, the timing of Brett bringing Felicity home: exactly fourteen weeks after her supposedly dead mother's due date—he would never let himself believe the truth.

So, Brett carried out a plan of her own. After reaching out to share what Thomas had told her and getting the truth from me, Brett moved me into the loft her parents had bought her once she finished undergrad—a loft Thomas had no clue about, and which Brett used as an Airbnb.

"Good day, and welcome to the Channel 2 Action News at noon," a woman's voice says on the television. It breaks both my memory train and Brett's mountain-gazing trance.

Felicity yawps into the monitor, waking from her morning nap right on time.

"*Our top story this afternoon: an abandoned vehicle was discovered near the Georgia/Alabama state line by an elderly man on a fishing trip with his grandson this morning.*"

Brett's eyes narrow and she crosses her arms as she turns to face the screen.

Felicity yowls again. Louder this time.

"*The white Honda Accord, which was missing a tag upon discovery, was reported stolen on the evening of June 3, and has been implicated in a hit-and-run accident involving a Marta bus that same day.*"

Felicity begins to cry . . . and suddenly stops when I walk in to scoop her up.

When we return to the living room, Brett is fixated on the car being hauled out of the river. There are obviously white Honda Accords everywhere, but something about that one—

A banner with the words **BREAKING NEWS** flashes big and bold across the center of the screen.

"*In breaking news,*" the anchor says, "*we've just received word* that the body found washed up near a riverbank here in Atlanta has been identified."

The camera zooms in on the female anchor.

"A mere four days ago, Josephine Jones discovered a dead body in the Chattahoochee River near where she'd pitched her camping tent in the woods."

"It was the scariest damn thing I'd ever seen in my life," the woman says, appearing on-screen. "Been having nightmares ever since—"

"Wait a minute . . . I know that lady," I say as I enter the room with our baby girl on my hip. She tucks her face against my neck and shoves her two favorite fingers—the middle and ring of her right hand—into her mouth.

Brett crosses her arms. Nervous tick. "You do?"

"Yeah." I step closer to the screen to get a better look. "I used to see her sitting outside that convenience store where we stopped to fill up on our way out of town."

"Weird," she replies. "You think she committed the murder? Feels a little convenient that she just stumbled upon a dead person, doesn't it?"

"Mama!" from Felicity (and mumbled around her fingers).

"I doubt it. She's usually zoned out. I really only noticed her because she was wearing three shirts, hot as it was. Pretty sure I gave her five dollars."

"Well, that was nice of you."

I shift my attention to Brett. The woman who kept me alive when her Jekyll/Hyde husband wanted me dead. Who actually showed up for me and took care of me and made sure I got to keep my baby girl this time.

She places her palm against her collarbone as the news story rolls on, and I blink; for half a second I see a different hand. Smaller and lighter-complected. Micah used to cover her collarbone when she was anxious.

Had *she* really been the person who catalyzed all this? This escape to the mountains and incessant watching of the news to learn whether a girl who supposedly looked like me was dead? Had Micah really just *shown up* on Brett's doorstep? What had she wanted? How had she found out where the McIntyres lived?

"*It can be hard out here, you know?*" the woman, Josephine, continues on-screen. "*I seen some straaaange things in my day, but that one certainly took the cake.*"

"*Did you recognize the name when you heard it?*" the reporter asks.

"*Naw. I don't really do much listenin' to music these days.*"

The program cuts back to the anchors:

"Mama!" Felicity signs for milk more forcefully, lifting her head. A chubby, spit-covered hand lands on my cheek.

But, like Brett—who Felicity refers to as *Moomie*—I also can't look away from the TV.

A new photo appears on-screen.

And Felicity points.

"Dada!"

It's a miracle I don't drop her.

"*Ms. Jones's mention of music is relevant because the washed-up body has been identified as that of a music-industry rising star, reported missing just four days ago . . .*"

MONDAY, JUNE 9

Lyriq

"... ONE THOMAS JEFFERSON McINTYRE, *the A&R executive said to have discovered hip-hop's latest global sensation, Lil Aylie—*"

I turn the radio off. And smile.

"'Bout damn time."

I've got the windows down and the sunroof open. It's hot, but the fresh air blowing in feels good against my skin.

For the first time in a long time, I truly feel free.

Getting here hasn't been easy, obviously. The night everything went down almost didn't happen. Cuz for a minute, I was admittedly doing a little too much: texting from Felice's flip phone *and* showing up at his house *and* asking questions about shit I wasn't supposed to be aware of ... It was only after I pulled back from the in-person aggression that my original plan experienced a breakthrough.

Three days after I started texting "Jeff" from Felice's phone—

Heya stranger. Miss me?

—I got a reply. Can't say for sure what made him respond, but I'm guessing it had something to do with me pulling up and spooking the shit out of his wife (and child).

All I know is when I got to back to my car after the son of a bitch rolled up strong, threatening my life and shit, I checked the flip phone. A message had come in at 10:41 p.m.

New phone . . . who dis?

(I shit you not.)

I laid it on heavy from there. Texting multiple times per day, using language from their earlier messages so it sounded like her. I figured even if she was dead and he'd been the one to kill her (and stolen her baby?), suddenly getting freaky-ass messages from a woman he'd clearly developed a *thing* for would at least shake him up enough for me to get *some* sort of info out of him.

Didn't take long for him to start flipping the fuck out. Come to think of it, the doing-too-much might've worked in my favor because dude was totally giving *if unhinged was a person*. ("You killed my baby, you dirty whore!" had been my favorite of that response batch.)

But the wildest part was when he claimed to have had an epiphany and "realized" I was "actually Felice's spirit communicating from the great beyond to provide an opportunity for confession and forgiveness of sins." (Like, he literally texted that. I have the receipts.)

Then he started telling me all *kinds* of wild shit.

As much as I did what I did in Felice's honor—he admitted that his "tour de force" had been having her and "the unborn child she'd conceived when I railed her catatonic body" killed and disposed of (a *real* piece of work, this guy)—by the time he'd finished listing all the other "sins" he wanted to have wiped off his slate, I knew going to the police with the text thread wasn't gonna do the trick.

The only place Thomas McIntyre deserved to go was hell.

Besides, he'd completely lost his mind by that point. On the morning I suggested that "we"—Felice and Jeff—meet so I could "provide the necessary closure and freedom" (figured I might as well play along, right?), he initially replied that he needed "a pass for one final cardinal sin." I had no idea what the fuck *that* meant, but a few hours later, there was a new text: **It is finished.**

Dude was a goner.

Then I sent the coordinates he'd previously sent her, with a suggested time.

That must've freaked him out: took him two hours to reply. **I'll consider it**, is what the message said.

But I knew that motherfucker would show up. He'd shown his whole damn hand.

The shovel wound up coming in handy: I dropped the handle into his path as he barreled his way into the small clearing, and he went sprawling. Face in the dirt.

I jumped on his back and got the rope around his neck . . . then pulled and squeezed as tight as I could . . .

Unfortunately, wasn't *quite* tight enough. Homie popped up, and next thing I knew, I was riding his back like a damn cowgirl gone wild.

Then he did that thing they do in the movies, and he slammed me up against a tree. If I hadn't hit my head, I prolly would've been able to hold on, but the shit hurt like hell, and I dropped. I was in the process of shaking the stars from my eyes when I heard *"YOU!"* in a low growl. He was halfway across the little clearing, maybe twenty feet away.

That's when I realized my wig had come off.

"You dumb bitch!" he shouted then.

(A little uncalled for, but go off, I guess.)

"*She* put you up to this, didn't she? Told you she stood me up in this exact spot? FELIIIIICE!" he shouted into the sky, a whole raving madman. "Where are yoooooou?"

When he looked down at me again, I could tell he'd *really* snapped, and I was in serious trouble. He was gonna charge, and I wouldn't have time to get up. As he took off, I felt around on the ground for my rope—

My hand closed around a perfect-sized rock just before he reached me.

As that first blow connected, a car alarm went off in the distance.

"THAT'S AN INTERESTING SHIRT," Dr. Chamblee says when she sees the beat-up ash-gray Metallica tee folded on top of my clothes pile. It's from a 1993 tour around Europe, if the graphic on the back is accurate. "Can't say I had you pegged as a heavy-metal girl."

"Pegging isn't really my thing, Doc."

She smirks. "Don't be naughty, Ms. Johanssen. I'm at work."

I can't help it: I laugh. "The shirt was a gift from a homeless lady."

She shakes her head and pushes the button to lay the exam chair back. "I'm not even gonna ask," she says. "Let's just get you checked out. This is all very exciting, no?"

I smile.

The *this* she's referring to: I'm here (and happy) because today's the day she and the plastic surgeon will both examine me so I can schedule my reconstructive surgery.

It's almost too crazy to believe. The morning after my . . . *forest encounter*, I was digging around in my purse, looking for my phone when I found the letter I'd pulled from the secret mailbox at Tink's. On it was a bunch of jumbled letters that were pretty easy to unscramble, and once I did, it led me to the back entrance of an adorable little house in Lindridge where there was a dead potted plant to the right of the door. Beneath the false bottom inside the pot was a ziplock bag. And inside that ziplock bag? Fifteen-thousand-nine-hundred-and-seventy-three dollars.

I didn't make the appointment until the following day, though. Friday.

When I walked into the club a few minutes past three—about an hour after the day shift ended—Clutch passed me a note. "From that tall, brown, and handsome little cherub who kept coming in here lookin' for Charm," she said, shaking her head. "That poor little lovestruck puppy child."

It was straight to the point. *Please text me when you get in. Have something for you from a friend.* With a phone number.

When I met him in the parking lot thirty minutes later, he didn't even get out of his car. Just handed me a leather pouch—like the kind you get from the bank—through the passenger window, saluted (little weirdo), and drove off. *Loan payback with interest* was scrawled in black marker on one side of it.

It contained twenty thousand in cash. All in hundred-dollar bills. I almost cried.

"Now I need to warn you," Dr. Chamblee says, tugging me out of the memory. "This is not an easy surgery, and recovery is going to be rough. We left as much skin as we could, but we'll likely have to take some grafts from that big ol' booty."

"I really can't stand you," I say.

"Mmhmm. We both know *that's* a lie." She turns to head to her computer.

The surge of emotion I feel is unexpected . . . but I don't resist it. It's actually kind of . . . pleasant.

Makes me feel real.

Alive.

I shut my eyes and let the tears run into my ears. Which is low-key nasty when you think about it, but whatever.

"Hey, Kia?"

"What's up, babe?"

"Will you call me Micah?"

"Hmm?"

More tears fall. "My first name. Micah. Will you call me that from now on?"

She turnes around. "Of course I will, Micah. It's pretty, like you."

She comes over with a box of tissues.

"Oh, fuck you, bitch," I say.

"Time and place, baby girl."

"Thought you were 'at work'?"

"It's too bad you aren't . . ." She licks her lip.

"Oh my god, get out."

She laughs as she raises the exam seat, and then heads for the door. "I really do miss seeing you dance, girl," she says. "You were a miracle then and now. Your plastic surgeon will be in shortly."

TUESDAY, JULY 1

Charm

I FEEL SILLY ABOUT IT—especially since this whole thing was my idea—but once we're in front of the house, I'm afraid to go to the door.

"You good?" Dejuan says from the driver's seat. "We been here like four minutes and you haven't moved."

I grunt.

"Maybe it's a lil different back in North Carolina, but down here, you can't just sit in folks' driveway without getting out the car. People shoot first and ask questions later—"

"Can you come with me?"

His whole face—and boy, is it a glorious one—goes soft.

Can't say I hate dealing with a boy who's genuinely sweet on me.

"Of course I will, D. Lemme come open your door." And he gets out.

There'd been a lot of moments like this over the past four weeks. When I was struggling something major, and he was there for me.

And he never complained. When I couldn't get out of bed for the first five days, he brought me food and water, and he spent as much time as he could by my side. When I'd call him at three a.m. because I'd had a nightmare, he would come straight downstairs to hold me. When I told him, through tears, that I couldn't do darkness anymore, he went away and came back with Himalayan pink salt night-lights and plugged them in all over my apartment.

That last one had been what made it click: he really did care about me. Which some part of me obviously knew deep down. Getting myself out of that trunk had been hell, but once I did, Dejuan was the first person I called.

Lying there naked—still don't understand why Thomas took all my clothes off, though I try not to think about it too much . . . no parts of me hurt, so I don't think he'd done anything to me—waiting for death to come for me again had been the longest stretch of time I'd ever experienced. When I'd reached *sixty* in my seconds count, there were two *zoooooms* in quick succession, but they sounded far away.

Then silence.

As in . . . no more footsteps.

I shut my eyes again and held my breath. Counted to ten.

Still nothing.

So, I sprang into action. Step one involved getting my tied hands in front of my body. I was thankful for my flexibility and core strength. (Also: if he was so convinced I was dead, why the hell did he tie my hands together anyway?)

For step two, I had to use my feet and legs to try and shift the bag closer to my hands.

Step three: find the zipper to the shoe compartment at the bottom.

Step four: get my hands past the journal and ziplock bags and find the spare key fob I'd pocketed when I saw it in the kitchen drawer at the McIntyres' the final time I took care of Felicity.

Step five was physically the easiest, but mentally the worst.

Because I couldn't remember which button on the key fob would open the trunk. I shut my eyes and pressed the one closest to the free edge . . .

The horn blared. Loudly.

Car was locked, then, at least.

I held my breath and waited, feeling around on the fob. There were four rubbery buttons total. The top three were in a clustered little family, but there was a span of smooth plastic between them and the bottom one . . .

Which I thought meant the bottom one was the trunk.

I was wrong.

As the alarm began to blare. I pressed every button. *All* the buttons. Press, press, press, press, press, press, *press*—

The trunk latch popped free with a *thunk*.

Without a single thought, I shoved the lid up, threw my leg over the side, and climbed out—

And immediately collapsed. My legs had fallen asleep.

I heard a car zoom by, and though I couldn't see it, I knew there was a road close. So, I exhaled and pushed myself to my feet, now covered in gravel dust. I yanked the ziplock bags out of the way—the green-tinged faces of unimpressed Benjamin Franklins staring up at me over and over was a little jarring, especially since it was my second time taking a bunch of money that didn't belong to me, but I shook it off. I hoped by the time Thomas realized ten banded stacks of hundred-dollar bills were missing from the locked cabinet in the master bedroom closet—another easy-ish lock to pick—I'd be long gone.

I turned off the alarm, shut the trunk, unlocked the doors, and got inside.

Pressed the button to start, clicked the gear shift to reverse—

Something lit up on the passenger seat beside me.

My cell phone.
The incoming message was from Dejuan.

> Not sure if you're getting these
> now, but if you are, please
> thumbs up or something so I
> know you're okay . . .

I plugged the address to his house (and my apartment) into the GPS. Then hit the call button.

The phone connected to the car's Bluetooth, and when his voice came out of the speakers? I cried like a baby. Especially since the first word from his mouth was my name.

MY CAR DOOR OPENS, and his hand appears in front of me. I take it and let him pull me out of the car, grabbing my favorite Old Fourth Ward Farmers Market tote bag on the way.

The walk to the front door is terrifying, even though I know Thomas doesn't live here anymore. Or at all. I felt bad about it a little bit, but I'd rejoiced inside when Dejuan came and told me his body had been found.

The closer we get, the more the doubts pour in. Is this even a good idea? Yes, I want to apologize to Ms. LaBrettney and return the stolen key fob (not that it *went* to anything . . . Dejuan helped me bail Tink out of jail the morning after my whole trunk ordeal, and *she'd* helped me get rid of the car). And I was dying to see Felicity—that little girl had become such a light at one of my darkest times.

But what if Ms. LaBrettney didn't want to see me? What if she was angry?

"You gonna ring the bell, or should I?" Dejuan asks once we are standing on the doorstep.

I take a deep breath and reach for the button—

The door flies open.

"DAMARIS! Oh my god!"

Before I know what's happening, I'm wrapped in Ms. LaBrettney's arms. It feels so nice, I shut my eyes for a moment.

But then she says, "And who do we have here?" at the same time another voice says, "Who's that?"

When I open my eyes, I freeze.

There at the other end of the entryway is my sweet Felicity. But I can't even smile at her. Because she's propped on the hip of a woman I've never seen before.

Except . . . it feels like I have. Feels like I see her all the time. She stares, and I stare right back.

It's like looking into a mirror.

"Felice, my love, this is Damar—" But Ms. LaBrettney stops short because the woman is coming towards me, brow furrowed, but with awe in her eyes.

"Yo, the resemblance is absurd," I hear Dejuan say from somewhere behind me. But he sounds far off. All I can see is the gorgeous woman and the baby girl . . . who, in the woman's arms, also looks like me.

And then she's right there, mere feet away. She hands Ms. LaBrettney the baby and takes another step closer.

Before I realize I've even moved, my hand is closing around something in my bag. When I pull the journal out, the woman gasps and covers her mouth.

When we lock eyes again, mine instantly fill with tears.

"Lady Luck?" I say just as she asks:

"Where'd you say you're from again?"

EPILOGUE

AFTER

TUESDAY, OCTOBER 14

❝ EXCUSE ME? LADY JOSEPHINE?"

It's so rare for me to hear someone call my name, I think I might be dreaming. But the voice comes again...

"Lady Josephine, it's me." A warm hand wraps around mine. "I've been searching high and low for you."

It takes some effort—I've had a bit to drink, and everything's a little heavy—but when I get my eyes open, there's a woman squattin' down beside me.

Real pretty young thing. Redbone gal with bleach blond hair cut close to the scalp like a boy. Big ol' brown eyes and full, shiny lips. Real curvy-like too. *Hourglass*, they called the shape back in my day. Titties look 'bout ready to spill out her top, but that ain't a bad thing. "What's that you said?"

She smiles. "I'm so glad I found you!" Squeezes my hand a little harder before letting go to reach into her handbag. It's one of them Louis Vuittons. Always wanted one of those.

"I'm sure you don't remember me, but some time ago, you really helped me out." She lays something in my lap. A folded T-shirt. "You let me borrow that a few months back," she says, gesturing to it. "It kept me out of what could've been a world of trouble for me."

I stare down at *Metallica*. Never quite knew what that was—I got the shirt from a giveaway bin at the shelter some time ago. But fuzzy bits of memory drift through my mind. There was moonlight. The sound of the river. Darkly stained fabric. A metallic tang in the air. A strange fire.

"You was searchin' for *me*?"

She looks me in my eyes. Almost brings me to tears, it's been so long since somebody did that. "Been searching for a while," she says. "I have something for you."

She holds up an envelope. "What's in here is yours to keep no matter what, and it'll get you some shelter for a while if that's what you choose. But I was also wondering . . ."

I feel her hand on my shoulder.

"Do you want some help, Lady Josephine?"

I can't do nothin' but stare.

"I know you don't know me from a can of paint—"

I hoot. "Ain't heard that one in a while!"

She smiles at me again. "Glad to bring you some joy, Ma'am."

Ma'am!

"I'd like to give you a little more, though . . ." she goes on. "I don't know your story, but I have a friend who helps women such as yourself get back on their feet. If nothing else, you'll have three meals and a hot shower each day, plus a nice bed at night so long as you follow the rules. Think you'd be interested in that?"

She goes in her bag again and passes me a little pack of tissues. That's when I realize I've begun to cry. "Why, yes. I think I'd like that very much."

"I'm so glad to hear it." She smiles again. Real, real pretty smile.

A car playing loud rap music turns into the parking lot across the street, and she looks over her shoulder. The neon lights cut on: BOOM TOWN in glowing green with the shape of a woman holding a pole between the two words.

She faces me again. "I gotta go prep for my shift—"

"Oh, you're a dancer!" Dunno what makes me say it, but she smiles again. Even bigger this time.

"Yes, ma'am, I am."

I drop my voice down. "Tell me your given name. I won't tell nobody."

She laughs. "It's Micah. Micah Michelle Johanssen."

"Oh, that's a pretty name!"

"Thank you, Lady Josephine. I appreciate that."

"You're quite welcome!" Real pretty indeed, this gal.

"I'm going to let my friend know you're ready to go, okay? She'll be here to get you in about an hour, so don't go anywhere. Her name is Tink."

"I'll be right here."

"All right. I'll see you soon."

As she crosses the road, I open the envelope. There's more money in it than I've seen in a real long time.

And except to wrap my new treasure in my T-shirt, I don't move.

Because one thing about me, Lady Josephine? I try to do what's right, and I'm a woman of my word.

THE END.

ACKNOWLEDGMENTS

IT FEELS ODD TO immortalize the following words by putting them on paper, but I was nervous I wouldn't make it through this book. The world has been uncomfortable, life is strange, and it was quite the leap for me as an author whose name is most frequently associated with (oft-banned, but still) bestselling children's books.

This . . . was clearly not a book for children. So, I first have to thank my agent Mollie Glick for believing I could pull off this expansion into the adult fiction space and going hard in the paint to get it sold for me. Thanks also to Yahdon Israel, the amazing editor who purchased it and spent countless hours trying to help me align the vision with his knowledge of the adult fiction market and our shared love for Black people and Black culture in a book that juggles a number of easy-to-fumble topics. And crucial to helping me avoid those fumbles: Chanel Craft Tanner. If not for her careful eye and rich expertise, what I meant to be a powerfully feminist exploration of Black erotic dance—and the lives of women who choose it as a profession—might've done more harm than good.

Also supremely thankful to have such an incredible support system: Brittany—who gifted me the notebook and put "Write that next bestseller" inside the cover in her unmistakable scrawl. Angel—who kept me fed and watered and encouraged and loved on as I researched and wrote and edited and edited and edited. Casey Kelly—whose excitement and staunch loyalty gave me the boost I needed when my confidence was flagging. Morgan Menzies—who helped me announce the existence of this thing I'd been working on in secret for two-plus years.

To Steve Johnson: thank you for answering my random texted questions at all hours of the day and night. To Dr. Tracy Brinson: you were the first person I showed my initial pitch deck to, and your enthusiasm from that moment made me want to nail it. And to LeKeith D. Taylor: thanks for letting me steal your name, my guy.

To the team at S&S—I haven't had the pleasure of meeting all of you as of the writing of this letter, but Chonise, it's such a serendipitous pleasure to work with you. Danielle: from JUMP, you've made me feel like I truly have partners in promoting this thing. And to Stacey Sakal . . . by far the most validating copyediting experience I've ever had as a Black woman who leans pretty hard into AAVE both in my daily speech and in my writing. THANK YOU.

To the readers: thank you all for either coming with me over to Adult Land or for picking up this book (and potentially deciding to read some of my stuff for children and/or give it to your kids).

Lastly, I have to thank my own kids: thank you for being so damn expensive, thereby keeping the fire lit under Mommy's ass to continue churning out stories.